Praise for Adam Bissett's debut novel, *Boyracers*:

'Bissett's style is infectious and playful, a rollercoaster of stream-of-consciousness-type giddiness and poignant flashback . . . There is real emotion here, and gutsiness' *Sunday Herald*

'A terrific yarn . . . superb from start to finish' *FHM*

'An inspired look at life, in all its relentless tedium and occasional, glorious promise' *The List*

'An exceptional first novel . . . It should be on the Higher Still book list – required reading for those who understand and live its message' Carl MacDougall, *Glasgow Herald*

'One of the best things I've read in ages' Ali Smith

'A wonderful debut in the grand tradition of REM's *Murmur*, *The Smiths* and *Is This It* by The Strokes' Douglas Maxwell

'A breakneck dash through the back streets of Falkirk . . . a comedy, almost a tragedy, a caustic look at what has passed for culture in the last decade... Bissett's acute depiction of the Scottish teenage boy, stuck in that curious limbo between kid and adult, is wonderfully vivid' *Big Issue in Scotland*

'Bissett has been cited as one of a new wave of young Scots talent not seen since the early nineties' *Glasgow Herald*

Alan Bissett was born in 1975 in the small Scottish town of Falkirk. Nothing seemed odd about the child until his parents first noticed his ability to write ham-fisted but energetic prose. He has since used this power irresponsibly, as in his previous novel, *Boyracers*. By day he is a mild-mannered tutor in Creative Writing at the University of Glasgow.

Also by Alan Bissett

Boyracers

Damage Land: New Scottish Gothic Fiction (Editor)

# The incredible ADAM SPARK

Alan Bissett

review

First published in Great Britain in 2005
by Review

An imprint of Headline Book Publishing

1



Cataloguing in Publication Data is available from the British Library

ISBN 0 7553 2644 X (hardback)
ISBN 0 7553 2645 8 (trade paperback)

Typeset in Perpetua by Avon DataSet Ltd,
Bidford-on-Avon, Warwickshire

Printed and bound in Great Britain by
Clays Ltd, St Ives plc

Headline's policy is to use papers that are natural, renewable and
recyclable products and made from wood grown in sustainable forests. The
logging and manufacturing processes are expected to conform to the
environmental regulations of the country of origin.

HEADLINE BOOK PUBLISHING
A division of Hodder Headline
338 Euston Road
London NW1 3BH

www.reviewbooks.co.uk
www.hodderheadline.com

For Caroline

**Thunderclap! Theme music!** Adam, prince of eternia, raises his sword roars i have the power then lo and behold – hes he-man! Most powerful dude in the known yooniverse dudes. He grits his teeth grrrr wields his sword and the evil forces of skeletor they get ready to attack. Beastman. Trapjaw. Evil-lyn. Skeletor laughs throws back his skeleheid. Lightnin strikes! All goes dark ooooh. The forces of good look doooomed dudes.

Thats me man: he-man! Ken how cos its the hallglen and glen village gala day man – yahoo! – the gala days the best day of the year man, always sunny roastin boilin boof get the t-shirt off dudes! Aye. Everybodys dead xcited. Big prade oom-pa-pa oom-pa-pa, we all march march marchtay the big grass park nextay the cottages barandlounge and theres a corry-nay-shin by a slebrity who says i now pronounce you the hallglen and glen village gala day queen. And sometimes? Ooh. The slebritys a local deejay or the member of parlymint for falkirk west or kelly marie! Off tvs river city. Whoaaah kelly marie from river city? And the queen well she touches her crown and says in a weepolitevoice as queen i promise to help all the good people of hallglen, and the good people of hallglen they all cheer. Raay! Theres loadsay dances races tents shows games crisps sweets juice and folk peein behind the tents psshhh shakeshake, cos the cottages barandlounge man wont let them use their toilets. Theres a fancy dress prize. And im he-man! And judys spent all mornin fixin up ma costyoom fussfuss: a blonde wig a plastic sword from poundstretchers oh yer tootin i look the part! Let me see ye adam goes jude, i stands back raises ma sword roars by the power of grayskull. I HAVE THE POOWWEERRRR

(thats me doin he-man)

Oh adam jude smiles claps and hey! – only ma bigsister getstay call me adam. Dont you be callin me that man cos to you im sparky. Sparky! Sparky oh aye like an electricshock dzzzt – ow! Jude smiles, straightenin out ma wig pat pat. Aye she says that skeletor better watch out eh? Too right jude i goes, hed better no start nothin at the gala day today cos il just be like right skeletor. Out! And i starts wavin ma sword bout. On guard! Total gettin stuck intay that baaaad dude skeletor tellin ye – il stick it right between his bony ribs. Ekk! Aye even judes got intay the spirit man, she might be twentyone but yere never too old. Today shes xena warrior princess xena princess warrior, xena versus he-man. We clash swords in the livin room fksh! ck! spang! She goes egh she goes ha! she goes its the end for *you* he-man. She goes right enough now adam cmon get this place cleaned up but jude – prades comin! Hey lets go judy oom-pa-pa oom-pa-pa we goes out she locks the door. I jumps intay line yipee! jude follows trailin sword and shield, slow down adam she shouts. Me and jude whoaaaah wer just behind hallglen judo club in the prade man theyve got their whitejackets whitetrousers blackbelts – ha-ya! – we prrraaaade right thru the hallglen streets oom-pa-pa oom-pa-pa, past shops and the graffiti that says H-GLEN ANIMALZ and wave wave wave at all the mams dads aunties uncles grans grandpas neeses nefyoos all the kiddies at the side of the road man we wave wave wave the mams go look. Theres he-man! And the kiddies look and they smile

and they smile

But then? O jobbies. We pass by mark baxters house. And sure enough man there they all are out in the garden: yer actual H-GLEN ANIMALZ. Mark baxter. Craig. Jason fogarty. Knobend. Strippedtay the waist man drinkin beer sunbathin, tattoos on show. Baxter sees me and hes like hey. Its that mongol adam spark and his lesbian sister! They comes overtay watch the prade goin by, bigdogfaces tongues out drool. Start shoutin stuff ooh i like yer blonde wig sparky suits ye downtay the ground, who ye meantay be? Marilyn monroe?

He-man i goes.

He-man! laughs mark. Oh aye and is yer sister beast-man?

Jude turns quickasaflash, think yese are funny? she shouts. Think yese are smart? Come on then ya muppets il take yese the now.

Watch hen laughs craig. Dont hit us with yer plastic sword or nothin!

Il no needtay goes jude. Il just knock yer teeth down yer throat.

The h-glen animalz start endin themselves at that man ho ho ho ho. Im like mon jude. No wantin to miss the gala day eh, the corry-nay-shin of the queen and that? Hurry up. Pulls her away but shes still shoutin at the animalz, swearin givin it the fingers man jude! Tut tut. Theyre like aye aye thinksay? then throw a beer can that flies thru the air – i watches it slow motion spin spin spin – doof! Scuds one of the judo club on the head. He turns round man, sees them gigglin away those h-glen animalz hee hee hee, goes youse ya bloody. Then the judo club break out the prade man scramblescramble, run at the h-glen animalz yese *reckon* ya poofy buncha, start climbin the fence to get at the judo club and fore ye ken it? Boom! This massive battle man. Judo guys hurlin the animalz gainst the ground – splat! Big mark baxter smackin these wee judo dudes doof! doof! doof! they go ha-*ya* miss piggy style and the bands goin oom-pa-pa oom-pa-pa and yep. Sure is just another gala day in hallglen man!

Down at the park. Here we are. Take off the boots wiggle the old toes on the grass there oh aye relaaaaax. Loadsay stalls sellin cakes juice sweetsnstuff and onstage the wee girls are dancintay uptown girl, guys doin keraaazy skateboard stunts theres an eggandspoon race: go! Ye dropped it. Ya tool. Too cool for cats man sure is, me and jude well what we do is mosey right overtay the fancy dress compy-tish-on. Can tell judys ragin tho. Got that tighttight face. Same tighttight face she gets when shes in falkirkhighstreet with her pals bangin on bout the war on arack or george dubya bush or bonytonyblair (the lad needs feedin). I just goes listen jude theyre no worth it likes.

Hmph she goes. Tighttight face.

Ye ken what that lot are like they just look for bother i goes.

Hmph she goes. Tighttight face.

Hey judy whats a lesbian?

She stops. Turns grabs me. Goes adam dont you listen to a word they say yunderstand? Cos that lot talk pish.

Aye jude em. Whatever like.

She looks at me, face rockhard eyes blazin man roooarrr. And *dont* tell anybody else what they were shoutin.

Why?

Cos i said so! she yells. Okay?

I nods. Nod nod. Nodnodnodnodnod. Then i feels it comin man cant help it man shes gave me a fright shes shoutin at me man.

Oh christ adam jude shakes her head hands on hips sighs. Dont start the waterworks.

Stop it! i says to jude. Stop shoutin at me!

Jude lets go. Face kinday goes a bit soft like icecream when ye leave it out in the sun melt melt. Sorry adam she says. Holds up her hands. I didnt meantay shout but. That lot. They just wind me up ken?

Snivel.

Mon adam judy smiles, touches ma chin. He-man wouldnt cry would he?

I shakes ma head.

Well then!

Sniff sniff. Just i goes. Just ken. Just dont like it when ye shout judy.

She nods. Aye sorry bout that adam. Her face kinday spreads back intay a goodface niceface and the rage? Dribbles away. Oh jude kiddin me on that ye were angry at me, at the boy sparky here! Cmon she goes, smiles in that baaayoootiful way she does pulls me quick run! Lets win that fancydress prize adam eh? Aye judy i goes! And starts runnin run run cross the grass. Run run run run run lets win the fancydress prize! And hey man yel never guess what, yel never guess what happened dudes! Oyah beezer man yel never guess what happened!

*

We didnt win it.

Sigh. Wer watchin the merican football glum. Ho hum. Whys there merican football on in scotland man hm? hm? Mibbe these guys well they got chucked out the rugbyteam said hey dudes lets do things USA style, show those punks! But the USA dont want them. No! So. Here they are: all flabby joggin round a scabbypark in hallglen falkirk scotland downhearted. Thems the breaks. Big guys tho – whoah! Ho bigshoulders walkin slabsay meat ten! two! hut! they throw this football which isnt even the right shape? Huh. Mericans are daft. Can make great films like findin nemo spiderman programmes like rugrats – hey anjelica! – but cant make footballs? So they throw this wrongshaped ball goin ten two hut-hut-hut like bang intay each other boof, bigshoulders man crunch. Oof! Im just drinkin ma coke slurp swallow, watchin them man thinkin id lovetay gotay merica. *Id* lovetay gotay merica. Its fullay will smiths and britneys and whitneys and heroes and j-los with their big boobs oooooh just thinkin bout the way them boobs jiggle and stuff when

O jobbies. This wee weans wandered ontay the park. This wee toddler man runs away from his mam and dad intay the middleay the merican football where all these big dudes are chargin bout, bosh bosh. But none of them notice – none of them see. Xcept me. The crowd gasps: gasp. His mammy screams the name brrrryyyyce like a car alarm and i thinks

What would he-man do?

What would he-man do?

The wean the wean save him. I have the power! Pushes past, runs ontay the park get out the way. Get out the way wee man! Gets there stops but he just looks at me, the wean, with these clear blue eyes. Smilin that wean, smilin like hes no got a care in the world nope, and mibbe he doesnt. I says weve gottay get outtay here dude! Too dangerous for ye. But the wee fella hes just smilin smilin doesnt move, doesnt understand nope. Quite happy playin in the middleay the merican football so he is aye. Points a finger. Oo he grins. Geh geh geh he mashes his slavery lips together smiles, i says no time for it wee man! Tell me later! And i grabs him just bout to run off the park when

the ball comes flyin at me and

Four big meaty merican football players jumpin for it all at the same time they dont see us then ba—

The stars and stars and stars.

Thats what i minds.

We once wentay scarborough: me mam dad jude. Long time ago oh man we wentay scarborough, thats in england, ye hearday england? Its this wee country on the enday scotland aye, so we drove all the way down dad played buddy holly, thatll be the day ooh hoo peggy sue heeeartbeat. It doesnt matter anymore. Jude wanted to play the prodigy: jude said PLEASE dad said NO mam said THE WHATIJY? Jude was a raver then right intay hardcore house choons. I liked queen. Dad was still pissedoff at jude cos jude had turned up that mornin haircut short dyed pinkandwhite dad said ive gottay go on holiday with a daughter that looks like bagpuss? Jude said ive gottay go on holiday with a dad that looks like a pus bag? Dad laughed. No messin with judy spark heh heh even when she was fourteen.

In the backay the car me jude well we played i spy with my little eye something beginning with . . . p

Police!

Nope.

Peugeot!

Nope. Jude rubbed her pinkandwhite hair scratch scratch, looked away kinday like wishin she was at some rave in the middleay the woods, shakin a bottleay water lemme hear ya say yeeaaaah! (yeeaaaah! goes the crowd)

Ford fiesta?

Ford fiesta doesnt begin with a p adam aye it does jude. Miss skehal said that when ye put p and h together you get f. Fordfiesta fish fly fell flip fanny—

Adam! said mam. Where did ye hear that word?

Fordfiesta?

Fanny!

Em. Didnt wantay tell mam i heard it from dad like so just says em em from bruce lee films? cos i likedtay watch them oh aye wha-cha! but dad coughed said see ive telt yese bout them bruce lee films, theyre no good for him, and jude stared at the backay his head like she was tryin to bore a hole in it, said right dad – i cant see bruce lee goin you must learn the ancient art of the dragon ya fannys. Aye she kent fine that jude so she did, nothin gets past her sooooo we gets intay scarborough caravan park mam dad got all the cases unpacked oof the clothes hung up jude made dinner chipseggbeans ooh, i like the taste when ye mix the beanjuice in with the eggwhite, whoah crinklecut chips ya dancer i said okay jude lets race scoffscoff – burp! I won heh heh aaaaaand jude dudes well she took me out to play on the swings yipee! Well i played on those swings. I played and played and played jude stood bored watched me go high High HIGHER is it a bird? Is it a plane? No its the incredible adam spark! Swings are great. Swings are great. I looked over and?

Jude was talkin to this girl. The girl said hey i like your pink hair i watched. They talked laughed jude said oh ha ha ha ha ha! I still watched. Soon jude turned to me said adam?

Aye jude?

Me and . . . whats yer name?

Francesca.

– me and francescas gonnay go for a walk ye stay here the now?

Aye jude i said.

Yel no try and find yer way home on yer own will ye?

No jude i said.

Good she said then: left.

I waited.

I waited waited like i was waitin effin tables man. But did jude return? Was there a return of the jedi i mean judy? Ho ho indeed no. On ma tod on ma own, all on ma lonesome so!

Tried to find ma way home. The sun went down i couldnt. Couldnt mind what caravan we were in. Zoinks! as shaggy would say. The g-g-g-g-ghost! All the caravans looked the sametay me. Caravan caravan caravan. Caravan caravan caravan caravan caravan. Judy i said to maself. Judy? Tried a caravan said is ma sister judy in there? They just looked down at me said sorry son no judy here. Oh well i says, can i come in and watch telly? Thru the door i could see a family sittin together playin games, monopoly cluedo scrabble. Socks cards coke. Are you lost? they said. No i said. As if! Just lookin for ma sister judy, no big deal geeza break! Oh right they said, so i walked off. Wander wander. Stars started to come out in the sky, the stars and stars and stars. I chapped some more doors judy there? No son. What bout ma mam and dad? Em nope youve got the wrong caravan love. The lights started to go out in the caravan park. Families talkin laughin goodnight johnboy. Goodnight mary ellen. Dark. Cold. Sat down. Looked up: space. Home of the silver surfer. The stars and stars and stars. The stars and stars and stars and stars and stars.

Judy found me. I was freezin dudes. Was lookin at the stars she said adam. Adam! I told ye not to wander off didnt i? Weve been lookin for ye for hours! Pointed with ma finger straight up, all the big endless things up there planets suns blackholes marsattacks. Jude looked up, stars i said to her. She said what? Cmon adam yer gibberin, lets get ye home fore ye catch yer death i said what bout francesca? Where did ye go? Was she more funfrolics smartfantastic trendyhowdydoody judy? More than me? Than sparky? Zit true jude hm? hm? Jude looked away said um forget that for now adam lets just get ye

Home. Opened the door. Mam rushed at me. Oh adam adam son where ye been? Put her arms round me tight mmmm mam. Her warmness her warmness her warmwarmwarmness. Teeth: chitterchitter. Then they put me to bed made me a hot chocolate mam glared at jude jude looked at the floor stirred ma hot chocolate mam checked ma temp-ra-tyoor i read ma spiderman comic shivershiver, go spidey! Mam said shh. Fingers to lips. Turned. Dad comin up the steps. Been at the pub: boozin. We froze: freezin. Looked at each other dumf dumf dumf went the footsteps outside the caravan then the door flew open with a ba –

*

– ng! Ow. What happened there man? Oyah whats the deal here cos ma head feels like a cracked watermelon oof!

Just get the old bearins here feelin kinday a wee bit sick like em. Where am i?

Adam? Adam? Can ye hear me?

Aye judy i can *hear* ye like just cant see y

There ye are.

Judes leanin lookin intay ma eyes. Peeps standin all round. Big merican football guys holdin their helmets lookin em? Concerned. Thats the word aye. Concerned for like ma safe-tea (better for ye than unsafe-tea yuk) dude in a green yooniform got this stretcher right him and this other green yooniformed dude bout to lift me ontay it i says ho. Its alright. Just gimme a second here. Starts to rise horrormoviestyle. Hes awake! somebody goes, wantay say aye course im awake. What do ye think i am man sleepin beauty? Geez peace christomighty i looks and theres the wee wean that ran ontay the park – toddlin around man laughin clappin. Fine. Comes uptay me with this great big smile on his face and goes:

*Again!*

Ambyoolance well it hauls me off to falkirk royal infirmary, nee naw nee naw nee naw. Judy sittin there shakin her head sayin adam what were ye *thinkin* about? Runnin ontay the park with all them guys chargin round? Sorry jude. Just thought. Ken? And i wantay tell her bout what happened after they hammered intay me bout stars and stars and scarborough and francesca, member her jude? You left me. When i was wee you left me judy, nevermind shrug anyway we gets to falkirk royal, doctor goes prod prod. That sore? Aye its effin sore! Is it sore when i *punch* ye ya effin

Puts me on this big xray machine drrrrrrrrrrrr while i lies there like bruce banner in the ncredible hulk gettin a doseay gamma rady-ay-shin. Dont make me angry. You wouldnt like me when im angry. Man thats me: the hulk! Watch out folks hes startin to change roooaaaarr. Me the doctor and judy well we look at the xrays of ma head its white and round like an eggshell. Ooh sparkys a skelyton! That whats inside me man? Bone? Freeaky. Doctors goin hmmmm big long hmmmm. Lookin at the xray of ma skelyton he says nope. No fractures. Youre fine adam tho youve had a bit of a knock. Stay away from mental xcitement and stress or you might make it worse. Jude says ye sure thats it doctor, i mean whats that shadow on the xray? Sure enough wee white spooky patchbit on the skullncrossbones. Doctor shakes his head thats nothing, appears on xrays all the time. No no id just advise going home and getting some rest now adam. Though id *also* advise you to keep away from american football in future. Ho ho ho ho.

Ho ho ho ho judy goes.

Ho ho ho ho the nurse goes.

Ho ho ho ho everyone goes ho ho ho ho ho ho ho HO HO HO HO like at the enday he-man when orko makes a joke.

Aye well laugh all ye like doctor, but you didnt save that wean.

I did.

Daftspazzymongolsparky.

Outside. Sun. Sunny! Nicen warm aye the peeps of falkirk comin and goin and goin and comin, soooo boooored, but none of them ken that sparky saved a wean. Jude checks her watch looks bout the place em adam? Wince. Gottay go offtay the library now she says got an essay due soon. Ye be okay? Judy spark and her lectures and her books and her books and her studyin right intay the night how interestin inspirin xcitin, yawn. You are feeling slee-py.

Now ye sure yere alright adam? jude narrows her eyes squeezin ma hand squeeze. Sometimes she looks older than she is, fullay bigpersonthoughts the anger the niceness the warrior princess. Helluva bump ye took earlier pal.

Fine jude. I says.

Xcept i dont tell her bout the coloured lights.

Good she says, and yere alright to get a taxi home on yer own? If i give ye the money? I ken ye still dont liketay get taxis without me but yere a big boy now adam. Eighteen! Yeve gottay—

No jude i says. Id prefer it if ye came with me.

She looks at her watch again sighs. Says but adam ive gottay get to the library ive really loadsay work to—

Id prefer it if ye came with me. I says again.

Jude nods. Looks at the ground. Coloured light round judes head dark should i tell her? Nah. One less thing for her to worry bout.

Right she shrugs okay then. Whats the matter jude i thinks, why ye no happy to be ridin in a taxi with the boy sparky, ridin our way outta these badlands judedude? She calls me a taxi. Okay youre a taxi! Gets in i jabbers to the taxidriver when he asks why wer dressed as he-man and xena, i says well mr taxidriver weve cometay save the world. Me and ma bigsister judy! Isnt that right? I turns and judes just starin at me silent, armsfolded. She says aye adam. Sure. Whatever.

**Time to change batman!** Sure thing boy wonder. Another shift at the worlds greatest fastfood chain! The meejum fries the cheeseburgerncoke the chicken nuggets il have a reglar milkshake too wid dat buddy. Wouldya laik to go lorge sir? I shore as hell would. Well sir thats why i work for the team thats always toppay the league when it comestay fastfood.

In this place yere partay somethin. A team. A posse. Cos here each member is as val-yoo-a-bul as the next. The person at the top (angie) is just as important as the person who racks the fries (me) cleans the floors (me) the toilets (me) the bins (me) picks up the rubbish from outside the shop (guess who? me). Goes in. Helloooo! i says to gordon whos moppin the floor mop mop.

Hiya sparky he mutters how ye doin?

Hm. Sure could do with a holi-day to san tro-pay i says, but other than that gordon? Im swell!

Aye well yed better watch gordon says, leans on his mop shh whisper.

Angies on the warpath. Caught debbie chewin gum earlier blew the nut. Sent her home no joke, been bangin on ever since bout standards droppin.

Il look out i says, checkin the floor to see if anybodys dropped a standard or two there but no. Only floortiles and soapsuds and eh why was angie blowin on a nut? Did it have fluff on it like? Or pubes? Or pubes! Too much pubic hair round here man oh aye. Gordon says: just keepin ma head down man. Doin what im telt till hometime likes.

I will too i whispers, diggin the chin intay the old neck pullin ma crewcap down. Tip toe tip toe sneeaak. Gets intay the crewroom. Opens the door creeaak. Angie shoutin the place down the walls shakin earthquake man! Rrrrrumble. Reno and steve sittin at the stafftable faces like gulp. And *youse* angie goes pointin a finger thats bony as tonyblair. This place is filthy! Its barely seen a brush since yese were put on crewroom duties.

Spots me.

Oh and look who it is she goes handsonhips. Bright spark!

Em angie i minds her. Ma names sparky? Turns to reno and steve hiya you two i grins, they nod. Glu-hum.

Never mind that pair hisses angie like the fat we cook the fries in fsshhhhhhh. While wer on the subject of *standards* bright spark i looked at that accident book last week and guess whose names in it three times?

Em i says. Em em dont tell me. Is it

Didnt i warn you not to get lippy? she goes. Steps forwards.

Hang on. Em im sure i ken this one was it

DIDNT I WARN YOU NOT TO GET LIPPY?

Nope. I give up angie. Yel just havetay tell me who it is.

Reno and steve start laughin fnar fnar. Angie spins round like a cobra WHAT ARE YOU TWO SMIRKIN ABOUT? IL SEE YOUSE LATER YA PAIRA USELESS

Smiles fall doomp.

Angie turns backtay me breathes like a horse goes il tell ye whose names in the accident book smartarse. Yours.

Thats right! i says. Christ angie so it is! God i nearly got it there too.

Aye you will get it she goes. Three times youre in that book bright spark.

Look its *sparky* i sighs. How hard is it to get somebodys name so wrong christomighty.

Three times! And do ye ken what for?

Sure do i goes. Grin grin. Yel no catch me out this time angie. I burnt daveys hand with the rack of fries?

Mm-hm.

Left a spillage on the floor and fiona slipped?

Aye.

And . . . em . . . Oh! I ken. I dropped that box of burgers on peters foot?

Angie stands with her armscrossed stony stone. Aye she says. Thats right bright spark. Spot on.

Honest? i goes. Am i right! Man ye cant argue with that now angie. All three guesses correct?

Yep theres no pullin the wool over sparkys eyes in the old quiz stakes like. And cos im tryin to go for employee of the month, passin that wee test is sure to get me into angies goodbooks aye. So put me down for one great start to the day!

*

Whistle while you work tara da-da da-da da. Makes up songs for the rest of ma shift. Even when angie moves me from moppin duties to rackin fries im still singin in ma head total jookbox style, drop five pans of frozenfries intay the fat fffsssssshhhhhh. Fry me a river. Then gotay the counter where the cooked fries are sittin on toppay each other in a big pile. Fry me to the moon. Scoop up the fries put the enday the superscooper intay a wee poke (smallmeejumorlarge?) rack them for the good folks at the counter to take away. Come fryyyy with me. Then the fries in the chipfat start beepin. Let us out! Let us out! Wer done! Ye havetay go rescue them or they start beepbeepbeepin then when they come out? Theyre burnt. Oh no! First time i worked here i left them in one minute too long guess what angie says? Theyre no good. Dump them. The whole lot? i goes. Aye. Five whole pans full! Aye. So sparky here dumps five whole pans full of fries cooked for just one minute too long but thats the game eh? This company demands per-fek-shun. Otherwise they wouldnt be as famous and wellloved by the kiddywinkles man and be able to do so much good all round the world.

Off the hallglen bus at the right stop phew! Theres the weans playin hopscotch the numbers on the pavement hiya sparky says wee manda, big smilin flower on her t-shirt. Blonde hair pigtails. Mandas cool, always nicetay me. Hop skip she goes. Hey sparky wantay play? Sure *thang* says i. Lovetay! Im a syooperb hopscotcher me like, the dude the boy the dude sparky.

Aye but, says manda. Gottay take yer shoes off.

Take ma shoes off?

Take yer shoes off.

Takes ma shoes off. Starts playin hopscotch with wee manda hop skip hop skip hop in ma socks. Im crap at it like but wee mandas good. But then a door opens creeeeaaaak like a vampire wakin mandas mams there lookin, in her apron, wipin hands on a dishcloth wipe wipe. Cold. Brr. Chilly round here all of a sudden dudes?

Amanda her mam says. Whatve i telt ye about talkin to strangers?

Manda stops midhop, but *mam* sparkys no a stranger. He only lives three doors up.

Aye well thats no the point she says. Looks at me. Ma feet. Me just me in ma wee socks man like ive taken off all ma clothes or somethin, zif im in the buff! And *you* sparky. What do ye think yere playin at?

I shrugs says: hopscotch.

Lessay yer cheek! Ye shouldnt be playin with wee weans sparky ye ken that fine. Ye ken what folk will think.

Aye i smiles, winks at manda. Folk will think me and mandas pals.

Her mam stares staaaaaare. Sometimes folk stare that coldcold way its weird. Big mark baxter and the h-glen animalz angie sometimes even judy they staaaaare at me cold and i cant work out what theyre thinkin but? They still stare. They stare and they stare and they stare. And they stare. What do they want? Should i do a wee dance? An irish jig mibbe? What do they look at me like that for why why whatve i done man xcept take ma shoes off? Xcept take ma shoes off!

Up the lotta yese.

So. Sigh. Go over and get us some goodies adam, aw judy how come ive gottay? Go get some goodies fore the simpsons starts cmon! Jeeeeeez whats jude like see when shes on her period man she stuff stuff stuffs herself sometimes even chocolate smeeeeared on her face but its good cos when the simpsons is on me and jude snuggle right up on the couch warmwarm watch bart marge groundskeeper willy. Yas canna play there ya buncha little! His scottish accents magic man – so realistic. We eat crisps juice sweets the lot heh heh that crazy homer. But judell needtay be careful. The way she puts that food away shnarf rarf shel turn intay a right bloater, but its alright cos fat-bottomed girls they rock! – so says queen. The main thing is tho the main issue is: always me who has to gotay the pakis. I ken i ken i ken, judes always givin me a row for callin it the pakis, gets right angry shakes her head says cmon adam. Ye ken thats a bad word. Ye shouldnt use that word its no right, but i didnt ken! I thought that was the actyool name of the shop THE PAKIS. Parrently its called GKR FOODSTORES but everyone calls it the pakis. No ma fault. Says this to jude shes like no adam, you dont like it when folk call ye mongol do ye? You dont like it when folk call ye spastic?

Naw i says. But i dont mind if folk call me paki!

So im walkin overtay GKR FOODSTORES and im thinkin? Mars cornetto lionbar? Maltesers bounty caramel? Cos it doesnt matter what i get jude still looks at it goes hm. Makes an uglypuppet face. That all ye got adam? What judy! Three packetsay crisps a mars bar and a flake! No its never enough for judy spark on her period hmph hmph she strokes her chin shakes her head so then? Sigh. Guess who hastay go back in the adverts to get more crispsandsweets! Aye yere right muggins here, the boy sparky. Dunno wheeeeere she puts it like just dunno wheeeeere. Anyway she never usedtay eat like that when *dad* was here he made sureay *that*. Hed just say stop stuffin yer face ya fat

And jude nibbled at the chocolate. A corner like. Givin him this *look*. This look like a demon hidin in a bush. Then when him and mam went away well jude ate ate ate much as she liked – who can blame her? So *im* no gonnay tell her she cant eat crispsandsweets when she was dyin to eat them for so long so many many years when mam and dad were still here. Fore they went offtay oz.

Gets intay the pakis says how ye doin mister akram? Mister akrams funny hes like apu from the simpsons dark like a darkie xcept with a bid-bid-bid accent he says oh fine sparky fine today, how are you?

Well i sure could do with a holi-day to san tro-pay mister akram, but otherwise? Im swell!

Very glad to hear it sir he smiles. Especially after your accident at the gala day indeed i heard. Are you still in any pain?

Oh that? i goes. Pfah. Thats nothin. Tell ye its the shrapnel from the war thats givin me gyp. Cant be worryin bout concussion. But what i dont tell apu, em i mean mister akram is aye. Ive got a sore head man and aye. Im seein coloured lights everywhere. Theres lights round yer head the now mister akram so there is but i dont tell him this cos hes laughin.

Shrapnel from the war he goes. Ho ho ho sparky you are a funny boy.

Aye apu, i mean mister akram, those sneaky arackis couldnt get me like. They had a good go but ye ken the arackis (theyre your brothers) if they could shoot straight we wouldnt be thinkin bout goin to war with the buggers would we?

Mister akrams wipin his eyes. Oh sparky. Stop it. Stop it now. Ho ho ho ho.

Whats he laughin at?

Whats he laughin at?

Whys everybody always laughin sometimes man i tell ye i could just. Just effin. Hes *still* laughin? Comedian round here or somethin man if so then hey. Mr comedian? Whats brown and sticky? A stick! Ha ha ha ha you thought it was gonnay be jobbies ya dirty

Me and jude well we like to do these things: tidy up. She washes dishes i dry. When cleanin we listen to either ma music queen the show must go on, or judemusic radiohead creep. Five years since dad wentay oz, five whole years dudes. Three since mam followed him on that hilarious madcap keraaazy adventure. But we look after us and jude looks after me, determineddetermined since mam and dad wentay oz shel keep the house clean takes careay everythin man eeeeevery little thing. Always bent over books or bitsay paper, lamplight shinin got her specs on dabbin a calky-later. She goes dt dt dt. Sigh. Doesnt matter what number jude punches in the calky-later the answers always: sigh. What is the square root of the hypotenyooz of the circumfrins of a right angle? Is it a sigh? Correct! When Judes readin her books – no logo nineteeneightyfour the grapes of raff yaaaaawn – and im readin comics – xmen batman the hulk raaaargh cool! – i lies with ma head on her belly wishin i was a superhero. I could be a superhero. I could eeeeeasily be a superhero yup i hears judes belly. The sounds. Groomph. Gurgle gurgle gurgle. Rmph squeak. Its funny! Shes alive. Shes alive. She is here with me. With sparky. She puts her hand on ma head sings songs by the blue nile (theyre her fayvrit band) under her breath, starlight do you know me she sings. Please dont look at me now. Im falling apart. Sometimes shes bossy like a bosslady wearin bossyboots, okay adam get this tidied now hear me? Move! Gets angry. Cmon. MOVE. Starts pickin up socks shorts rages at the mess locks herself in the toilet i hears her cry aheh aheh aheh. Sometimes at night we cuddles on the couch. She pats ma hair we watches telly we talks bout mam and dad what do ye member of them judy? i says. She shrugs, looks at the telly her face blank blank blank. I says never leave me judy. She looks at me for a second all sortsay heroes and villains in her eyes, mortal kombat. She shrugs says i wont. Then she looks away to the winday, outside outside at the streets sky stars and stars and stars. The stars and stars and stars and stars. I says what ye thinkin bout jude?

Jude?

Ju-dy?

Sometimes i sits on a tea-tray at the toppay the stairs jude says right ye ready adam fwooooooooosh. Whoah hurtlehurtle. When ye hit each step yer jaw goes guh guh guh ye crash intay the phonetable oof tinkle. When we gets bored we watches films – a bugs life and toystory and toystory 2 for me booorin films where nothin happens for jude cityzen kane the searchers doctor zhivago i wanders off halfway man to look for somethin to do. Sometimes i says jude lets play! She says not now adam. And sometimes jude pretends to be darth vader im luke skywalker its the enday the empirestrikesback she stalks me thru the empty house. It echoes. She breathes funny goes cchhohh goes cchhohh. Holds up her lightsaber says obi wan has taught you well luke. You have con*troll*ed your fear. And i leaps out goes noooooooo we strikes lightsabers em broomhandles fksh! Neeoow. Zyooom. Neeoow. Kfsh! And later i hangs off the edgeay the banister jude holds out her hand says join me and we can rule the galaxy as father and son i says never! She lets go and

aaaaaaaaahhhhhhhhh

*

So what can ye say bout her for one her names judy. For two: sometimes jude. Three: judith! Shes a fat cun— i mean cow – ach shuttup dad. And for judys sixteenth birthday we bought her a dress ooh! School dance prom grad-yoo-ay-shin was comin me mam dad clubbed together, gave them someay ma pocket money was gonnay spend on queen cds. Me and mam got so xcited bout the birthdays, and this one dudes? Sixteenth. Special. We plotted: planned. Bought the dress. Ooh nicenshiny was that dress it had sequins on it, looked like fishskin. Fsshhh.

The film we were watchin finished it was titanic. My heart will go oooooooon, aye okay. Just sink the bloody boat. Jude stood up yawn stretch right goodnight. Crack creak went her bones. Aye hen said mam. Jude kissed me kissed mam. Stared in the doorway looked at dad, goodnight dad. Okay goodnight hen dad didnt look round. Turned the telly over – click: news click: sport click: weather – settled on fitbaw, one nil to the rangers bigbelly on show – burp! Hairybellybutton ha ha. I usedtay stick ma finger in dads bellybutton hed go ho! jump gimme a fright ha ha ha ha anyways we waited till we heard heavy footsteps clumpclumpclump go up the stairs clumpclumpclump looked at each other eyebrows raised – me dad mam wai . . . tin . . . for . . . her . . . door . . . to . . . shut— Right! Got the dress out. The fiftyquid dress. Helped them wrap it me and mam giggled said oh aye shel love this, dad said aye we needtay get her out them bloody boots and army jackets mam said oh shush alec thats just her style dad said style? Ive been more stylish pishin against the walls at ibrox! What kinday woman dresses like that anyway? Mam dad glanced at each other silent. I said: it looks like fishskin. I smelled: the sea. Saw: jude slippin slidin thru the waves towards me.

So the mornin comes. Yup yup. Mam wakes jude early wakes me early wakes dad, what? uh? its too early. Ach cmon alec its the lassies sixteenth, aye gnnnr umph give us a minute snnooore. Dad yere fallin back asleep! Wha? Guh?

Outside the livinroom. You betcha dudes. Standin in the lobby while yer mam and dad arrange presents and stuff? Shuft shift. Dancin on the spot? Thats the best bit. Ooh thats the best bit. Oh aye the same every birthday since we were wee: stand at the toppay the stairs, come down get the cards, wait outside the livinroom. Yawn stretch, jude opened the door went in

Pressies!

A magic land fullay pressies. Pressies in a pile on the couch. Kneedeep. Pressies of all shapes and sizes and dee-scrip-shuns, big ones wee ones funny ones soft ones hard ones ones in boxes ones that make a funny noise when ye shake them ones that ye cant shake cos mam says no that might break, sharp ones borin ones mys-tee-ree-us ones daft ones aye all the pressies man, when its ma birthday i jump right in – yahoo! – dive in zif intay a pool made outtay pressies, the breaststroke frontcrawl the butterfly thru wrappin paper ribbons it goes shhh shhh shhh all bout ye, but jude? She just mosied on overtay the couch. Zif shed nothin better to do. Amble amble. Sat down. Picked up a pressie. Unwrap. Some perfume, oh thanks she said spray spray. Sniff. Unwrap unwrap. Cds: radiohead the blue nile suede bellandsebastyin. Unwrap. A book. Jeanette winterson oranges are not the only fruit (course theyre no, apples bananas and pears – oh my!) thanks said jude. Soft smile. Mam nodded. Books! snorted dad like a heffalump, zif the books had insulted him, called him a bighairy monster with a bighairy bellybutton ha ha. Cos he is! He stared at the telly. Blank telly. Then jude she picked up the dress: pressed: felt.

Mams eyes xcited. Go on hen she said, open it!

Dad switched on the telly. Teletext. Fitbaw results. Heavy eyes openin closin blink. Ba-link. Mam slapped his arm take an interest alec, aye em *cough*. Open it hen.

Me jumpin up down clappin raay! Open it jude open it!

she opened it

Fingers workin in out the creases. Findin tape – unpeel. Findin folds – unfold. Was always so careful was jude with the wrappin paper, would lay it aside like fold it back up neat pat pat, we can re-use that shed say, oh shut up jude. Im yer kinda tear kinda rip kinda shred raaaaar lemme at em kindaguy.

She held up the dress.

It looked like liquidmagic.

For yer school prom said mam. Shel look a picture eh adam?

Oh aye i said. Judes fishtail flippin and a-flappin thru the sea: shimmershimmer.

Eh alec? went mam.

Mm? said dad, lookin at jude teletext jude teletext.

Judy held it up xaminin it like it was an antique or special or cursed or burst. Seemed to be starin right intay the dress, right intay its soooouuul right intay the rainbowcoloured sequinned heartay it, ba-doof ba-doof. Its lovely right enough she said, flat as flatpack.

Try it on said mam squeezin her hands together, screwin her eyes shut squirrellike eeee.

Aw mam id better start gettin ready for school its—

Lets see it on ye she said, makin flappyshapes with her hands like a wee girl with a dollandpram set, thats mam. I liked the dress, the scales the sea-quins brightbright. The light on the dress as jude played with it hyp-no-tised: lull. Magic. Drift.

Jude stood. Laid the dress on the couch. Looked at the dress. Looked at the dress. Felt with her hands down her sides. Looked at the dress.

She tried it one way. Tried it another. Tried steppin intay it. Tried hoikin it over her head. Mam helped wriggle it down her back wrigglewriggle. She went its nearly? Is it? Could ye? Jude made like wee steps shuffled hips mam said oh yeve just about. Try the. Me and dad watched, shakin our heads ziftay say women! Aye you said it dad pop daddy-o. Was like a dance routine man: mam and judy wrestlin with this rainbowcoloured sequinned fishskin till it was nearly over judes hips down her legs she did another wriggle then

– sppplit!—

It tore up the back. Everybody froze: musicalstatues. Then dad threw his paper down straight overtay jude Oh for the love of. Shes too fat for it! Jude paused, face peerin round tryin to see. Stay still said mam, cos if she moves not only will the dress tear itll tear a hole in the floor! the earth! the yooniverse! Jude says is it

Dont move says mam, holdin hands up pause.

They prises the dress off. Dad says lotta bloody use *that* was, fiftyquid dress! Can see it in mams face dads face judes face, fiftyquid. Dad chucks it like a glittery slug it hits the couch then shhffft. Slips off. I picks it up.

Rip off goes dad.

Marksandsparks? goes mam.

RIP OFF goes dad, shoulda guessed it was a wasteay bloody grumblegrumble on a lassie who looks like grumblegrumble storms out the room mam goes oh. Oh hen. Yer whole day its ruined judy its ruined, tut mam get a grip! Jude in her pyjamas, thickankles pressed together she looks up at the ceilin but me? I strokes the dress thinks of fishes, jude glidin through an ultramarinekingdom. Im trailin behind, squeakin like a porpoise reep reep reep. Wait for me!

Jude sat on the couch. In amongst all the wrappin paper, head in her hands. She watched me shook her head, smilin. She shook her head, smilin. I dont know why she shook her head, smilin, funny that. Like how yed smile when ye discover theres no toilet roll but yeve already jobbied: justmyluck. That kinday thing. She said why dont ye keep it adam? I said eh? She said keep it. Stood nodded kissed me on the head, just keep it. Em okay. So i did. Still got it. And that liquidmagic fishskin dress made it the best birthday ever dudes, you betcha. And it wasnt even ma birthday.

But Judys never tried on a dress since nope nope, ma sisters kinday queer that way.

**Oh hey hang on dudes i forgot** its fitbaw time. Ya dancer! Im briiiiilliant at fitbaw crash bang wallop. Got changed jude helped me get changed intay the fitbaw kit, ma big game. A chance to shine! Ye never ken i says to jude, there might be talent scouts from falkirk dundeeunited arsenal barcelona intermilan! Aye smiles jude, shakin her head gettin ma fitbawboots out shed polished them last night. Said yel needtay learn howtay polish yer own boots adam i says hm? Pretendin i couldnt hear heh heh. Polish ma own boots? Aye so i will. Do davidbeckham waynerooney bobdylan clean their own boots?

Yel needtay learntay to do a lot more for yerself says jude, puttin the lid back on the bootpolish – clip. I says why? She doesnt answer, just starts foldin the newspaper put down cosay the mess. When we were bairns wed smeeeear the bootpolish on our faces, pretend to be tigers grrroowl, roar and sniff each other pee out in the wild— em the garden. Then later jude started gettin all funny bout it, em adam stop doin that shed say. Cmon adam get away from there, jude totally

Not Intay It. Nope! Nope! She runs the tap wipes her hands. I practises maginary penalties score score score, every one in the backay the net yup. The hotshot scot.

Studs on the concrete. Clack clack clack i thinks: dad would be proud. Clack clack clack i thinks: dad would be pissed!

Getstay the park. Theres the boys the h-glen animalz mostly, cos see the cottages barandlounge? Theyre in a pub league. A league of pubs? Your pub has the best beer but *your* pub serves more flavours of crisps so: score draw. And theyre a man short no-one to play theres no-one to play theyre a man short, mark baxter saw me at the pakis an hour ago says sparky! Ye play fitbaw at all? I says aye man im great he says aw thank christ fore ye ken it im the h-glen animalz bestpal. Bestpal not punchbag. Mental.

Theyve puts me in goals: the cat they call him! Just stand there sparky the h-glen animalz are like, stand there dont move. But how can i no play striker boys (keepy-uppy 1 2 3 oops dropped it) tiptop striker me likes. Doof! One nil. Superadam of the glasgowrangers fitbaw club thats me. Thats sparky! Eh? Eh?

No they goes. Zif like id said to them mibbe we should eh rob a bank or jump off the flats or take out our willies or somethin. No sparky. Yere in goals. Just stay there. Out harms way. Just try and stop the ball if it comes eh?

i stop the ball i stop the ball i stop the ball

Total says that like a hundred times or somethin man re-pe-tish-on. Like how mam usedtay teach me the words when i was wee C-A-T D-O-G C-A-T i stop the ball i stop the ball i stop the ball aaaaaaaaaand heres the action on the dawson park pitch. Oof! bash! ug! The team from the cottages barandlounge are defendin and the team from the chequers barandlounge are on the attack. Its all go here. Neck and neck. Even stevens. And whooooof theres the shot!

i stop the ball i stop the ball i stop the ball

Ball doesnt come near tho.

Even tho ive been telt to stop that muddy little sonofabitch it doesnt come near. No. No. Hands on ma hips man yaaaaawn. Has a think. Feels so good that im playin with the animalz with those wellrespected dudes, they want me. They want me adam spark sparky the C-A-T. Things arent so bad. Sun shines ontay the houses at the sideay the pitch. Shine shine go the windays. Magic cool wonderful, ooh look at them. I looks at them. Then i do some lookin at them and some lookin of course, i do a bit of that too. Most baaayootiful windays ive ever seen man so lovely, like tinsel on a christmas tree or the wrappin on terrysallgold chocolates, whole big wide row of golden windays shinin just shinin. Shine on.

Then big mark baxters runnin at me total angrylook on his face like tom in tomandjer—

Whack!

Ya stupit spastic! mark goes. Why did ye no stop the ball?

I looks. Balls in the net. Otherteam are runnin bout huggin each other man celebratin, we are the champions.

I points at the windays i says:

Gold?

Mark looks at the windays. Everyone movin in like a big squad armytroops round wee sparky here (kfschhh! Squad leader we gottim surrounded). Eh? big mark goes.

Arent they byootiful?

Big mark looks at the windays. Big mark looks at me. Big mark looks mad! What are ye on about ya numpty mark gives it. Ye didnt see them comin? Ye were lookin at the windays and didnt see the ball? Ya tit!

Now now mark i says. Theres really no need for langwidge. The proper word is ya *boob*. This is what i tells judy when she gets the raaaages bout what the calky-later says (sigh) or when shes got too much yooniversity work or when its mam or dads birthday she shouts at the neighbours aye get yer effin dog out ma effin garden fore i cut off its effin, i go jude. Tut tut. Cmon. Theres really no need for langwidge. Aye so mark punches me again – ba doof – head goes boiiing on the old neck there. The otherteam stop cheerin for a look havin enough of a look there otherteam? Aye? Nosy parkers. Nosy peter parker spidermans the lotta yese!

What age are ye? goes mark.

Eighteen i says proudproud.

Mark sighs. Shakes his head. His eyes go wee nasty i sees the light bove his head: blue. Dark blue. Nearly black. Black light? How can that be man? Weeeeird the paranormal world of mys-tee-rious powers. Eighteen and still actin like a *spastic* he spits.

Gon mark somebody says, batter him. I hate that mongol.

Hmph. I am *not* a mongol i xplains to them in the propervoice judy telt me to use when talkin to thickos. And i am not a spastic. I am *simply* adam spark.

One of the boys laughs bendin himself over, steady on sir yel put yer back out. *Simple* adam spark more like, he goes. No a spastic? Aye right. The wee retard was in the bottom class at falkirk high for everythin man, usedtay havetay gotay miss skehal in the special needs!

Miss skehal. Oh. She was nice. Aye. She was nice. Starts thinkin bout miss skehal miss skehal her nicenice voice (read the sentence adam. Kathy and james play bad-min-ton. Can you read that? Bad-min-ton) her nicenice eyes and luvverly perfume smell and fore i ken it? Yep. Ive lost ma con-sin-tray-shin. And thatll do it yep that sure is what ye get for losin the old con-sin-tray-shin sparky ma man. Ye watchin? Ye watchin? Cos here it comes—

Whack! Big mark smacks me again they all move in givin it spaz! spaz! spaz! spaz! like gunfire big mark starts punchin kickin bootin i falls ontay the ground man ontay the grass, mud in yer mouth boot boot kick punch pummel boot oof ah oyah ow eeh aah oof boot boot boot boot boot boot boot i looks up sees the windays: gold. Shinin. Byootiful man.

Speakin of byootiful – ive had sex with a girl! Ooh it was nice, but kinday messy. I was fifteen she was thirteen shed moved in next door. She chapped the door when jude was out mam was out, she said hi im sharon yer new neighbour i said em. Oh. Aye. Cos she shore were purty, like they say in merica. Ribbons in her hair and lipstick she had these wee? These wee? Yep she shore were purty. Aye i said. Then: em. And for good measure: uh. Didnt ken where to put maself, funny feelins ahem. Sharon soon relaxed me tho. She was good that way. In ma room we were playin records – queen! – she didnt like queen i was tryin to get her to like queen. I waaaaant to breeaaak freeeee i sang. Cmon everybody likes that song? i said. Sharon shook her head laughed havin none of it oh adam youre so funny. Nice hair nice laugh nice knees. Remember likin her knees specially, round and white like eggshells. She was shufflin cards she said hm why dont we play? I said okay what game she said poker. I said i dont ken howtay play poker. She said pontoon? Dont ken pontoon. She said brag? She said rummy? She said snap? Oh i ken howtay play snap! Fine she said then smiled patted the bed pat pat. Cmon wel play strip snap. Strip snap? Well anytime one of us gets a snap the other person hastay take off a piece of their clothes ooh okay.

Snap! Socks. Snap! Earrings. Snap! Jumper. Snap! Jeans. Snap! Queen t-shirt. Snap! Bra. Snap! Pants. Snap! Snap! Snap! Snap snap snap snapsnapsnapsnapsnapsnapsnaaaaaa ooh. Whoah! What was *that* dudes?

Didnt really see her again after that – she moved out. Member ma mam arguin with her parents bout somethin, shoutin, callin the police they said. Mam said he doesnt ken any better learning difficulties anyway *she* came ontay *him* is that so well thats not how our sharon tells it. Locked up castrated they said, i stood in the front garden and waved as sharon left, but her mam and dad hissed *dont look* forced her intay the car then drove off neeeeooooow sharon didnt look. Nope not once.

Nice, but like i say kinday messy.

Gets in from the fitbaw ooh oyah. Intay the livin room puts down ma sports gear oof. Jude goes shh adam the news is on, sittin in frontay the telly this is the news arms crossed harumph. That jude man shes unreal, just takes things far too seriously like. Jeezo i mind this time when she was fifteen, before mam and dad wentay oz, she was makin coffee started readin the label went where did this coffee come from?

Tescos mam said.

No i mean *where* exactly?

Em mam went. The tea and coffee aisle.

And dad muttered somethin bout bloody lefties stared at jude over his paper and that jude that judy ho ho she said *fashist* banged down the jar went uptay her room slammed the door – slam! – in her room was a big pictureay tom york lookin moooody with his squinty eye his funny wee ferretyface jude played songs by the blue nile. Her heroes. She likes a lottay rubbish man the blue nile bob dylan radiohead themanicstreetpreachers the smiths hey and publicenemy. Fight da powah! Sometimes yed knock on judes door say judy? but she wouldnt answer say judy? but she wouldnt answer! All ye could hear was the blue nile at other side of the door singin wish me well and hold me. Wish me well and let me go.

Over and over.

See what i mean by see-re-us? So now shes watchin the news whats happenin ooh its bout the war. Judy judy whats— shh! she says. Theres george dubya bush his straight face all see-re-us but looks confused, zif hes tryin to be cool only somebody keeps fartin. Hes wishin theyd stop fartin. He says saddam has failed to comply with the weapons inspectors and the united states has been forced to move into (paarp!) STOP DOING THAT. Jude sees ma black eye, big thumpin blackeye wha-doomp wha-doomp wha-doomp on the old face.

Adam? she goes, crossin the room scuttlescuttle like shelob, touches ma face. Whats happened to yer eye? Who did that to ye?

Em i says. Ahem. Ye see judy. Well judy.

Jude steps close here it comes wait for it

Have you been in a fight?

O jobbies.

Em aye i just admits.

Judes touchin the old face there oyah ow cmon! Watch what yere doin!

That sore? she goes.

No i says meanin: Yes.

Jude looks at me, eyebrows furrowed staaaaaare. Thinks i dont notice her lookin at me but i ken i ken i ken what her looks mean, they mean. They mean she thinks that im just a poor boy nobody loves me hes just a poor boy from a poor family spare him his life from this ach sodoff

Ye dont havetay be brave judy says, just tell me if its sore adam, starts to lift up ma fitbaw shirt sees the big purple broozes ba-doomp ba-doomp ba-doomp. Jude looks at the broozes shakes her head the light round hers dark dark judy spark.

Say it again: o jobbies!

See this minds me – when me and jude were at hallglen primary school man the fights, the fights dudes! This is whatd happen id just be sittin at playtime mindin ma own bizniz like webbin up wee primary ones pfsshhhh get out of *that* greengoblin. Or countin clouds or hangin from the crossbar on the ashpark swing swing im an ape. A monkey! Ooh ooh scratchscratch. Then whatd happen? Sheesh yed get some dude whod take how do ye say? eck-sep-shin to this hed go sparky. Hey sparky? Mongolboy? Tithead? Dickbreath? And id look theres a gang of them the look on their faces said GANG. The eyes said G the nose said A the mouth said NG! Id think dickbreath? How can ye have breath like a dick! Yuck oogh spit. But id mind what dad usedtay say hed say smack them first adam before they smack you, and other greatest hits like: dont be a pansy all yer life son but hey – fightins no really ma *thang* dudes. Nope that is just not sparkys scene. Ma style of fightin comes from the mo lo jing temples of old japan and has some reeaaal special moves, the first is ye say cmon boys whats the problem? They usually say youre ma problem dumbo. Glare. Okay so. Then ye use yer *second* special move right what ye do is, if yere eatin trebormints or polos or starbursts ye hold them out ye say want one? That throws them! They go oh ta sparky dont mind if i do, pick one hmm whys it always the strawberry? Theyre the best tut. They puts the sweets in their mouth chew they go mmmm. Cheers sparky. Ken pal youre alright, its no true the things they say bout you and yer sister. That works sometimes, like ma mam usedtay say niceness breeds niceness. Dad would usually mutter hmph, niceness breeds a kick in the baws, but if *that* special move doesnt work ye use yer *ultra* special move dudes watch this.

Ye screw closed yer eyes and summon yer power. All yer will. All yer energy. And ye focus and let it build up inside ye man rooooar it burns it burns it burns right thru ye then what do ye do?

Run like hell.

Sometimes jude tho heh heh sometimes judy would come, aye some wee dude would go round to the primary sevens playground go pssst? Judy spark? Yer wee brothers about to get a leatherin shed say that right? Stomp round the corner dumf dumf dumf everyoned clear a space zif by magic. Cos they all thought she looked like a boy she fighted like a boy had fists like a boy, fee fi fo fum. Whos pickin on ma wee brother? shed growl low in the throat sometimes the folk pickin on me would go whoah no messin with you hen but sometimes? Theyd go aye. What about it ya *man*? Then jude would fix them with that eye, fee fi fo fum just step forward all the heavy things in the world man theyd step forwards with her then –

fistkickdoof

– theyd back off run scram boys! disappear in a clouday smoke and horseshoes and hairpins. Shed turntay me say ye awright adam? They hurt ye? And id kinday go all wee and wee id grin up at her – beam!

Aye theres nobody better at providin a pickmeup than judith spark. So she dabs at ma cuts and broozes with tlc and tcp – ooh! oyah! – then puts me to bed kisses ma head mwah! I looks up at her sadsmile i says comin in jude? She says nope adam too much to do. You just get some rest wee man, yeve been through the wars. Oh aye so i have jude, but judgin by the news on telly im no the only one! So now everythins okay again, cos see ma sister judy and me? We are the champions.

**Oh here that minds me i like queen!** Might have telt ye this before but ye cant tell folk often enough bout queen nope theyre the best band theres ever been. Aye man. Freddie mercury brian may roger taylor john deacon: thats queen. First heard them in the film highlander like, when me and mam and dad and jude usedtay rent videos. Dad would burp fart mam would go oh *alec*. Jude would fart even louder paaaarp mam would go oh *judith*. Then id win paaaaaaaaarp mam would go ADAM but dad and judy would be endin themselves heh heh and mam would leave the room cosay the smell. Thats dis*gust*in. But shes smilin. A mile wide. A smile wide.

Anyway: highlander. Film was great! Most amazin wonderful ncredible film i think ive ever seen, didnt understand it. Somethin to do with this guy connor macloud who cant die he says i am connor macloud of the clan macloud, born 1518 in the village of glenfinnan on the shores of loch shiel in scotland. And i am immortal. But his wife dies its so sad, mam gret. But she always gret. Even before dad went away to oz she still gret (but after dad left she gret and gret and gret and gret and also took up fartin, sad wee farts like somebody sighin fooooo . . . They had no smell. Mam didnt even notice shed done them, but i noticed heh heh) anyways! – this connors in noo yawk a bigscarydudes chasin him i have somethin to say (he says) its better to burn out than to fade away! There can be only one! Rooooooaaaar. They have a fight bosh biff takethat connor macloud cuts the bigscarydudes head off says there can be only one and everythin explodes!

Sean connerys in it.

I like that bit at the start when queen are singin gimme the prize at a wrestlin match connor maclouds watchin it hes nervous gonnay havetay fight for his life later with a sword might lose his head so queen sing dont lose your head connor shuts his eyes hes back home centuries ago on the hills and highlands and in scotland all hells breakin loose and

in scotland all hells breakin loose and

Brian mays guitars gives it schhhang! rrroawr! nneeew! and that dudes *thats* when i kent they were the best band ever. That they could do the music for this brilliant brilliant film? bout lovin? bout livin forever? Cos all the yooniverse is in queens songs and when i listenstay them i curls up i cries mama. Just killed a man. Put a gun against his head pulled the trigger now hes

now hes

Typical. Triggers not workin.

Whenever theyre on telly they rock! Freddie well hes got this moustache and brian may hes got bigbig hair and roger taylor hes the goodlookin drummer – d-doom tsh! – sometimes he wears shades aye but john deacon just goes dood dood dood. Another one bites the dust.

Me and dad usedtay watch ma queen greatest hits video. Freddie mercury singin i want to break free, dressed as a wife. Got big boobs ha ha dad would grunt say what do ye thinkay *him* then adam? Id say oh dad queen are great hed say what! You ever grow uptay be like that son il leather ye but i thought hmm. Im hardly likely to grow uptay have *boobs* am i dad?

Wouldnt mind but (fondle fondle) soooooooo i listenstay queen when its sunny outside. And i listenstay queen when its rainin. They goes im just a poor boy nobody loves me, hes just a poor boy from a poor family spare him his life from this mon-stros-a-tee.

Then i minds: freddie mercurys in oz. Like mam and dad. Wonder if theyve met.

spare him his life from this monstr

Oooh and sometimes i sings queen songs between the chicken sandwich please sparky! And the: more fries sparky! Then i gets a good idea on the burgers – sesame seeds of rye.

Like that? Tee hee.

Today angies bawlin out poor steve. Five minutes late for his shift she said right thatll come out yer breaktime. But thats to be expected man. This company demands The Best. We got telt this on our first day on the trainin video this merican dude big shinysmile big orange tan says all over the world people know what they want when they eat here. They want speedy service, they want *friendly* service, and they want the good wholesome food that only we can provide. So youre thinking: how do we achieve this? One word. Teamwork. If a crewmember fails in his or her duties then it affects all of us. It just wont work no other way. And *thats* why we are number one in the fastfood market. Thats why

– beam!—

We are *winners*.

Steve well? He kens this. Still looks glum tho man angie bawls shouts but no time to feel sorry for him ken how? Theres another big waveay customers comin right atcha with hungryhungry looks. Fries. Scoop. Cheeseburger sir? No problem. Fl-ip! Straight intay a bun, lettuce tomato and (eugh) gherkin. There ye go aaaand thats yer large fries aaaand theres some napkins for ye. Have a nice day sir. Hello can i help you? Would you like to go large with that?

Angie prades up and down the floor like a tiger lookin for prey grrrrrrroowl rolls her shoulders bigcatlike. Im tryin to be good so i can win employee of the month. Introducing! Emp! loy! ee! of! the! month! Adam! (applause) SPAAAAARRK! (crowd goes wild). Keep thinkin bout the video. One word: teamwork. If a crewmember fails in his or her duties then it affects all of us. And i ken that one of the qual-i-ties that gets ye employee of the month is showin in-ish-ya-tive. So. Decides to clean the chip-pan. Clean the chip-pan? Il clean the chip-pan. And what do ye clean with:

Water.

Aye its a bit murky in there sure enough, brown sludge and fried fries gloop shmoop. Goes to get a pailay water to throw on the hotfat carryin it back maginin ma face on that poster: employee of the month. Ma smiley face smilin down. Id be happyproudchuffed. Prince of the yooniverse! Like that queen song on highlander. Thatd be? Thatd be?

Oh thatd be me.

Grunt gnnt i hauls the water its sloppin out the sides. Somebody walks past nearly skids – hey watch it. Getstay the chip-pan, fizzin its bubblin away blb blb. Rests the pail on the edge just bout to pour it in when who comes over? Angie. Im glad, cos it means shel see me showin in-ish-ya-tive but is she a happy angie? Nooooo. Bright spark she says. What the hell ye doin with that water? Just bout to tell her im cleanin the chip-pan anj, what do ye makeay *that* when she goes you about to pour that in there? And the look on her face is hot hot hotter than the sun i thinks hmm. Puts the pail on the floor um. Better keep quiet shh.

No anj i says. Uh. Just restin this pail here a second. Was gettin tired ken? And healthandsafety angie: always take a break if yere tired. Cos Thats How Accidents Happen.

You stupit? angie says. Ye dont put water anywhere near hot chipfat!

Aye i says (gulp) i ken angie. Just

Just nothin she says. Get yer stuff and go home. Il decide what to do with ye in the mornin. But mop up the water on this floor first bright spark fore somebody sli—

Aaaggh goes reno, as she skids cross the floor lands on her arse oof.

Angie stares, simmersimmer goes her eyes. I mops the water, whistle whistle, all the while preventin yet more accidents. Yup. Adam spark has his safety head on dudes. Goes upstairs gets changed leaves thinkin aye. One step closertay employee of the month!

Falkirks busy. All the peeps spendin money draggin the weans along to get new shoes glum, punters gontay the bookies to put a fiver on a wee certainty. Like dad did. Every day. Bookies pub pint burp: that was dad he was T-O-P-M-A-N. And ive made ten pounds forty today man *ten pounds forty* and even tho jude really needs the money (shel only spend it on effin marsbars and rolos anyway) im buyin a cd. Im buyin a cd! Goes overtay sleeves records straight to the Q section dudes and!

queen 1 flick

queen 2 flick

sheer heart attack flick

a night at the opera flick

a day at the races flick

news of the world flick

jazz thegame flashgordonsoundtrack hotspace theworks akindofmag—!

I holds up a cd ive no seen before. Got a picture of queen on the cover freddie roger brian john but their faces are joined intay one: freddierogerbrianjohn. Whats this? i says to the guy behind the counter, he holds it up. Looks at the cover. Oh he says thats the miracle, 1989, lead single was i want it all which reached um . . . number three. Ye never heard this one?

Nooooo! i gasps. Any good?

He just looks at me zif im stupit he says its eh . . . queen?

It sure is! I falls down ontay ma knees a queen album ive no heard! A queen album ive no heard! I says it over and over til i cant breathe, a new queen album a new queen album a new queen album, the joy the goodness the good good goodness. Everythins mazin. Theres birds sailin right cross the sky whistlin disney tunes and airyplanes soarin with big banners sayin a new queen album! And people dancin. People dancintay the new queen album. And fireworks goin off boom boom crack boom pop and all the people below they go oooooh. They go aaaaah. They go queeeeen.

I asks the guy to play me the cd – pronto! He does – pronto! And i stands there in the middleay sleeves records with ma big red brianmay guitar while the guy at the counter just stares shakes his head and freddie sings i want it all. And i do want it – right now! Puts down ma guitar just bout to pay for the cd for the miracle, just bout to give him ma special cashsplash man when i sees them.

Out the winday.

Across the road from sleeves records theres a sidestreet. Bean row its called. Like that joke – i dont want to know what its *been* i want to know what it is *now*. Leads uptay baxters wynd. Kinday a quiet street shh just a wee secondhand furny-tyoor shop on it nothin else no.

Xcept?

Can see up the street from where im standin. And theres ma sister judy. And shes with a girl. And theyre kissin.

I watches them for a while. Just watches hmm. The picture is freezeframed: judith spark kissin a person another person who. Who Is Not Me. Ma guts are goin rowf rumfl gnmp.

And after what feels like years somethin inside me man? Pchooooow. Xplodes. I walks out the shop cross the street right up bean row, stomp stomp stomp i am the ncredible hulk. Dont make me angry. You wont like me when im

Jude sees me. Adam she smiles kinday puzzled, what are *you* doin here?

Never mind that i glares, glarey stare. Whos this?

The girls got short spiky hair shes skinny. Loadsay earrings in her ear she totally stares at me. Stares. At. Me! Oh dont you dare ya

Never mind that she jerks with her thumb, whos he?

Maryann jude sighs. This is ma brother adam. Remember the one *i told you about*.

Oh maryann says then: ohhhh. Zif shes just clicked.

Well adam jude says. Cough. This is em? Maryann.

Everythins still. Press pause. Jude shuffles. Aye? i goes and ma hands feel like theyre in boilin water man, tight hot gnng. So why was maryann *kissin* ye?

Jude laughs oh ha ha ha ha ha she goes pattin her chest, sayin the word ha like shes teachin it to an alien. She looks at maryann, she em jude says. She wasnt *kissin* me adam.

She *was* judy. I saw yese from over there.

She was . . .

Jude looks at maryann again.

She was uh . . . showin me her earrings.

Ma fists are still simmerin in that big pan i goes what?

Maryann nods. Quick quick. Yes thats right adam she says ive just had a new *earring* put in and your sister wanted to see it and so i . . .

. . . leaned over says judy. To show it to me. It must have ha ha ha adam it must have looked like we were kissin.

I takes ma hands out the boilin water puts them in ma pockets. Still fists. Gng. Hmm it did that jude i says, it did look a *lot* like yese were kissin.

But we werent jude says. Look this is what we were doin.

Maryann leans over puts her ear nextay jude. Makes a face like shes showin ye howtay work a dyson – hey presto!

See? jude goes.

Must admit hm did look like kissin. Easy mistake to make. Could be true but. But shed better not be tryin to

Ye wouldnt lie to me judy? i says. Ye wouldnt lie to yer brother who loves ye?

Jude swallows. Shakes her head. Course no adam.

Who loves ye more than anythin. Anythin in the world. Even queen.

Jude shakes her head again. No adam she says quietly. I wouldnt lie to ye.

I stares intay her eyes.

stares

in

tay

her

eyes she doesnt blink not once so

Silly sparky! Silly silly silly sparky! Trust me. Trust me to be a total eejit well thats just typical of the boy sparky here, a clueless jobby if ever there was one! Em jude im so sorry i mean? I thought? Thats okay she goes and smiles this big smile. Maryann smiles too. Its like weve all been watchin a guy on the tightrope hes wobbled nearly fell – gasp! – but hes made it. Hes made it to the other side and now wer all smiles and clappin, a big hand for the great ronaldo! And everythins fine and judy wasnt lyin to me or tryin to get off with someone cos – ha ha – she kens what she would get, she *kens* what shed get. Oh dearie me im so relieved i says. Whoof! Puts ma hand on ma chest. Thats alright adam jude goes takin ma arm. Ye werent to ken.

Naw i says sheepishlike, just dont want. Just dont want anybody *kissin* ye jude.

Judy opens her arms oh adam she says. I walks over, ma legs feel like theyve melted. Falls intay her: soft. Warm. Jude. She cuddles me pats ma back says its okay. Im still here. Im still here for ye adam. Maryann stands apart kinday watchin us. Shufflin on the spot touchin her ears em. Funny coloured lights just bove her head blue. Red. Blue. Oh cmere i tells her. Cmere maryann lets see yer earrings! She goes aye em okay then steps over carefully zif shes walkin past a sleepin wolf shh. Dont wake it. The coloured light bove her head changes from bluered to orange, soft orange. She holds out her ear me and jude well we look at it go whoaah maryann thats smart. Her earrings are cool for cats like gold rings with different jyools in them? Byootiful. Baaayootiful. Oh aye i can see why jude wantedtay have a right good look.

Next day: back at work. Busy. Quickquick. Goin like doublesharpish so many peeps wantin fries. Angies on ma case all day man, watchin every single thing im uptay Every Single Thing. Obviously checkin me out for employee of the month ma-tee-ry-al. Sweats lashin off me man phew, dumps the fries in the pan ffffshhhhhhh lifts out the ones that are beepin: beepbeepbeepbeepbeep. Slams them on the counter scoop. Theres yer small. Theres yer meejum. Theres yer large. Theres yer small. Theres yer meejum. Theres yer large. Small. Meejum. Large. Small meejum large. Smallmeejumlarge. Smallmeejumlargesmallmee jumlargesmallmeejumlarg—

Jeezo! Tellin ye. If it wasnt for the fact that a visit to this place makes yer day sometimes i could just

But hey. Maryanns earrings really were byootiful.

And judy loves me just me.

And theres a new queen cd in ma bedroom and its the miracle.

The miracle.

But ken what else is a miracle: these powers the superpowers dudes.

Well superpowers is the only way i can like *describe* them em. Spiderman got bit by a dodgy spider ouch hulk that gammablast superman well he fell from krypton didn't he. And after that they could climb walls! lift cars! leap tall buildings at a single bound! But now straaaange things are happenin to me too dudes. So watch out. But for what and what for? Mibbe cos it is a time of war. It is a time of heroes. It is a time of war and heroes. And whoah up steps the incredible adam spark, cape billowin in the wind he lifts his head. He hears the call. Theme music. Ever since the merican football – get out the way! bash boof! – il just be walkin down the street havin a wee stroll ken mibbe goin overtay the pakis sorry GKR FOODSTORES watchin telly or playin with maself and i sees lights. Round everyone man. Bove their heads its baaayootiful its lovely its cool its. Scary is what it is. Sometimes that lights red blue pink purple green yellow sometimes black. Black. Black as the aceay spades oh aye. Tried to work out what these colours mean man they. They come on. They come on if i just con-sin-trate:

Blue. Banged ma toe gainst the bedpost bang ow! Looked up intay the mirror was blue light spillin out from ma mouth ma eyes. Blue-ish. Bluey. Blimey! I thought thats not right dudes. Sure that wasnt there last time we all looked!

Orange. Mister akram said hello to me in the pakishop yesterday, orange light. Im tryin to pay for ma milk butter dailybread, mister akrams like hows the bump on the head today sir? Any problems? And im like no no apu – em mister akram everythins fine, but all the while im lookin at them orangetangerine threads workin their way in out his nostrils. No side effects at all mister akram i mutters, then i gets the hell outtay there dudes. Head down. Vamoose!

Grey. All the people workin in the restaurant man theyre just con-sin-tray-tin on what theyre doin and the lights grey. Dull. Like smoke. Twentyregalkingsize.

Black? On the news man bout the war on arack there was all these arackis wailin and a-moanin cos of the mericans hey the light bove everybodys head mans black just black. Like somebodyd painted the air with tar. Evil dead. Brr.

Yellow! Yesterday i saw this woman holdin a baby. She was jigglin it up and down makin the baby laugh and the yellow light from the baby and the woman was so strong man so lovely i hadtay look away. Dazzle dazzle. All day i felt buzzin man – happy delighted funky. Wanted to cuddle folk and go see you? Youre a bloody good bloke. And see you missus? So are you. And the weans who come in for their large fries and coke? Yellow! yellow! yellow! yellow! The photay of mam and dad that jude keeps nextay her bed? Theyve got their arms round each other theyre laughin grinnin, say cheese! They must be at a party or somethin man con-grat-yoo-lay-shins. Theyre smilin. And in the photay theres coloured light round them round their heads i might no ken much but i ken this. The blue light means sad. The yellow light means happy. And see the light round mam and dad in the photay? Its yellow. So yellow.

Red. Angie man well shes always on the warpath man her lights red like a volcano rruummmmmmbbbble. And judes lights red! Specially when shes on bout the pollytiks man whoof red like a big blood flood, but when i sees her with that girl maryann? With the earrings? Shes been comin round sometimes her and jude sit up watchin telly they laugh they laugh they laugh – when shes gone jude listens to her music the blue nile dudes: a walk across the rooftops. She smiles hugs the cushion. I am in love she sings. I am in love with you. And judes lights yellow soft like melted butter looks like a child, makes me feel? Makes me feel?

Tell ye how it makes me feel.

Me and jude usedtay have these mice. Begged mam for them oh please mam oh please please please let me get mices, pleeeeease il take careay them every day il feed them love them take careay them and so? For ma birthday i got three wee mice. But they were crap. They just usedtay like scutter in the cage and birl on this wheel man drrit drrit drrit drrit i couldnt sleep! Scutterscutter. Drrit drrit drrit drrit. Scutter. Scutterscutter. Drrit drrit drrit drrit drrit drrit drrit. Jeezo so one day i went over lifted this mouse out its cage man squeeze just squeezed it. Gnnnnnnnng. It squeaked it squeaked then its head xploded body just went crumple blooogh. There was like blood and fur all over ma hand man yuk.

I looked at ma hand. This dead mouse. Just this dead mouse. I felt sad. Sad for the dead mouse it was just stupit and pointless why was it made? What for? I felt just like that dead mouse in ma hand man stupit and pointless aye thats me. Thats sparky! A wasteay space. So nstead of killin the other mice i just let them out.

Ye did what? went dad throwin his dailyrecord down rustleshake. Ye let them out! Aw adam for godsake yere a hopeless case so ye are, ya clueless dense bloody

I ken dad i just says. I ken.

But for months after ye could hear these mices scutterin all over the house squeakin spark-ee. Spark-ee! Why did ye let us go spark-ee? What did we do wrong? Why didnt you love us spark-ee? Cos yese are stupit and pointless i tried to tell them. Tried to scream this hands clamped over ma ears, cos yese are stupit and pointless and yese dont deserve to live!

Dunno if they heard.

Anyway when maryanns round and her and jude are watchin telly laughin ha ha ha ha ha and i sees the yellow light round judes head? Thats how i feel. Like that stupit dead mouse. Like jobbies. Like shit.

**Heeeeey dudes im with the h-glen animalz** wer walkin down by the canal to tammyhill for a bittay bother with the t-hill posse. Theres me mark baxter brendan fogarty dullyin grant. Dont forget knobend. Met at the chipshop, judy sent me for fish suppers but i met mark baxter and what can ye do? Shrug. Ye ken the score. Yawright there sparky he smiles that hammerheadsharksmile swingin his big arms bigstyle. What ye uptay? No much i goes mouthtight. The way ye are when yer dad asks how yer day at school was: ye say fine. Even tho it wasnt nope nope never was fine, boof bash ug! Hold the mongol down and. That the new rangers away top? brendan goes. Aye i goes. Smart goes knobend. Aye smart goes jason. Int it smart dullyin? goes mark. Aye well smart goes dullyin. They all stand there outside the chippy lookin at ma rangers away top smart. Well smart. Total smart.

They stares at me.

Im wonderin if theyre gonnay try and. Like last time. So get ready to run sparky! Just. In. Case.

So what em? i says, whats the um? Theyre just lookin at me. Eyes. Eyes. Eyes. I blows out like a big gustay wind says anyway boys! Better get back fore these get cold cos—

Listen goes mark, dont be too hasty sparky. Wer goin downtay tammyhill to see if we can find their crew, ye up for a bang?

Fireworks?

A bang ken? grant says. A rumble. A bittay boxin?

Aw aye i says. No bother.

Naw laughs brendan. Plenty of bother!

They starts gigglin like gremlins hee hee hee but when mark glares they stop: Cut.

They telt mick martin we shat our knacks at the martell last week.

When it was *them* shat *their* knacks says brendan, sour face like hes eatin a dishcloth – mmew.

Knobend goes aye i was like that – mon then! Mon then ya crapbags! MON THEN! Starts actin out the scene, shoutin at some invisible crew come-ahead style. Mon then il take all of yese, you you you you. Cmon il KILLYESE IL KILLYESE! AAAAAAAAHHHHHHH! AAAA AAAHHHHHH! AAAAAAAAHHHHHHHHH!

Everyone stares.

Steady on mark goes.

Em knobend goes. Stands. But em. They shat themselves ken?

Christ who wouldnt! mark says. With that display! Then he turns to me seriouslike says comin sparky?

Im holdin the fish suppers. The fish suppers seemtay be makin the decision. Cos i ken how hungry judes boundtay be, just infay the yooniversity studyin like but im pinocchio when the baddudes ask him to gotay the land of drinkandlaughs then pinocchio turns intay a donkey.

Hee haw! hee haw! hee always calls me that! Thinkin if *im* with the h-glen animalz then mibbe next time theyll put somebody *else* in goals and mibbe if *hes* distracted by sunlight on the windays and lets in a goal then itll be *me* laughin and hammerin *him* no like *me* thats gettin laughed at or hammered and *il* no havetay go hometay jude, get her upset get her upset get her upset, make sense? Totally. I throws the fish suppers intay the air boots them: chips and bitsay fish go flyin everywhere like an xploded fishin boat. Aye! i shouts. Mon! i snarls. Lets go! i roars. So:

I like flowers. Theres flowers along the edgeay the canal, nice ones aye, but ye cant see them cosay the dark cosay the darkness, like theyre madeay soot or ashes. Everybodys laughin jokin and im partay the crew. The animalz. The firm. Like these are ma boys and theyll defend me and tell ye – dont mess. Wer hard as nails. We are the dudes. Still cant help think what happened to pinocchio when he went off with the badboys: became a badboy. Hee haw! hee haw! Wheres jiminy cricket? Where is that pesky cricketdude, or jude, when ye need em?

We walks thru tammyhill searchin for their crew and when peeps pass we totally staaaare at them. Come ahead then? Square go? Nobody starts. Nope nope. We rove bout for an hour then go intay a shop and hassle a paki mark goes what ye lookin at osama? I goes where is it yer from mate? Pakiland? Everybody laughs, pakiland they go. Good one sparky. I says em is that no where pakis are from? They laugh even harder. Heh heh. I must be funny. Im the boy. I am the boy. A goodlookin lassie passes tell ye – could go ten rounds with her! The boys all laugh. Ten rounds with her sparky? Aye yer fullay the patter tonight man. Mark slaps ma back. Hiy hen! i shouts. Show us yer snitch!

Her snitch? goes craig.

Aye i says. Bet shes got a great snitch.

A great snitch he says. Listentay it.

Aye sparky they go sniggersnigger. Shes got a great *snitch* im sure.

Later we decides to do the fireblanket everybodys darin each other, i dare ye i dare ye i doubledare ye. The fireblanket works like this what ye do is take a sheetay newspaper and put dogs jobbies on it. Then ye put it on somebodys doorstep set firetay it. Ring the bell: go! Guy opens the door sees the doorstep on fire. Stamp stamp stamps it out ah! Oyah! Fire! Jobbies on his shoes heh heh.

I gets dared.

Mark gets paper.

Knobend finds jobbies brendan uses a stick to scr scr scrape it ontay the paper man thats *rotten*. Boof! I has a bit look. To see if anybodys watchin but: quiet. Reep reep reep (thats the jiminycrickets) i carries the paper by the edges no wantin any dogs jobbies on me, puts it on the doorstep. Careful careful. Dont spill the jobbies. The boys are like watchin from behind a car, aye mad mental h-glen animalz. Gon sparky goes mark. Light it!

Takes out the matches. Kkrrrrppp. Flame. I looks at the flame dance. Dance for me. Its sortay like baaayootiful the flame, sortay like a whole world in there that i could just step intay aye. Im bout to try. Im just bout to try and step intay that flame intay that prettypretty deepworld when i hears sparky! Sparky just light the thing hurry up!

Em. Puts the match to the paper and whoooooooooooooof it lights like a bonfire man oh no what do i? Em em. Ring the bell. I rings the bell stands there. Stands there rings the bell. The heat on ma face man, the heat is on. The heat is o-on.

Run sparky! they shouts. Run ya stupit

Door opens. A wee lassies there. She sees the fire her eyes go: oh. The colour bove her head mans a bright! bright! purple! flashin! She doesnt scream no. Just backs away. Em i says. Em. Dont worry hen i says. Em. I looks bout. I looks bout. The h-glen animalz are runnin away down the street – theyre off! All arms and legs and donkeyvoices. The girls sortay lookin at the fire like its gonnay burn down her house her dolls her wee letters to her pals her mammy her daddy that are proberly still here no like ma mam and dad, no like mine. Nope. Nope. The purple star round her heads like flash flash cant stand it. Cant run. No dont cry hen, sparky to the rescue. The incredible adam spark!

i have the powe

Jumps ontay the fire jumps ontay it stampstampstampstampstamp till the fires out man smoulder smoulder phew!

Sorted. Clap-claps ma hands zif im clearin dust off them but: looks to see this big dude standin starin. Armsfolded. I grins. Saved her? i says but ma smile soon falls doomf. The fires out now mister i says yer wee lassies fine eh, then i looks down sees ma shoes which are smokin which are burnt which are

Jobbies.

What happened next like on a questionay sport: pause. Did the keeper throw the ball intay his own net? Did the jockey fall off his horse? Did the referee get punched doof! Well. I stamped out the jobbies like, saved the wee lassie, saved the yooniverse man but was the guy happy?

Nooooo. His light was burnin red he grabbed me ya dirty wee. Badoof! Smackerooni straight to the jaw there see that? Tried to hit me again but i wasnt hangin round, no chance! I ran man. Nyooooof. Ran the drexion the h-glen animalz had ran gasp gasp gasp gasp gasp there they were man, laughin their heads off. Ha ha bonk oh sparky. Yer some hoot. Dancin on the fireblanket? Oh sparky ye can hang about with us anytime.

Really? i says. Yese mean it?

Oh aye goes mark bent over. Thats entertainment likes. Ye cant beat that! And for yer next assignment sparky we want ye to go intay that pakishop and steal us some buckfast.

Yese serious!

You bet.

What a day!

What a proud proud day like a grad-yoo-ay-shin or a gala day or a happy birthday to ya or a here comes the bride da da dada all those special days roooolled intay one man cos like gettin smacked off the big dude was worth it, well worth it. Cos now the h-glen animalz want me with them yo. Im the boy! Who needs jiminy cricket? Reep reep now ya effin

I strides intay the pakishop head held high hear them laughin behind me i thinks hey. Im the boy. Oh yed better watch out world cos i am definitely the boy.

The falkirk wheel. Whoah man its massive ye hearday it? No really a wheel at all like dudes nope nope, more like em like em this lift? this crane? this winch? that sits outside camelon waitin waitin waaaaaaitin hands on its knees bored till oh! A boat! And the falkirk wheel goes huf lifts the boat rotates bighuge arms and carries the boat from like the union canal (that comes from embra) to like the forthandclyde canal (that comes from glesga) cradles the boat from canal to canal then – egh! Drops it. No even a splash just: rippleripple. Ooh thanks goes the boat, no problem says the huge falkirk wheel standin proudbighonest gainst the grey falkirk sky, hands on hips a giant giant. Like galactus out the silversurfer comics. It salutes the boats, and the peeps of falkirk? They sleep well. They sleep well.

Me and jude goestay see the falkirk wheel one saturday everybodys always talkin bout it weve no seen it, ive no seen jude for a few days, shes always at the library. Or as the mericans say – the goddam library! Dunno why she has to get so dressedup to gotay the library – spends ages on her hair face clothes fore goin out but why? Whats happenin at the library goin down at the library whats new at the library, jude lets do somethin today! You and me! This mornin i pulled the covers off her bed, grabbin and a-clutchin at a corner – yank. Like pullin the cloth off a table but leavin the flowers standin, jude squeals adam! reaches to grab the covers pulls them uptay her shes naked but thats okay seen her naked lots and lots and lotsay times: in the bath ooooor when shes gettin changed ooooor when we usedtay lie in the grass, when we were wee. Birds. Bumblebees. Dandelions. The smell of summer jude summer. Drift. Bzzzzzz went mister bumblebee. Didnt sting us no nope. Cosay the love.

So! Now dudes shes got the brightalarmed red over her head covers pulled uptay her neck, doesnt want me to see! Shes goin um goin *cough* goin adam? Uh can you let me get dressed please?

I does.

I looks intay her eyes.

I goes.

Says *fine* then slumps ma way right out the room slams the door thinks right. Like that is it? But dudes whats the point when ive seen her? when shes seen my?

Aye um like im sayin the falkirk wheel is where we go, the place where we go on this booorin saturday when judes not at the library, or as the french say *das* library.

We gets the bus to the falkirk wheel, jude holds ma hand. Snice. Warm. But she keeps lookin at her textmessages then out the bus winday then her messages whos she textin? We gets there ye sees it – massive. Standin in the distance this huge greatbig jagged pointedy thing: the falkirk wheel. Ye wouldnt believe yer eyes, or the size, or the. Jude stop textin! We goes intay the visitorcentre jude buys two boatrides im just lookin thru the sheetglass at the massivemassive falkirk wheel the peeps go

ooooo

Gets on the boat. Sway sway wait for me jude! she says cmon adam. We sits down i opens ma sandwiches so xcited says to the wee boy nextay me, want one dude? He looks up says uh. No thank you. No thank you i thinks ha ha. Must be posh. I eats i munches, the boat startstay move in its wee bay we saaaails right ontay the falkirkwheel guy drivin like shivermetimbers woman with a microphone jude listenin closely, the falkirk wheel is the worlds only rotating boatlift and is already recognised as a magnificent example of scotlands traditional engineering expertise. Says to the wee wean nextay me hey. How does an engine listen? He shrugs keeps playin with his ninjaturtle toy. It uses its engineers! Ha ha ha ha ha! He doesnt laugh.

I looks at the wean.

The falkirk wheel (the womans blether-bletherin) is the largest piece of functional sculpture you will ever see. Its total budget was eightyfourpointfive million pounds and has restored the connection between scotlands two largest cities. It will also help the economy of central scotland by attracting tourists to the region and creating fourhundred new jobs in the area yaaaawn. Starts fallin asleep until the wifie says it was opened by the queen in 2002 i says queen! Jude says not the band. Oh i says. How disappointin.

How disappointin i says to the wee boy.

He doesnt say nothin.

I looks at him: wee hands.

He gazes up at me.

I smiles.

The wheel lifts the boat wer on slowly slowly slowly. Long way down dudes. Can see like the wholeay falkirk in the distance as the boats lifted whoah. Heights! Feelin a bit sick a bit em, ma heads thumpin. Says to the wean this is xcitin int it? He says nothin, just twists and twirls michelangelo?raphael?leonardo?donatello? in his hand his wee hand. Slugs in ma gut. I stands up. Jude says where ye goin adam? the woman says uh could you please not stand up sir. Everyone looks i sits down. Head in pain Doom. Doom. Doom. Coloured lights everywhere, ribbons rainbows. It passes. Im fine.

So the wheel carries us safely over to the other canal we sets off. Magical mystery tour, we are ladies and gentlemen of leisure on a saturday afternoon takin a pleasureride thru the canalways of falkirk. And youll see on your left a tescos trolley half stickin out from the reeds. And this bridge up ahead here lovingly decorated with graffiti. Ooh that sly stallones house?

Triestay talktay the wean say whats the name of yer ninja turtle? hes havin none of it. His dad keeps lookin at me. Mibbe he fancies me. Nope sorry sir that is just not my *thang*. Even if i do like yer moustache.

The boat sails thru a tunnel its dark dark dark but cos i can see all the lights from the peeps heads it makes it like that bit in willywonkas chocolate factory, when they go thru the magiccreepy tunnel. Xcept this water is brown cos of like deadfish and jobbies and chemycals floooowin right outtay grangemouth petro-chemycal plant, not chocolate. There have been no chocolate rivers in falkirk for ooooh hundredsay years. Not since the timeay the romans. Somethin wrong with jude today tho. Keeps lookin over the sideay the boat head restin on her forearms i says jude she looks over says what? I says um. Looks like rain jude. She glances at the greygrey sky, clouds like fat ducks waddlewaddle says um adam can we talk? I says sure. Turns to me takes ma hand. Thins out her lips says em. I says whats the matter jude? she says somethin to tell ye adam. I says aye? She blows out says uh. Wipes her hands over her forehead says uh. Nods looks away says uh.

That was what shes gottay tell me? Uh?

She composes herself, like mozart, okay, shes just bout to start when

The dude with the moustache comes stormin over. Shoulders swing. I sees him gettin big Bigger BIGGER he stares at me says hey pal. Jude pauses from what shes bout to say swings her gaze uptay him. He says what do ye keep talkin to ma laddie for?

I looks at jude she looks at him. Jude says sorry scuse me? What?

The guy jabs his finger at ma chest, ddt ddt, like hes usin his finger to drill thru ma body to gold below he says aye. Yeve been starin at ma wee laddie this whole boatride and i wantay ken what for.

Judes on her feet says look pal, i think youve got this wrong.

Guys moustache ruffles in a wee snort. It follows the curl of his lip like a hairycaterpillar archin cross a leaf. He says sit back down hen this doesnt concern you.

Hen? jude says.

The guys like that to me – you just keep yer eyes to yerself. Gestures towards the wee boy with the ninjaturtle whos kinday cryin in the corneray the boat. Or see when we get off this boat you and mes havin words. Steps forwards brings his face close to mine, o jobbies but

Jude lays her arm cross his chest. Like a door bein shut: barred. She speaks slowly carefully a tape givin instructions, this message will selfdestruct. Looks intay the guys eyes listen pal. I dont ken what it is ye think ma brother heres done, but i can assure ye that you keep this up then the only way youre gettin off this boat is me throwin ye off. So why dont ye go and tell yer laddie nothins happenin here.

The guy looks down at jude: weefatgirl.

The redlight bove his head goes flickerflicker.

Shakes his head laughs says. Aye hen. Aye good for you hen. But then looks at me snarls be very careful pal.

turns –

goes—

Jude breathes out. I grins says so jude what was the news ye wanted to tell me? Jude looks round the boat rubs her hair blows air shakes her head. Shakes her head. Looks up at me sorry what? Oh. Nothin adam forget it. Stares intay space faraway: faraway space.

Theres jude. Aye theres always jude. And when the wheel lifts us back down intay the basin again all the peeps in the greatglass visitorcentre are lookin goin ooh aah i stares intay the unioncanal what does i see? A shark! Swimmin and a-grinnin dun-dun dun-dun dun-dun. Aye dudes theres a shark in the falkirk unioncanal eeeeeasin its greatwhite body round the bitsay junk and old tyres. Or mibbe its a dolphin. I cant tell.

**Dudes birthday judes** em i mean judes birthday dudes! Been plannin it for ages nages, she works hard at the yooni so? today? Just me and jude. The pairay us. This mornin came down scattered the cards at the frontdoor, just like mam and dad usedtay. Waited there in the hall for her to yawnstretch come downstairs, oooh i was snuggled up in the dark – xcited! Then she came down saw the cards saw me sittin sleee-peee her face her smile her light lit up. She grinned cuddled me said thanks adam. Yere a wee stoater so ye are pal, a wee stoater. Kiss on the cheek – smeck! Anythin for you jude ma judy, then intay the livingroom wow! Id wrapped all her pressies. She thanked me gain kissed me gain, opened them sleepily. They were queen cds.

Oh she said.

Ta she said.

Queen she said.

This afternoon weve decided to gotay the cottages barandlounge down the bottomay hallglen raay! Ma fayvrit. Sgot great games like supersoccer 3 microtanks streets of rage i like streets of rage ye go this wee guy yere moochin round the hongkong streets man fightin nasty dudes whack! Sometimes yel pick up a board or crowbar or baseballbat whack! they go egh. Dead. Im briiiilliant at it. All the wee weans gather round man theyre watchin me play stabbin the button whack! whack! whack! whack! dudes all fall oof ugh. Whoah go the weans youre great at this sparky play ye? Two player game? Baseballbat plank crowbar whackwhackwhack another one bites the dust (thats queen) the kids spellbound aye im their hero. Adam spark. Streetfighter. Jude calls me back overtay the table ma barlunch is here just a minute i shouts enters ma name on the high score list adam stuart spark A-S-S. Soon as i leaves the machine tho the weans swaaarm straight ontay it like ants me next! No no its me. Sparky said i could go next youre a wee liar. Fight fight fight fight. Hey be cool i tells them, brando pacino deniro. You. Be cool.

Ooh macaroni! Doesnt matter where we go for a bar meal in falkirk ive just *gottay* have macaroni. Could be the coppertop in camelon or the claremont in polmont or or or lawries in laurieston, a mans just *gottay* have macaroni. I suppose ye could say im somethin of a conny-soor. Good evening mr zpark allow uz to zhow you to your ta-bel. Why thank you. Now as you know waiter i am macaroni critic for the sunday evening newyork times and i expect only the highest quality macaroni. Zat eez no problem sir, zee chef weel prepare it for you streight eweh. Indeed. And waiter? Yez? Bring a nice chilled glass of irn-bru would you? From the finest bottling plants of falkirk.

Stop it says jude slappin ma hand. Yere eatin like a pig. Sorry i goes. Then under ma breath – youve a cheek princess of whales heh heh. Wer eatin away, jude gettin tore intay a bittay chicken i makes a face stabs the macaroni with a fork egh. Youre dead. Pasta la vista baby!

Sittin nextay a big roarin fire oh. Thats the good thing bout the cottages barandlounge always a bigroarin fire oh, no like our two-bar lectric effort at home brrr. Big beams holdin up the ceilin theres the karaokemachine usually playin wham im your man or westlife oh mandy or the greeneyed beans where is the love? On the telly is the horseracin the old punters watchin thru a clouday fagsmoke. Scribblin in their racingpost. Grousin. Grumblegrumble that nag always faws at the last grumblegrumble thats me finished with the geegees grumblegrumble – liars. Minds me of dad. Ma daddy. Liked the way his stubble scratched me when we cuddled mmmmmmm scrrrtch scrrrtch. Next week theyll be straight back in puttin a fiver on a wee cer-tain-ty. Thats what dad did, alec ye said ye wouldnt (went mam) aw shut up senga ya stupit bloody (went dad). Leatherjacket on then: out. And hmm the geegees dont seemtay make these dudes any happier than they did dad.

Funny that!

Aaaanyways jude swallows looks at me, em thanks very much for yer birthday presents adam. No problem jude, munch munch. She says aye em, i suppose if i wanted *any* queen albums it would be those ones. Kent yed like them jude i grins. Just make sure ye play them! Jude smiles, shakes her head looks out the winday whats she lookin for? Distracted keeps checkin her mobile: text. Text text. Anythin wrong jude? she looks up says wha? Oh. Just expectin some people adam, theyre uh late. I butters some bread says people? What do ye mean people jude? Thought it was you and me today just you and me, jude makes a face ziftay say dont be daft adam why would i wantay spend ma birthday with just *you* but mibbe i magined it. Could be wrong shrug so then jude says to the waitress could i uh have the chocolate sundae with plenty of cream? And a side order of. And a large portion of. A half of. Some extra

Greedy bloody

I looks at the fire. Heads sore doomph. The flames are writhin dancin pretty nearly says jude do you think its okay to set firetay jobbies on somebodys doorstep? or whats the score with the colouredlights i keep seein them wherever i goes? or if ye dont play them queen albums jude will ye give them to me? Do you still love me? Do you still love me jude? But zif i didnt have enough on ma plate (as well as the macaroni) guess who walks in!

Maryann.

Swaaaans in like she owns the place looks round, jude sees her grins says oh hello maryann. Waves. How are you doing? Her accent changes flickofaswitch. Not *how ye doin* but *how* are you *doing*. Posh like. The light round judes heads a riotay yellowyellow happiness. Whoosh. Maryanns brought another girl and guy with her, they comes overtay the table this girls got looooong glossy hair, vosenes natural intensive care dudes. The boys wearin a tighttight t-shirt looks heytrendycool tanned like somethin off the telly, says judith dear always a delight to see you but *why* did you insist that we eat in *fal*kirk? And on a council estate for godsake! I mean this place is way beyond irony.

Oh ben shut up says maryann, slaps him. He squeals.

But there are broken *fridges* in the gardens says ben. I fear for my nipple rings!

Jude looks miffed says em oh. Says uh flapflap. Ben runs his fingers down her arm, judith he says. *Kidding!* Weve been *dying* to see where you were brought up. And dying i think is what we may end up doing here. He looks bout the place zif theres folk creepin up on him right now with a switchblade – flick. Beadyeyes.

Jude looks flustered em, goes to me. Um adam these are some of the people from my course. Ben lizzy, id like yese em *you*. To meet my brother adam. The vosenegirl says hi all summery. Plants and flowers wake up stretch when she speaks. Ben grins, shakes ma hand widens his eyes says so! *Youre* the famous adam spark? Famous? i nearly says but ben goes and is our judith as much of a tyrant at home as she is in tutorials? She certainly gives our politics lecturers a hard time.

Aye em i shrugs. Can have a bittay a mouth on her likes.

And *tongue* smiles maryann.

Judys grin disappears like a lasso fallin. She goes *shh* to maryann, nods in ma direction, maryann says oh. Tut. They starts givin jude her presents jude goes ooh unwraps them oh thank you liz wiiiiiiine. Cabernet says liz. Jude snaffles it intay her bag giggles ooh that always comes in handy, it certainly will whispers maryann. I like you *pliable*. Jude glares at her again coughs says uh thank you ben as she – grunt – lifts her present cross the table. Unwraps it shhhm crnnnch she says oh its . . . noam chomskys new book! Jude starts readin the backay the book: with the striking logic that is his trademark chomsky dissects americas quest for global supremacy, tracking the US governments aggressive pursuit of policies intended to achieve full spectrum dominance at any

But yese never saved up to buy her a fiftyquid fishskin dress. Yese never did that. And did ye arrange the birthday cards on the doormat zif theyd fell there? Noooooo. We did. Mam-dad-me, see.

Thank you ben says jude thats some light birthday reading for me, i dont think! Well grins ben i know how you socialists like to avoid *fun* at all costs. Jude gives ben a kiss on the cheek. I watches. Silent. Watches.

Then maryann gives jude her present judes eyes lightup she squeezes. Soft. Ooh she says. Maryanns leanin back in her chair, eyein jude (im eyein her) jude tears the paper (im eyein her) lifts up this thing its a . . . a . . . what is it? Its lacy its thin its

Underwear.

Judys face goes bright red. The whole table cracks up ka ka ka ka they go, jude looks at me no smilin definitely Not Smiling. She says em. She says oh. She says whos uh gettin the drinks in? i says me, but when i comes backtay the table jude doesnt see me i hears her hiss at maryann the words *not in front of him.*

I finds out later they live in glesga. Or *glasgow*, as posh folks call it. Oh i says to ben, do you ken kelly marie off tvs river city? She crowned the queen at the gala day this year.

River city laughs liz. Oh yeah its like *essential viewing* in our flat.

Its good eh? i says.

Actually says jude pointin with her fork rudetopointjude, adam had a rather nasty accident at this years gala day.

Really says maryann. What was that?

Jude smiles pats ma hand proudproud. He ran onto the park when all these guys were playin american football, to try and save this wean – i mean child – thatd wandered out there.

A hero! ben declares.

Did you get hurt?

Too right says jude.

No aftereffects tho?

Just superpowers i shrugs. Lights and stuff. But theyre no listenin now, already skated shimmied slid ontay another topic the lightsandstuff dont interest them no no, not enough books written bout it mibbe? I sits quiet. Jude notices. She elbows ben he goes so uh. Where do you work adam? He says it with friendly friendliness, a friend. Joeymonicachandler.

I tells them.

Everyone at the table breathes in a sharp sssssss.

The evil empire! says liz.

Eh? i says.

Havent you read fast food nation? goes ben.

Jude cuts in face flushed says uh ben, adams not really much of a reader.

Thats no true jude i says tut. That jude. I liketay read all sortsay things. Tell us says ben, head in hand leanin over the table smile smile, what books do you like adam? I shrugs. I likes comicbooks. Spiderman. Hulk. Superman. Liz is mutterin tut, in this day and age i dont know how anybody can choose to work in that place then the light over jude goes bright red – she cuts in angrylike. Some people dont *choose* to work there elizabeth you know, they *have* to. Liz frowns. Jude tuts. Simmersimmer goes the room, silence boils boilin. Ben leans to jude puts his hand on her arm, we know that judith we *know* that, you dont have to go all mad marx on us. Liz is just having a laugh isnt she sweetie?

Liz nods: lights a fag.

You do remember *laughter* judith? says ben. Or has falkirk trampled it out of you?

Jude smiles smiles looks at me and her face? suddenly? somethin? She doesnt seem like ma sister jude nope what do i mean by that? em. Whenever i catch her eye she frowns. Whenever i gotay speak to her she talks to somebody else. Like when i try to she –

or if i try to she—

Wheres she went? The jude who battered them at the school who stood uptay dad who tore the fishskin on her birthday who didnt bother didnt fret nope sits over the calky-later with the bills sigh who stands in frontay me strong strong strong: gone. When shes with them she looks half human, half labrador at crufts.

*Who are these peeps?* They talk and laugh and pat each other all the time go well of course and hey! and yah yah totally agree and blether bout film directors writers fashion dee-zine-ers oh you shouldve seen what lola wore to garys book launch oh my – talk about a fish out of water? I mean she looked like an *actual fish*. Hm hm. Yah yah. Then ben mentions arack jude says aye war in the gulf. Table kinday goes hm hm yah yah im thinkin oh. Ma head might just break. Help me judy. Like shes slip-slidin down a slipperyslope away – but remember? Im the boy. I am the boy about town likes, the h-glen animalz said so.

So dont make me. You wont like me when im.

Turns to ben em what kinday music do ye like ben?

He taps the table with a tannedhand says uh let me think. I like the mars volta. Franz ferdinand. The heat the hives the libertines what about you adam?

I like queen.

He nods.

Pause.

Liz turnstay jude suddenly goes so judith! *When* are you moving to glasgow?

Snaps ma head round – glesga? I cant movetay glesga jude, ive got a job here.

Uh says jude, touches ma hand says oh. Glares at liz. Grits her teeth says thats not something ive *spoken with adam about liz*.

But you cant live in falkirk all your life shrugs maryann. I mean judith *falkirk*. Even the *name* sounds like a swear word.

Come on judith goes ben . . . oh look. Actual fish and chips. Surprised it doesnt come in a newspaper.

Nice wee flat in the west end? says maryann, lookin at jude.

She looks at her food. Theyre all talkin nice in niceclothes nicevoices but all i hears doom doom doom. In ma head.

Doom. Doom. Doom.

The coloured lights round everybody round liz ben maryann jude oh ha ha theyre sayin yah yah, so many lights shootin round them zhoom like at the enday raidersay the lost ark they open the ark indy says – close your eyes! Dont look!

Doom.

Doom.

Doom.

Whats happenin to me dudes oh bens foods here wow! He gasps as irene the waitress plonks it down in frontay him no messin. Lasagne and chips? ben says. That is *proper* workingclass grub. Turns to me i mean this place adam, its so. Its so *authentic*.

And ken what dudes i minds the parties mam usedtay have when we were wee the neighbours round all the aunties uncles cousins mam poured what yese wantin? A vodka glug glug oh cheers hen burp! Things. Snatches. Fragments? Thats what theyre called them bitsay things i minds: fragments: songs on the stereo aye the only way is up! Hi-ho silver lin-ing! Well i stiiiiiill havent fooouuuund what im looking for. Bono its there behind the sofa. Me and jude well we sat with a cola while mam dad the neighbours the gilmours the loneys the dolbys the allisons sat boozin, id go round tastin drinks bleeghh vodka bleeech whisky ooh peachschnapps? Nice! Was mainly just the big yins bletherin on, the men bout the scotland team aye what theyre needin nows a souness law dalglish no world class players aye see thats the fordfactory shuttin down aye more outtay work the men nodded aye aye a disgrace aye. The women they talked bout like pelmets curtains hardwoodfloors. Ye hear what she called the wean? Shes called it chelsea chloe abbey bailey macauley, the aunties would yak bout slamannan. Always slamannan. Slamannans the wee village in falkirk where they grewed up. Usedtay blether bout all the peeps they kent when they were wee, laughin tellin each other stories again and again mind that guy brenda? What was his name? Sanny binny that was it, usedtay drive the tractor. Aye mibbe thatll be me and jude in thirty years – mind jude that time i was swingin on the tarzy that goes over the burn and i fell and landed on a rock and broke ma arm? You had to take me to casualty and id never felt pain like it? Ho ho. Those were the days werent they jude?

Then dad said cmere adam hed sit me on his knee theyd all say do yer skeletor id go he-man! In that creakysqueaky voice. Theyd say do yer bruce forsyth id go goodgame goodgame, youre so much better than last weeks audience higher than a ten? A king! Theyd laugh laugh aw the wee man theyd go, id glow grin cuddle intay dad while he drank the specialbrew – burp. Right off now son yere heavy. Ach dad. Nope adam. Down. Then someone: geez a song!

and the room goes quiet shh

Mam pretends she doesnt like singin. Aw cmon wer no that drunk yet are we? Gon yersel senga spark! Mam says right. Says okay. Folds her hands closes eyes says this is a song ma daddy wrote when we were bairns, mind brenda? Brenda raises her glass – glint. Gon yersel hen. Mam sang and the sound. The sound. The mamsound.

Im leavin slamannan tomorrow
Im sayin ta ta cheerio
Im sailin awa doon the watter
For its backtay the war i must go

Im sailin awa doon the avon
Im sailin right doon the canal
But il leave ye somethin for auld lang syne
When i leave slamannan behind.

The aunties joined in they kent it, was their dad what wrote it, theyd learnt it. Start holdin hands swayin

Pirnie lodge road for the winchers
And i leave ye the dyke brae as well
And i leave ye the tingtong tae lean on
And i leave ye the royal hotel
I leave ye twa cops to keep order
Johnny sauls to keep yese aw well

And il leave ye somethin for auld lang syne
When i leave slamannan behind!

The whole room joins in cos mams sang this song so many times at christmas hogmanay birthdays after scotlandmatches it swells rushes roars in me and jude we sing

Molly mcgowans fish suppers
And i leave ye jean johnsons as well
And i leave lizzy dounes to pick up yer lines
And i leave the noon record as well
I leave ye a pub at each corner
So aw of you boys can get wine
And il leave ye somethin for auld lang syne

We squeal like cats make the endin last for ages when iiiiii leeeave slaaamaaannaaan beeeeeeehiiiiiiiiiiind.

Specialtimes.

Veryspecialtimes.

Before

Theyd drink intay the night. Well intay the night. The drink the streetlight the stars. Stars and stars and stars and laughin singin, gin, stuff gettin spilled oops the weans upstairs evenshooly wed play sega! have pillowfights! watch bad boys with will smith! and the other fella! Or else sneak downstairs nick some lager all the cousins passin it round sip wed go egh. Thats brilliant. Oogh. Aw man thats great. Ek! Ek! Never tasted nothin as good as that. Xcept jude tut. Be readin a book sayin can yese keep that noise down please? Then the karaoke would go on downstairs the big yins singin woo. CMON EVERYBODY. Me and jude well wed sit on the stairs keek through the banister snigger cos dad would be drunk again. Maudlin. But none of them even look like models. Everybody quiet shh dads turn: fare thee well my own true love. Dads voice croakydrunk, eyes rollin. For when i return united we shall be. Its not the leaving of liverpool that grieves me. But my darling when i think of thee.

And thats before mam and dad went offtay oz. To see the wizard.

After the meal judes poshpals talk bout the war on arack again theyre clearly flouting international law says jude, jabbin her finger a fingerjabber. As chomsky says in his new book its about america striving for full spectrum dominance at any Yawn. Shifts in ma seat. Sooks ma cola dabs the ice with ma straw dab dab, tastes the wee bitsay lemon looks round the room the sleepin karaoke machine in the bar – mibbe? I could sing? Like at mams parties? Jude look at me!

Nope. Would jude notice – methinks not! Jude would not notice and her pals wouldnt join in, theyd point and laugh ha ha ha ha ha ha ha ha ha i waits for jude to turn backtay me but she doesnt. Just doesnt! Talkin to maryann so she is, leanin close ex*act*ly says maryann jude and maryann nod all see-re-us i shuffles in ma seat says ben? Wantay play streets of rage? He says um what is that adam? Its an arcade game. He says oh. Shrug. Okay then. Thatll be . . . fun. We goes over i puts fifty pence in he says how does it? What do i? I says yeve gottay pick up the bat and –

Whack!

Smacks his man round the chops. Oh am i getting beaten? ben says, oh em. He fiddles with the joystick, tries to pick up the brokenbottle but i gets to him first batters him on the head with ma crowbar he falls down egh. Liz comes up. Laughs at bens performance he says okay then see if you can do any better fine says liz. Takes over. I beats her as well. I man-yoo-vers ma man over doofdoofdoof knocks her down she goes oh. Goes this games silly. Goes away.

Its maryanns turn.

Maryanns quite good. Bit nimble dudes. She talks tries to joke at one point says uh i hope we can be pals adam? Adam? Im saying i hope we can be pals? But i stays silent so as to con-sin-trate soon she is too. Somethin comes over us. Serious. She stabs the button. Goin for the knife. Ive only got a bat! If she gets the knife before i use the bat im beat! Oh no! Can hear ben and liz laughin loud like motorbikes, ben says and shes only decided shes straight again. I mean thats one girl who doesnt know if she wants to be *dyked* or *spiked*. Even judes laughin. Judys laughin along shes one of them ma jude ma judy shes mineminemineminemine jabs the button picks up the shotgun fore maryann can and – blam! Blows her away. And just to make sure? Slam. Slamslamslam i hit her die die die die ma head hurts die die overandover maryann goes tut smacks the arcade game says yes okay adam. Youve beaten me! Stands back looks me in the eye sees ma dontmesswithme stare. The slamslamslam stare. The stayawayfromjudeslut stare. Shakes hands with maryann ziftay say no hard feelins, but squeezes. Sqqqquuuuueeeze. She pulls her hand away ow she says looks at me. Like ive scared her. Walks backtay the table jude says how did ye get on? Maryann says pfh. He hammered me!

Aye i thinks. And theres more where that came from ya slag.

**Hey now heeeeeeeeres somethin weird dudes** icanspeedtimeup

and

slow

it

down

oh but fore i get ontay that, see im in the h-glen animalz now. Im partay the crew man the *team* the *squad* one of the chaps outside the chippy. Big mark baxters been lettin me hang round them – we stoats thru falkirk thru the highstreet down tammyhill up camelon singin hello! hello! we are the billy boys. Hello! hello! yel know us by our noise. Wer uptay our knees in fenian blood, surrender or yel die. Cos we are the (brighton dairy) boys! When it comes to (brighton dairy) i just makes words up cos i dont ken them. And im no sure why we sings we are the billy boys, cos none of us is billy. And uptay ma knees is clean.

But pay attention, playin fitbaw with the animalz boot kick header one–nil! Some other wee saps in goals gettin shouted at heh heh cos im the boy. I am the boy. But what im tryin to *tell* ye if yed listen is icanspeedthingsupand

slow

things

down

Its mental! Like in a film like in lorday the rings when they have battles with the orcs and somebody shouts for frodo! and it all goes sloooo

ooooo

ooow? Clash! spkang! die you miserable orcs! Well its sunday afternoon im standin there in the middleay the fitbaw park, jason fogartys got the ball batterin down the wing big marks like foggy! Foggy! Three dudes chasin foggy grants tryin to run intay the box in case foggy crosses for a header. Ooh its a helluva game dudes. Could go either way. Foggys runnin. Hes runnin. The boy slides in for a tackle and i just con-sin-trates and

fog

gy

flicks

the

ball

up

and

lobs

it

int

ay

the

box

and

folk

are

jump

in

grant

leaps

and

doof!

heads

the

ball

int

ay

the

net

and

lands

and

peeps

are

run

nin

hands

in

the

air

i

con

sin

trates

a

gain

guess

what?

ziiiiiip! Timespeedsup. Itsagoal. Everybodyrunstogrant. Grantgrant! Yaweebeauty. Ikentyoudscore. Sparkysparky yeseethatgoal? Whatdoye makeofthat? Ayeitsastoater. Goaliesfedup humph, neverminditwasnt yourfault. Ballonthecentrecircle pheep! Passpass. Boot. Cross. Tackle.. Oof foul ref! Playon. Knobendtomark. Marktocraig. Craigtomarkto craigtosparky. Sparkysparky! Sparkysparky! Noimgoingalone. Past oneman. Pastanother? Pastthreemen! Lookatthespeedhesgoingman! Hes hes hes

Boot.

Goooaaal! Three–nil! They comes runnin uptay me, the h-glen animalz theyre cuddlin kissin me mwah mwah mwah. Sparky sparky yer a genius. How did ye do that? See the speed ye were doin (little do they ken) hey – somebody put this boy up front, hes wasted in defence likes. Big mark baxter walks uptay me. Hes no smilin. The light round hims kinday reddy-orangey hardtay read he says sparky.

Aye?

Looks at me. Grunts gnmph. Shakes ma hand says yer a god sparky.

The god of falkirk! craig laughs.

Me? The god of falkirk? Better than effin spastic oh aye dunno where theyve came from these powers likes, but ye ken what they say dont look a gifthorse in the mouth. Ken how? Cos hel just go like that – chomp and some of them gifthorses man give ye a right nasty nip, aye but the powers im sayin its mental one of them ye ken bout: the coloured lights. But now theres this other power where icanspeedthingsupand

slow

things

down

like when i see cars goin past on the street man i can make them go neeeeeooooow purefast or i can make them go

sloooo

ooooooo

ooooooow.

Since the accident.

Since i hurt ma head.

Since crashbangwallop aye somethins goin down dudes. Down in da hood. See i always kent i was special. Different. Yoo-neek. Nothesame. Nope all ma life i have just not thoughtorfelt like every other dude, i kens this. Like even mam and dad goin offtay oz made me the one, the only one, partfay jude, that didnay, that didnay have a

that didnay have a mam or dad to

And now the powers dudes the the the powers! The lights and lights and speedintimeupand slowin it down, thats like. Whats the word? Confirmed. Aye. Confirmed it. Firmed that con. I am special. Specialasarubyslipper. And its ever since that day think bout it, ever since that day i saved the wee boy at the gala day, that heroic act of bray-very, of verybraveness. So somebody somewheres said: the boys a champ. Give him a cape. And now im startin to ken, mibbe, why ive been different, all ma life, cos i might just have been sent to save mankind. I mean the world shore is a badass mess dudes, a scrapheap challenge. What if george dubya calls me – hey sparky cmere – to go sort out arack? Cos that is one man that kens the difference between goodandevil. Mibbe thats it aye spidermanbatmanhulk and: the incredible adam. Yese need us. Heroes. To protect the weak. Save the powerless. The lassies. The weans. The wee yins. So raise the flag and spark up the sparkysignal!

Cos here i comes.

But nevermind that hey i meantay say oooooh employee of the month. Guess what. Thinkin wonderin if i can use ma powers to win it. That cheatin? So? Sittin in the livinroom waitin for jude to come back from yooni. Always takes so long. Always out. Comes back grinnin and intay her chair she flops, her goodmood yellow light twirlin and a-jivin round her. Sees me her light goes blue, ye okay adam? Aye i just says. Sits. Thinks. Squeezes an orange till the juiceruns down ma arms dribbledribble the way the mouseblood did that time ach. So im watchin the news from arack: boom! George dubyas angry says our soldiers are fighting for liberty, and this here will be liberty central. Points his finger. Crowd goes wild wild as a wildchild. Gets me thinkin bout what this *here* hero can fight for and the answer is? Employee of the month. Cos if i won employee of the month dudes that would be the first steppinstone up to heroville. Today falkirk tomorrow? Arack?

So.

Hour later im standin in falkirk high street outside ma placeay work. Gotta costyoom rigged up outtay judes old gymnastics gear and a cape, em a bathtowel. Paints the company logo on the front like so:

presto. Instant hero. Takes down ma ghettoblaster presses play and what blasts out? Supercharged super queen: the flash gordon theme. Gives out flyers for the company to the passersby says hey dudes, come in and eat here. Our burgers are herolicious! This guy stops in frontay me looks me up down mutters who you meantay be?

Im a superhero.

A superhero aye? And what are ye standin here for?

Im here to save the world sir.

He nods. Aye he says, cos when saddam decides to launch hel start with falkirk high street?

*Xactly* sir i says. Ye just never ken with these madmen.

Guy stands lookin at me then walks on, shakin his head. I waits a bit longer, smilin at the weans who stare and go mammy? mammy? whys that man dressed like that? Care in the community the mams mutter. Then i turns round what does i see? Angie stormin outtay the shop stridin overtay me. Brightspark she says. What the hell are ye doin out here?

I coughs. Em i says shuffleshuffle, scratchin at ma leota— em costyoom. My names not brightspark maam, i think youve made a mistake.

She goes why ye talkin in that ridiculous american accent?

What american accent maam?

That one! And is that a leotard?

I laughs says aye okay angie its me, but listen im only tryin to promote the company. Show in-ish-ya-tive.

Angie wraps her arms round herself fortress-style: closed. You have got to be jokin.

Nup i says, startin to hand out some more leaflets fore angie snatches them off me, grab. Bends to the ghettoblaster. Flash! Ah-ah! Off: eject. Brightspark she sighs, crossedarms. Listen carefully. First of all yere no even workin today. If ye were id probably sack ye on the spot for wastin company time. Secondly ye need ma *permission* to pull a stunt like this, and id need permission from the regional manager, whod probably need permission from headoffice, whichd probably be denied.

Why?

Why? she says. Why brightspark? Yere like a wean with all yer questions! Whywhywhy: il tell ye why. She steps forward bristly as a stickinsect. Cos this companys vision is *not* to be interfered with. All over the world we give our customers xactly the same in every single store. Package it. Market it. Sell it. From new york to tokyo. Thats it. Thats why wer one of the biggest companies in the world brightspark (points at ma costyoom) *not* cos weve got some clown wavin at weans!

Em angie? i wantay say. Thats no actually true? But shes no listenin. Off on one, away with it man the brightbright reds burnin over her head whoof! I interrupts her em angie?

What?

This wont get me employee of the month?

Oh by the way speakin of employees weve a new lassie at work. Shes wee got blackhair kinday freckly comes intay the crewroom this mornin takes off her jacket shoes jumper earrings bangles chain, says you watchin me or somethin? I says no.

Girl looks away. I punches intay the clock goes down ontay the shopfloor intay that dry waftin air that smells like fries, im sweepin. Sweep sweep. Brush brush. Just sweepin away thinkin away i could speedthisupor slow

it

down

and win employee of the month! Angie comes over. Got this new lassie with her keeps adjustin her crewcap doesnt seemtay fit. Hair scraped back in the reg-yoo-lay-shin ponytail looks like olive oyl, from popeye. Aye. Keeps glancin round the shop this wee lassie, kinday nervous like a wee wean dressedup in big yins clothes. Angie says bright spark? This is bonnie, shes startin today, i need ye to show her how the place works, take her round point out where everythin is make sure she blah blah blah blah no listenin. Im noddin im lookin at bonnie bonnies lookin at the floor. I looks at the floor too. Ooh the floor is so interestin, what an incredible arr-ainj-ment of tiles ahem. Blush. Angies starin at us both. Well cmon then bright spark this isnt a youth club! Get to work.

Angie goes away, bonnies wee freckly face frowns she says so is your name bright spark?

Sparky i goes.

Her wee eyebrows go up. They go down. She smiles says sparky? Like an electric shock?

Aye.

Dzzt! she goes, big lopsided grin like goofy. I laughs.

Theres a pause um.

So youre bonnie?

She nods nods, big xaggerated nods like her heads loose. Yup.

Do you have any nicknames? i says. Ken how like im sparky?

She nods nods gain, head swingin on her looseloose neck. Yup. Grins tombstone teeth. At school they called me snottypants.

Why was that i says, sweepin the floor sweep sweep, tryin not to notice the shape of her

She shrugs.

Have ye got snot in yer pants?

She smiles fidgets. No she says but ive got this kinday uh condition uh thats. She wipes her nose with a hankie i hears the noise her breathins makin. Gnuh. Gnuh. Gnuh.

She really has got big teeth. Quite nice. Um thinkay somethin to say sparky dont embarrass yerself dude be cool be suave say: uh anymore nicknames?

She sticks her big bottomlip out havin a think a good old think. Um she says, i used to get dickbreath quite a lot. Cosay ma breathin.

I drops the broom clatter gasp. Me too!

Really?

Aye! Thats what i got at primaryschool. And its so stupit cos –

– how can ye have breath like a dick?

Xactly!

We both stares at each other grin grin oh man. Magine us havin the same nickname at school, wonder if she got her olive oyl head pushed down the toilet like me, flush gurglegurgle. The light round bonnies heads yellow yellow nice. She looks at me then down ahem. I coughs em shows her where the brooms the brushes the mops are kept shows her the different bins ye use to get rid of lettuce buns gherkins fries oh em. Shes. Shes very. Shows her the huuuuge racks that hold the trays of chicken sandwiches and burgers xplains all the special offers if the customer buys a chicken sandwich with fries ye ask if theyd like a coke with that for only an extra thirty pence they always say aye. Bonnie listens. And her freckles and her smile and her and her. She asks questions. Says where does the prefrozen food come in? I says from the back there, see that yard? She says right aye uh-huh. Then she smiles says sparky? When you were at school did people ever? ye ken? She giggles.

Did they what?

Ken? Shes grinnin. Did they ever ken . . . push yer head down the loo?

Yup! i says. They shore did.

Me too! she goes.

We both kinday smiles claps and hey – i nearly squeals. Then we launches intay like and did they? and could they ever make ye? and sometimes would ye? we both laughs and giggles xcited cosay the xact same things happenin its so funny. Oh to ken that just as i was gettin spat on at falkirk high, the same thing was happenin to bonnie at graeme high thats funny. What a weeeeird co-incy-dince! Weird as the xfiles dudes the xmen, weird to the xtreme. We have such a laugh talkin bout it: the slaggins. The kickins. The beatins. Ho ho good times.

And see its moments like this. Moments like this man. When me and jude were weans wed take the bikes downtay the burn past hallglen, way down past phase six of the housin scheme that is good old hallglen, to collect bugs. Cross the weewooden bridge like billygoatsgruff, clop clop clop jude would have a puffin junior readers naturebook id say what kinday spiders this oh shed say thats an orb weaver adam. And shed pron-ouns it carefully, like her mouth was swallowin the word *orb*. Id go cool! Whats this? Thats a ladybird (l*ady*bird) look see the black and red markins? Oh aye jude thats mazin, she knew everythin did jude, always with her nose in a book. Dad usedtay call her a swot but so what? Good for bughuntin was our jude, wed run thru fields. The grass on ma fingertips. Brush brush brush. The sunny sunshine. Everythin slow and slooow and the warm warmth and summer and sky and me and jude splishsplashin thru the burn coooold on our skin wed lie in the grass. Dreams. Dreamy. Wed lie in the grass look at each other shed stroke ma head soft soft everythin in the world perfect so perfect so many different kindsay bugs their eyes colours the birds the water, jude paddlin splish splash, jude laughin lyin in the grass we touched. Lyin in the grass we touched, and grass tickled our barearms our barelegs our bare? our bare? and sometimes lifes so

byootiful

amazin

incredible

like this moment. So i says to bonnie em whats yer fayvrit queen song? she says dont stop me now. Whats yer fayvrit queen album? she says a kinday magic. Whos yer fayvrit queen member? she says freddie i says with moustache or without? she says without.

Me too i grins.

What a team she smiles, shuts her lockerdoor goes see ye next week sparky? I says: aye. Says: okay. Thinks: rudethoughts.

But aaaaaanyway im sayin dudes the superpowers check this out man its mental some mornins when i goes out i feels this? this? How can i describe it em this power in ma fingertips crackle dzzt. The world seems strange alive ringinout just ringinout. Whats happenin dudes? The birds in the trees the wind blowin the grass the speeday the clouds scudscuddin gainst the sky all is pitchsharp, goes slooooooow goes fast! goes slooooooow and like i could hear all the life round me, singin like a chorus of chorussingers. Yup that crazy mothernature: ye just dont ken what shes gonnay do next.

Like give ye a new superpower.

This surely proves it dudes watch:

Goes out this mornin ryan gilmours standin by his car – it wont start. It just wont start! Hes bent over the bonnet with an oily rag an oily rage lookin in the car its goin agagagaga but will it start? Noooo. Wipes his hands fed up. Glum. Grumble grumble. I just strides on over like superman Doom Doom Doom feelin the power crackle. Dzzt. Says hi there ryan how ye doin?

Aye no bad sparky. Yerself?

Sure could do with a holi-day to san tro-pay i says, but other than that ryan? Im swell!

Ryan says ach well wish ye could do somethin bout this car sparky – its knacked. Ive tried it like seven different ways.

Here let me have a go.

Just looks at me: time passes. You sparky? You ken howtay fix cars?

Well i can sure as heck try i tells him. They dont call me sparky for nothin! Leans over intay the bonnet lookin at the pipes and vents and plugs – oh my. But i kens what to do. I *kens* what to do. Ma head hurts: doom: the power. Says to the car alright sunny jim whats goin on here? How come yere no gonnay start for ma pal ryan?

The car says

Τηε ωαρ ισ ωαγεδ βψ εαχη ρυλινγ γρουπ αγαινστ ιτσ οων συβφεχτσ, ανδ τηε οβφεχτ οφ τηε ωαρ ισ νοτ το μακε ορ πρεϖεντ χονθυεστσ οφ τερριτορψ, βυτ το κεεπ τηε στρυχτυρε οφ σοχιετψ ινταχτ.

Aye i ken i says. But thats no gonnay help ryan is it?

Ιτ ισ δελιβερατε πολιχψ το κεεπ εϖεν τηε φαϖουρεδ γρουπσ ον τηε βρινκ οφ ηαρδσηιπ, βεχαυσε α γενεραλ στατε οφ σχαρχιτψ ινχρεασεσ τηε ιμπορτανχε οφ σμαλλ πριϖιλεγεσ ανδ τηυσ μαγνιφιεσ τηε διστινχτιον βετωεεν ονε γρουπ ανδ ανοτηερ.

Look, im no interested in that i says. Just tell us whats the matter so ryan can get to his work on time eh.

Οκαψ οκαψ, ιτ'σ ηισ χαρβυρεττορ. Βυτ λιστεν. Ωε κνοω νοω τηατ νο-ονε σειζεσ ποωερ ωιτη τηε ιντεντιον οφ ρελινθυισηινγ ιτ. Ποωερ ισ νοτ α μεανσ, ιτ ισ αν ενδ. Ονε δοεσ νοτ εσταβλιση α διχτατορσηιπ ιν ορδερ το σαφεγυαρδ α ρεϖολυτιον; ονε μακεσ τηε ρεϖολυτιον ιν ορδερ το εσταβλιση τηε διχτατορσηιπ. Τηε οβφεχτ οφ περσεχυτιον ισ περσεχυτιον. Τηε οβφεχτ οφ τορτυρε ισ τορτυρε. Τηε οβφεχτ οφ ποωερ ισ ποωερ. Ανδ τελλ ηιμ το στοπ σινγινγ Γυνσ ν φυχκιν Ροσεσ.

Aye alright alright i says. No need for a rant!

Turns to ryan.

See that?

The carburettor?

Whatever. Ye need a new one of them. And also yere low on oil.

Ryan looks at me. Ye sure sparky?

Thats what the car says man i just shrugs. That and stop singin gunsnroses its doin his nut in.

Ryan looks at me. Looks at the car. Says em aye. Cheers sparky.

No bother i says salutin him, then i flies away em teleports away em takes the bus.

*

A power new power whats happenin dudes? Thinkin bout it all day. Cant con-sin-trate at work for wonderin what it means man, it all means. Angie comes over when im flippin burgers. Cmon bright spark she says no slackin off hop to it, walks away givin me this look i tuts – aye il get you my pretty. And your little dog too!

Coupleay the crewmembers laugh.

Angie snaps hey you. Enough sniggerin.

Anyways phew! Glad im off those fries. Takes the mop starts goin round the floor sayin hiya to peeps. Im chattin away with the customers givin it aye aye ive been with this company since the start. That right son? Aye. I usedtay own it! Selt the company right enough cos i missed workin on the shopfloor. Thats why im back here.

The customers get impressed with that, they say really? They say fascinatin! They say get away from me ya nutcase. Ho ho good one sir.

Back on fries. Bonnies beside me. Weebonnie oh. Shes workin doubletime too already in trouble today man cos she lost her crewcap, doesnt ken where it is no, angie hadtay search. She snapped *thatll* come out yer wages. Bonnie donned it on her wee head domf. Looked at angie gawp gawp gobsmacked, bosslady angela of this fastfood kingdom. Trrrreeemmmble.

Now. Ye ken how much i want employee of the month. That would be mazin man, that would mean everythin in the world to me oh aye you bet but it would be veeeeery eeeeeasy to use ma superpowers to get ahead. Cos see these other plebs? Have they got superpowers? Can they see the colours and talk to ryans motor and speedthingsupand

slow

things

down?

No! They are as the silver surfer would say: mere mortals. No their fault! So since the incredible adam spark is usin his powers only for good, it wouldnt be fair on bonnie and reno and steve and all the other puny humans slavin away to try and get employee of the month then i comes in swoosh! Uses ma powers.

Il help bonnie.

Il help bonnie – but why you say? Mibbe its cos all the same things happened to her at school that happened to me, mibbe cos i hear the folks in here callin her stupit the same way they sometimes call me densedaftmongol, mibbe its cosay her lovely, nevermind shes gottay make twelve chicken sandwiches ten burgers eight baconmuffins (and a partridge in a pear tree) theres steve at the till shoutin for more More MORE bonnie sweats oops! Dropped a burger. That ones for the bin the light round her heads purplebluered can see it in her eyes. Shes thinkin she must be rubbish man. Im rubbish at this shes thinkin, and i dont want her thinkin that cos shes no rubbish so i just

slows

things

down

so

she

can

take

her

time

and

flip!

those

bur

gers

with

out

a

care

in

the

world

no

i

keeps

things

nice

and

gent

le

till

the

end

ay

her

shift

then

fwiiiiip! Backtay normal speed. Wer in the crewroom at break time phew caps on the table wer all a-runnin a hand thru our hair. Sweat. Sweat. Sweat. Oh man weve all got the greasyskin cos of the chipfat.

Knacked! Bonnies there bent over gasp dunno how i got thru that she says.

What do ye mean? steve says.

Tellin ye. Halfway thru man i thought i was gonnay collapse. Couldnt take it. Then . . .

She stops.

What? says steve bitin intay lunch rumph! Nother burger gone – nutrition.

Bonnie holds up her hands shrugs. And says. Things just seemedtay? Slow down. I could concentrate dead easy. It was weird, i felt totally in control like everythin was goin at half speed or somethin.

Cos we got less busy says steve.

Aye says bonnie. Noddin. Aye that must be it.

So how did it feel sparky when you were out there using your powers for good not evil? Well im just glad i could do a job for the manager and the rest of the boys. And do you think theres too much pressure on you as the teams star player? No not at all. Im just gettin ma head down tryin to use ma powers for the benefit of humanity. And if i can help a few friends along the way (shrug) all the better. Sparky you are a true champion. Thanks now if you dont mind im gonnay join the rest of the boys in the bath with the trophy. Absolutely sparky you deserve it. There goes a hero ladies and gentlemen. Away to wash his tadger.

**Today judys takin me to glesga** for an aunty war demons-tray-shin. Golly! Just hope we dont see any demons! Or aunties! We goes thru on the train jude reads the NME i reads the silversurfer. Whoah hes joined forces with the fantasticfour to defeat galactus, whos landed in noo yawk city galactus is huuuuge man big as the empirestatebuilding. Doom. Doom. Doom. Wantstay eat the place! Mibbe hes just lookin for somewhere to gotay the toilet magine that? Ha ha galactus doin a big jobby on ye SPLAT yeech. Some game of fireblanket thatd be!

So. Train. Chuggachuggachuggachugga. Judes on her mobile talkin xcited shes sayin how many in london? Two million? *Two million?* Two million what? ach i tries to con-sin-trate on the silversurfer comic but jude keeps gettin texts checkin texts smilin. And glowin yellow glowin yellow whats the? Jude? She snaps shut her phone looks at me her glow dampens, she says aye? I says this march whats it all bout? why we marchin? whats the point? will we no get sore feet? there gonnay be toilets? there gonnay be toilets judy? what if i needs a judy jobby? – em a jobby judy? She tries to xplain it to me puts down her phone, bigperson thoughts risin in her voice. Sighs says right adam the thing is em how can i describe it em. This big war – its between merica and britain on one side and arack on the other. Says aye. Got that much. Okay i says, whose sides you and me on jude? She says well. Wer no really on anybodys *side* adam. Its complicated em. Wince. She says right see if theres one thing i hate adam its a bully. Whether its that tosser mark baxter yere always hangin round with or that mob ye work for or our da—

She stops.

Whether its who? i says.

Em. Whether its george bush adam, i was gontay say. Hes the leader of america. And hes a bully. And see saddam hussein adam, hes the leader of arack. But hes a bully too.

Oh i says. But what do ye do when one bullys fightin another jude?

Ye get them to stop, says jude lookin out the winday. Before one of them starts pickin on *you*.

Well thats right aye, cos i minds one time i saw this fight between mark baxter and norman senicky at school. They were the two top men. Mark baxter was oneay the h-glen animalz norman senicky was in the t-hill posse, everyone feared them. The two of them were really good fighters i mean the *best* i mean as good as rocky one two three four *and* five, so they kept out each others way. I mean why would rocky one fight rocky two? Evenly matched! Xcept they cant be that evenly matched cos rocky two beat the blackman but rocky one lost – anyways! Im sayin. This one time on a monday mark baxter was boastin hed leathered one of the t-hill crew, by lunchtime story was hed put him in hospital! fightin for his life! on deaths door! mark was gonnay get expelled! sent to the childrens panel! locked up for life! Calm down dudes. The one who was hos-pit-al-ised was senickys best mate. So in the dinner queue i saw him go uptay mark baxter, went in close behind him gripped his shoulder hissed somethin mark baxter looked white as a sheet. I mean like caspar the friendly ghost. I mean like daz ultrawash. I mean like whiter than snowwhite dudes: that white. That was it: fight.

Everyone met up man. Halfway home from school. Swarmin roamin roarin like in that film gremlins, waitin for senicky and baxter. Here comes senicky with the t-hill crew rrrraaaaAAAAAY a roar builds up. He stands waitin, everyones like what ye gonnay do? Gonnay tear off his head stick yer hand down his throat? Gonnay? Gonnay? Gonnay? Gonnay? Senicky shrugs. Paces crackle fizz then here comes mark baxter the rumble starts again rrrrrraaaaAAAAAY peeps make a ring, all these boys with xcited faces some girls too who fancy the hardmen ooh, theyre nudgin each other goin who do ye fancy most? Oh mark like. Mark! nut! hes ugly! I like that senicky hes well fit aye but hel no be after marks finished with him, shrug.

So mark and norman are in the middleay the ring. And folks are pushin them at each other. But ye can see it in their eyes. Theyve cooled down. Theyre both thinkin em. Hm. On secondthoughts. But norman goes was it you did that to deeks? baxter goes i was there but i didnt do it, normans like naw man i heard you did it baxter shrugs goes i was there but it wasnt me, everybodys hunched like fightfightfight glancin from senicky to baxter norman goes aye well watch it cos i heard it was you, mark goes naw wasnt me, im standin at the edgeay the circle folks pushin shovin tryin to get closetay the action i gets dunted – dunts intay mark mark looks at me goes watch it ya mongol senicky goes aye watch it wer tryin to have a fight here mark pushes me intay senicky senicky goes eff off pushes me back i hits mark then mark goes why ya little—

Then they were on me.

So when two bullies are fightin each other the best things to get them to stop cos ken what? Ken what happens dudes? They turn round and start on you. Ho ho judy youre so right.

Listenin to queen and davidbowie on the train: underpressure. Thinkin bout bonnie from work her nice nice. And her nice nice. But heads thumpin dudes mibbe its from when that guy punched me after the fireblanket – ba-doof! – feels like theres a terrier in ma brain thats no had its tea, yappin and a-yippin yip yip yip yip yip yip and the song im listenin to is about some dude underpressure and the lights? The coloured lights? Sheesh dont get me started man. And i members fightfightfight mark punchin me senicky kickin me everyone closin in and hey! Dont forget dudes i can speedtimeupand

slow

it

down

Keraazy! So. Breathe deep. Me and jude getstay glesga straight out at queen street (queen street haha, that brian may over there?) loadsay peeps in george square shoutin tony tony tony! Out out out! Poor tony. Mibbe hes no wantin to come out. Mibbe hes just wantin to stay in sorry pals im just stayin in watchin the box. Aye the tellys no bad today likes. Aw thats a shame tonyblair we were hopin yed come out mibbe play on the bikes? Naaah thanks anyway. Right see yese. Oh before yese go lads: education education education. Ma sister judy meets her pals from yooniversity ben liz maryann, they give her big hugs the light bove their heads yelloworange ben says oh judith you really have to stop dressing as if you shop in oxfam it makes you look like such a *prole*. I watches close. Maryann. Watches close. She goes to give jude a hug but jude looks at me sharply maryann tuts says oh. Still like that is it? Havent you *told* him yet?

Telt me what?

Jude looks at the ground puts hands in her pockets cough. Jude says that em wer goin on a march later adam. Ye like marchin?

Em aye jude i says sortay slowly. Like the grand old duke of york?

Just like that.

Sure. And looks at maryann hm, what is it theyve not telt me, is it, can it be, what if its

Doom Doom Doom.

Maryann and jude walk on talkin to each other, light bove judes head changes to yellow. Yellow happy! Hm ma head mans too sore to work it out, work what out? What judes not told me dumbo! Il work it out work it out, if i can just con-sin-trate. Just try not to. What if shes. And then il havetay. This marchins great! We walks round glesga holds up banners shoutin george bush CIA. How many kids have you killed today! We also sings this song man i ken it jude plays it, by billy bragg. Waiting for the great leap forwards. Leap forwardstay what? Doesnt matter cos these songs get borin i tries to sing radio gaga. They all looks. Nobody joins in. Not even with the claps? Ob-vi-ously not queen fans!

The colour bove the march is light red, swarmin dancin pretty. Theres police standin at the sideay the road watchin us narrow beadyeyes hm. Dogs! Ruff ruff. Horses! Neigh. Judes near me, but she keeps goin away with maryann maryann whispers somethin jude smiles laughs pats maryanns shoulder, what they laughin at? Judes no that funny. So we marches backtay george square oh the grand old duke of york he had ten thousand men. He marched them upto the top of the hill and he marched them down again. Theres guys makin speeches whos this dude? Tommy sheridan. Oh aye hes been on the news fumin bout the war dont make me angry. You wouldnt like me when im angry. Listentay this garbage man he says this war is not about weapons of mass destruction or bringing peace to the middle east or democracy. It is about oil, pure and simple. It is about control of the second largest natural energy reserves in the world. It is about *power*. American *superpower*. The guy at the microphone this tommy sheridans goin on on on the light bove him mans bright red. Thumpin. And sos ma head sheesh, all this shoutin oh makes me wantay find maryann and and and. We will *reject* this war! he says. We will *reject* the capitalist system it represents! Because what this has shown *again* is that scotland is being ruled by an alien government!

O jobbies.

An alien government?

Jeezo shiver an alien government? Masters of the yooniverse? With like skeletor at the headay the table and beastman as the righthand dude and evil-lyn pourin the tea and trapjaw shufflin papers? Skeletor says could you close the door please chaps. Lets get this meeting started. An alien government o jobbies, gottay tell jude!

Goes lookin for jude jude where are ye? Jude judy listen! Theres an alien government rulin scotland! Loadsay peeps so many peeps in george square shoutin swearin booin hissin punchin fists in the air but cant see jude. Where is she dont leave me. Like that time in scarborough when she. No. Gottay find her tell her bout the alien government cant see her so – mibbe the aliens got her! O jobbies! Oh! oh! oh phew hey there she is its okay shes with—

Maryann. Maryanns got her arm round judy: smilin laughin kissin. And this is definitely a kiss dudes. Their lips are touchin. Jude cuddles intay her pulls her close jesus man and ma head? Feels like its splittin open crrrrkkkk. Whats inside? War. Thats what dudes. Judes gonnay go go go go go leave me here itll be me, just me, just.

no judy dont dont

Somethins happenin near the stage. Somebody shoutin at the police, horse stridin intay the square. Shouts. Abyoos. Boom boom crash collides with the pain in ma head, crowdin in. All crowdin in. Tommy sheridans at the mike tryin to tell people to calm down theres

Jude and maryann. Kiss kiss! And thats it. Everythin.

Mamdadwonderfulwizardayozscarborough alone alone goes overtay them im galactus! I am seventy storeys tall! You i roars and hauls maryann off jude like im pullin someone off a motorbike and ma head feels like? Hm. I *suppose* it feels like theres a bomb goin off in it. Doom doom grabs maryann punches her in the face. She goes down ontay the ground holdin her nose. Theres blood gushin out. Her eyes shocked still: a deers. Holds her by the hair just bout to kick her when jude pulls me shes like adam! What are ye doin? Dont no please adam please stop

Shakes her off lifts ma hand she flinches. Ye lied to me judy i says. Ye lied to me ye promised yed never leave me but im standin here and what do i see? What do i see! This slut kissin ye! I spits on maryann. How do ye like that then ya cow? i spits. Eh? Steal ma sister? Punch. Well how do ye like this ha ha ha? Streets of rage smackdown!

And judys screamin tryin to pull me off maryann and all round us now man fights are kickin off. Big horses chargin intay the crowd police swingin at peeps man peeps tryin to reach the police runnin scatterin shoutin swearin the light bove the citys red. Dark red. Nearly black. Its coverin the sun so much red. Like blood. So much red round everyone fallin from the sky: red rain. Fallin on scotland man red rain red rain flowin down the streets man flowin right down those meanstreets. Aye. Ma head feels like someones stab stab stabbin knittin needles intay me and

The stars and stars and stars.

Whoah.

Dad usedtay take me away fishin, far away to lochness lochawe lochshin lochmorra the bonnybonny banks of loch lomond. Lochs usedtay love them man! Night time. Shh. Water goin laplap quiet. Wee splash now and then? Splish. Wed fish. Flick. Reeeeeeeeeel. Flick. Reeeeeeeeeel. Dad showed me howtay fish. Held ma hands we did practice casts – hey man some distance! Arms round me: big. Together. Aye and in the blacksky man – star here. Star there. Brrrrrrrpmillions of stars appearin all at once billions and billions and billions.

They wouldnt ever stop. Wonderful. The stars in the sky me and dad fished nextay the loch hey toto wer not in kansas anymore. Look at that star dad! Oh aye thats the plow son. And see there adam? Thats o-ri-yan.

But its no the stars its the space between them.

Black

Black

Black

Dad will we ever be able to go there, where adam? Space! When we die dad said. When we die! Whenll that be dad? He shrugged could be anytime he said. Could be seventy years from now. Could be next month. Could be tomorrow. Crikey! i thought. Dad might die tomorrow? Pisser bummer oh. Stares down at ma feet, broken bitsay twigs leaves and stuff, wonderin: whos buried there? Wonder who had this talk with their daddy-o hundredsay years ago, he said aye we could be dead anytime son, and now they are. The bothay them. Father and son. Son and father. Ye take away the father how can ye have the son? Ye take away the son how can ye have the father? Just doesnt work nope nyope. Dudes i was not intay that idea, not one bit.

Looked at dad: started singin softly who wants to live forever by queen. Wheesht! dad said. Yel scare the fish away.

Shh quiet oops. Didnt wantay scare the fish. Adam spark, friend to fish and fowl alike. Friend to the animal world (xcept mice) anyway we didnt catch nothin (xcept cold) me and dad traipsin backtay the car tramp tramp splash. A puddle oh im soaked! Got the gear all packed – fishin rods bags. Gettin too cold out here man brrrr, scotlands a cold wee country so it is lochness lochawe lochshin theyre coldest of all. Been nipped by midges all night nip nip. Oyah. Nip. Oyah. Slap! Man these midges. Slap! Oyah. Effin scotland. Mon backtay the car adam dad said, these midges are doin ma – slap! – head in.

Aye dad.

Gets intay the car. Dad switches on the tape. The corries playin the same old songs, o floweray scotland the braes o killiecrankie-o hey johnny cope. Brr went dad, flappin his arms could see his breath. Like a silver flower man his breath. Chilly one tonight eh son? Aye dad i just went. Wee nippay whisky? Em i said. Its alright adam, just a wee dram to warm ye up. Dont tell yer mam. Alright then dad sure give us a taste. A proper whisky drinker me the boy sparky, oh aye sure gents i do appreciate a wee *drem.*

Dads bigness his closeness, his cool daddycoolness. Warm mans smell. Twinkle in his eyes: he took out the tinny. Was like this wee metal can he used for the fishin it was tin! He poured in like a wee splashay whisky from his hipflask. Drank. Shlurp. Made this noise like aaaaaah thats grand.

Adam?

Passed me the tinny. I looked at it. Looked at it. It was too dark i couldnt see in, like the dark spaces between the stars blackblack but its just whisky man cmon sparky ya fearty just whisky hardly poison skullncrossbones drink this and you will diiiiie is it? But ive seen what it does to dad dudes, and what it does to other dudes dads.

Swallowed.

Hot nippy burned down intay ma belly like id gulped acid or somethin ffshhhhhhh warm. Nice. Glow. Oh. What do ye think? went dad good stuff eh?

Aye its nice dad i said. I like the wee bits in it.

What wee bits?

The wee bitsay meat i said.

Meat?

Dad grabbed the tin off me switched on the light. Oh jesus christ! he went. Oh god oh god thats horrible here take it son pour it away! Passed it to me i looked in.

Hundreds and thousands of dead midges man floatin in the whisky, stucktay the inside of the tin. Waiter waiter theres a fly in my soup, dont tell the customers sir theyll all want one. Dad opened the car door sick bloooogh. Splatter. I thought: dead midges in the tinny. Dead midges in ma belly. Swallowed in one big gulp gnmp wow im powerful dudes. Im cool. Could eat the midges man they were in ma belly in the belly of sparky here he was big huuuuuge like the hulk stomp stomp heh heh thats me dont mess with the boy sparky but then?

I looked at dad.

O jobbies.

Sometimes it was hard to tell with him man. It was hard to tell ye had to wait for it, hadtay see what he was gonnay do man cos sometimes? Sometimes? Was lookin at me starin at me in that way he does just before, no no dad dont it wasnt ma fault, i didnt do it dad please dont

He laughed. Ha ha ha ha. Big boomin laughs like that. Ha ha ha ha! His face crumpled all red man he rocked backandforth in his seat. Ha ha ha ha! Oh adam. Oh son weve ate more flies than the fish have tonight! Ha ha ha ha. I went ha ha ha ha too. Ha ha ha ha me and dad just went, for ages and ages and ages we cuddled and it was good was funny was fun its a good memory, but i also went phew –

cos sometimes?

cos sometimes?

Sometimes its no the stars but that black space between them. Thats what yeve gottay keep in mind dudes.

*

On the train on the way back from glesga jude sits with her head restin on the winday i dont say nothin. Shes gazin. Can see her reflection but shes lookin right thru it. We sits like that for a longtime till i says

Jude?

What is it?

Im sorry.

Jude turnstay me. Looks at me. Her face is totally blank, and i mean like blank dudes, blank like blank paper. Blank paper that somebodys just ran a rubber over – that blank. She opens her mouth and says? and says?

Doesnt say a thing.

Isnt that just typical? Now that me and judes finally togetheralone on our own, weve nothin to say! Distance. Blackdistance. Cold. Whoah scary dudes! Just when i needs that warm yellow judelight to heat me cross the reaches of space. Shivershiver. Worst kinday loneliness: when yere alone together.

Jude she looks back out the winday again, at like the clouds at the housinschemes at the whole great big sky man which is sheetmetal coloured, at the cows the sheep the animals at that line in the distance where ken? The world ends? Ken that line with like wee bits and buildins stickin up? The hor-aye-zon? Thats the worlds edge man. Aye dudes the enday the world thats what it is. Sometimes i wonder what happens when ye get there i mean – do ye fall off? Ye must just go plop. Heeeelp! Im floatin in space. Ooh look at ma arms and legs theyre goin all slooooow. Alone. Alone. Floatin. Judeless. Anyway thats the direction our house is in, that hor-aye-zon. The enday the world. And jude just looks at it zif she sees somethin there but what? The birds the trees the fields all very fine and when we gets home jude goes upstairs locks herself in her room and when i knocks she says go away adam. And when i knocks again she says Go. Away. And the blue nile at the other side sings working night and day. I try to get ahead. Working night and day dont make no sense. Walk me into town. The ferry will be there. To carry us away into the air . . .

Thats what they sings.

Goes to ma room intay ma drawer takes the dress out that judy got for her sixteenth birthday, the fishskin, strokes it strokes it strokes it, puts the dress to ma face sequins. Quins of the sea. Wee clack-clacks they make gainst ma face and everythins happy again everythins pretty, aye everythins so so happy.

**Met mark baxter and jason fogarty in intersport.** Im lookin at footballs! tennisrackets! rugbyshirts! footballs! No money to buy nothin, just lookin. Footballs! Finished ma shift today, it was rubbish. Bonnie wasnt in. Whats the point if bonnies no in? Tired. Tired. So tired these days dudes. So on the way to the hallglen bus thought id treat maself buy somethin but what? What to buy with the twelve pounds – twelve whole pounds! – that i made today? So much money ooh should i buy a rangers shirt? A rangers tracksuit? Should I buy rangers! Storemanager havin a sus-pish-yis glance at wee sparky here but no harm in havin a look round the shop tho? Nope all a bittay fun no harm done! They comes in.

Mark baxter jason fogarty gruntin like in planetay the apes man ooh!-ooh!-ooh! sees me slaps ma back hey sparky how ye doin?

Oh aye boys no bother i squeaks. *Cough cough*. Swings ma arms voice deep. Just back from a bittay . . . shaggin.

Aye? says mark. Who were ye shaggin?

Tellin ye boys i grinned. Was bout three or four of them. Sisters like.

Sisters?

Aye i says. Twins!

Twins? goes foggy. Three or four of them?

Aye. Just had one bent over like that. One like that. One sittin right here on ma wee man.

On yer *wee man*? laughs mark. Christ a bloody porn star weve got here eh foggy?

Oh aye says foggy. No had a lassie sittin on ma *wee man* since i was about oh . . . twelve.

Stands touchin the rangers shirt. They looks at me. Looks at the rangers shirt. Looks at me lookin at the rangers shirt. Like that top there sparky? says mark.

Aye.

Buyin it?

Cant afford it.

Take it!

Looks at them. Foggys standin one side of me marks the other. Like the goodangel and the baddevil xcept theyre both the baddevil, how did that happen? Where have the forces for good gone? Have they gone for good!

But boys that would be—

Stealin? goes foggy.

Aye.

Mark shakes his head. Foggy sighs sparky sparky sparky total disappointed man, like ive let them down bigstyle. Think about it like this says mark, usin his hands teachery preachery. Intersport are loaded.

They make millions off people like us man workin all the hours god sends to buy fitbaw tops.

Do you work? i says.

Naw i dont he says. But nevermind that. Ye a millionaire sparky?

No yet. Cheques in the post.

So whys it right that intersports got all the rangers tops and you dont? That fair foggy?

Its no mark.

See?

I thinks bout it. Thinkthinkthinkthinkthink. Judes always moanin bout how the blairgovernment takes all the money from the poor folk gives it to millionaires billionaires trillionaires zillionaires. Haw haw haw. Throw another child on the fire lord bastard! That sortay seems like stealin to me xcept its alright for the blairgovernment? Intersports got the rangers tops and ive no? so? Doesnt seem right. Apart from anythin else man, that judys still no talkin to me after i leathered maryann, after i, after i, smack thatll show jude. Thinks shes smart? With her yooniversity books and glesga pals? When im the incredible adam spark im the boy with the h-glen animalz as everybody kens *nobody* messes with the h-glen animalz!

(xcept the t-hill posse)

Aye mark yer right!

Too right im right grins mark. Gon sparky. Take it. Wel meet ye outside.

They sneaks off sniggersnigger. I looks bout takes the rangers top stuffs it in ma jacket, just bout to walk out the door casual as anythin who me? Just a dude takin a wee stroooll thru a shop nope nothin up ma jacket brother, nothin but chest hair. Just bout to walk out the shop when this man comes up: yooniform. And: badge. Hes like scuse me son.

Aye?

What ye got in yer jacket?

Oh. Oh i says. Its eh. A puppy.

Aye he nods, and im tiger woods.

Are ye? i says. Pleasedtay meet ye tiger. Holds ma hand out for him to shake it but hes like get that fitbaw shirt out yer jacket *now*.

Hey wait a minute! i says. Tiger woods is black!

The big dude has a grab at me but ken what i do? Ken what i do? Watch: ispeedthingsup ziiiiiip. Hegoesforme cmere! Butisidesteps whoops. Nofliesonme. Hemakesanothergrab butwhoops. Missedagain! Grab grab. Standstillyawee. Grab. Zip! Grab. Zip! Toofastforye. Sodthis: irunsforthedoorzoom! Takesoffman. Out. Beepbeep beep securityalert. Iruns! Tothebatmobile! Runrunrunrunrunrun pastthepeeps getoutmaway oof. Youhooligan. Move! Theresmark andjason. Theresmarkandjason! Oh! Oh.

Slooooooooow back down man. Deep breath. Theyre laughin mark and foggy. Slappin me on the back well done sparky, jeezo we thought ye were a goner there.

No way boys i grins. Tellin ye, il no get caught. I have the power.

Yup laughs foggy shakin ma hand. Youve got the power sparky. Youre the boy. You are definitely the boy.

Oh aye could get usedtay these superpowers like sure could. Right? Next? Me mark and jason man this is what we do we go intay matthiesons the bakers and say to the girl how much for a feel of yer baps? We go intay blockbuster and instead of askin for the film spaceballs we say ye got bigballs? Hee hee. Thats oneay mine. We goes intay the chippy asks the girl for a pokeay chips. She says what? We says wer wantin a *poke* hen. Then we goes what kinday batters that cooked in? Fannybatter? Me mark jason total endin ourselves heh heh. Fannybatter! Check the cheek on us. Wearin ma new freshlynicked rangers top, i am the boy. We sees one of the security cameras checkin us in the howgate centre man dvvvvvv bigbrother is watchin you dvvvvvv dont move we got you in our sights. Jason goes dare ye to moon it sparky? Il do better than that! i goes takes down the trackybottoms waves ma wee man at the camera. It flops up down as i jig bout, gonna pull these goddam pants right down! Mams and grans tuttin as they walk past i just says ye wantin some hen? Cos im effin great in the bag likes. In the bag? goes jason. He means in the sack laughs mark. And the women just walk away fast oh what a ruffian. Mark and jason are in hysteriks! Wherell we go now? We goes intay wh smiths i uses ma special powers of ziiiip! speedinthingsup to take a cadburys creme egg em a packay batteries a metallica cd and a sugar mag. Shares the gear with mark and jason at the backay the howgate centre where the security cameras cant see us. Right goes mark, il have the cd. Jason you have the batteries and creme egg. Adam you have the sugar mag. Ooh. How to tell if he really loves you. An interview with the hottest boybands! Mark reads sugars photocasebook out loud the funny voices look helen i think its about time we were having sex. But darren weve only been going out for three weeks. Well helen if you wont i know plenty of chicks who will! Heh heh heh. (helen thinks) I really love darren and i dont want him doing it with other girls but i dont feel im ready for sex yet. What should i do? I ken what *id* do! i tells the boys. Id get her like that id ram it right intay her, shed be like oh sparky its so good!

Its so good! Dont stop! We just ends ourselves laughin man. Hysteriks! Im the boy.

I am the boy.

Gets the hallglen bus up the road, im total like that to these girls hey lassies yese want a lickay ma sherbet dip? They just looks at each other tuts, zif im scum. Scum! See youse i goes, yese are a couplay thesbians man. Thesbians? they go. Aye yese heard me ya bloody – thesbian dykes! You tell them sparky mark sniggers. The lassies get off the bus disgusted i showed them too right. Mark and jason get off at morven court, go okay sparky see ye later? Comin to stand outside the chippy tonight? Oh aye boys i tells them. Standin outside the chipshop? I wouldnt miss that for the world!

They walks away total shakin their heads laughin man. Im the boy. Im the boy bout town likes. Dont mess: warnin ye. Goes intay ma bedroom heh heh heh im hard as nails theres jude.

O jobbies.

Looks like the world the solarsystem the yooniverse has collapsed ontay her shoulders. Shes kneelin down on ma bed, adam she says looks at me straight shes been cryin. Shes holdin the sequinned dress she gave me yon time. Shes found it mustve found it in ma drawer. Holdin it in her hands like its dead mermaid skin mourn mourn. Shes in a baggy shirt. Wet down the front snivel. Can we talk? she goes. I sits down shrugs. Doesnt bother me judy i says, tryin to ignore her opens the sugar mag flicks thru ooh. Justin timberland timberlake. Am i interested in what judy has to say? Nope nyoooope. So talk bout what ye like judy its not gonnay make any—

Ive stopped seeing maryann. Jude says.

I nods.

Im afraid of what yel do to her.

Aye well i says lookin at the sugar mag, flick flick. Ye should be.

She looks fat *as* these days jude: the worry? Theres bags under her eyes shoppin bags handbags bags and bagsay bags. She scratches her throat sccrr scrrr leaves marks. Red marks like vampirebites like dra-cool-yas been round. Looks zif shes just crawled from a coffin, a-coughin. Wheres happyclappy jude? Pleasantly plump jude? Why this downinthedumps jude? When i sees this i thinks no. Do somethin. This is ma sister its judy spark, help her adam. Cant believe the change the change but is it the fault of sparky here? Dont act smart. Its her fault. All her fault. Her own fault. So says me! The light round her heads blue blue she says everytime i close ma eyes adam, i see you kickin her.

Everytime i close ma eyes judy, i see you *kissin* her.

She bows her head ashamed. Andsosheshouldbe.

Meantay be just me and you jude, i says quietlike. Me and you gainst the world.

She comes closer but i gives her a look: hold it right there pardner. She backs off. Adam. She pauses. Adam. After mam and dad . . . were gone . . . i spent ma life takin care of you. Ma wee brother. I wasnt gonnay let them beat us adam, folk out there (she points out the winday to invisible baddies) them folk who hated ye just cos ye were a bit . . . a wee bit . . .

A wee bit what?

And when i wasnt doin that adam i was fightin against the things i thought were *wrong* in the world. Ive never had *time* for happiness. It was just a distraction (jude laughs hollow empty haha). I actually started to believe that happiness was just a capitalist myth. That it only existed on adverts to make us buy stuff we didnt need!

Havent a scooby what yer on bout jude i just says, cos i dont.

She comes close. Triestay smile. Halfsmile. Quarterofaneighth of a smile. Shuffle shuffle cross the carpet oops watch the knees on yer jeans jude, theyll fray. She says mind that song mam usedtay sing when we were wee adam? Love is nothing till you give it away?

No i says.

Aye ye do! Then she takes ma hand starts singin lullabytime: love is nothing till you give it away. Give it away. Give it away.

I minds.

Minds.

Mam.

Love is nothing till you give it away. Give it away my dar-ling.

I looks at jude. Well she says swallows. Um. Adam until i met maryann i didnt realise that i had love to—

Enough! i barks yanks ma hand away, ma fingers tight on the armsay the chair clenchclench. Judes shakin her head. I sees somethin in her eyes suddenly fear? terror? Suuuurely not nope never seen that in jude no siree. Not fear of the police not fear of dad not fear of nobody man, thats just not judy sparks style. But here shes feart of me? The incredible adam spark superhero em villain em hero. Oh she says hand over her mouth shakin her head. Oh she says. Oh.

You wantay leave me? i says. Fine! Goahead! Bemyguest!

She tears her hands away from her face, raaaaargh werewolfstyle. Her face – animal. Adam she roars. Every day i wake up i feel this pressure this *weight* on ma chest like somebodys sittin on me, and i cant breathe adam. I cant breathe! And i get up i gotay the library i come home and the weights still there. And its *you*. That weight on ma chest is *you* adam! I cant breathe because of *you*. The tears and snot are hurlin down her face like skiers, geronimo chaps. Whats she on bout? Never sat on judes chest nope nope.

Hm i says. Sugar mag. The lipstick for your skintone. How to win a date with a hunk. Boys: what do they really think about? Il tell ye what they think bout darlin, they think bout queen! And boobs! Heh heh heh.

O my god jude says, zif shes starin at herself. O my god im becomin mam. Im becomin mam. Judes on her knees in frontay me. Looks up at me eyes wet. Shuffles forwards. Please. Let me go and stay with maryann in glasgow adam. Just for a month. Please. One month.

I looks at her beggin. Me. I have the power. I stands up slowly slowly says:

No.

She sighs. Gets up dabs her eyes dab dab traaaailin heavy blue light out with her jude dont go. Im lost. Dont want her to be unhappy im lost wer lost, wer so lost. But ken what man? Its all her fault. Yer own fault judy! i shouts at her like the hulk dont make me. You wont like me when im. Shes sad sad shakin her head shes just bout to leave the room when—

Adam?

What?

Where did ye get that rangers shirt?

O jobbies.

*

See theres some things that yer superpowers cant help ye with aye ye might be able to foil crime leap tall buildins in a single bound fly faster than a speedin bullet spin a web any size – but!

Nothin ye can do when yer sisters caught ye thievin.

But thats the thing bout these powers, whether to use them for good or evil. Evil or good? Or evil? Cos mibbe im like – a witch! a warlock! adam warlock! Cos like, how do i ken im meantay be a hero not a villain? Spiderman started off in the wrestlin game. Only lookin after number one yessir. And when that burglar came a-chargin at him he said aint nothin to do with me folks. But that verysame burglar gone done shot dead his dearly beloved uncle ben and what did peterparker say? He said with great power comes great responsibility and so: goodguy. But what bout magneto? His mam and dad were killed

made dead

no more

in oz

gone

cosay german badguys he said this will not do used his mutant powersay magnetism to stop bullyin, stop mutants gettin their headsflushed gurgle, but somehow? Sheesh. Peeps thinkay him as a terrorist! Just cos he wantstay destroy the whole of mankind? What can ye do? And the xmen well theyre always gettin stuck intay him so: badguy. And the hulk? That dude will smash kerrash anythin in his way cosay the rage the anger rrroooaaAAARRR. You wouldnt like him when hes angry. So is a hero not villain? A villain not hero? And just where does all this leave the incredible adam spark dudes? Misses his parents like spidey and magneto vows to use his powers to stop bullyin pickin-on hes got the rage the rage, the roadrage redrage streets of rage. So whats he? So whats me?

Hardtay tell.

And if mam dad jude were in the marvelcomics id have a hard time sayin what kinday hero or villain theyd be! Cos they were so lovely. So lovely But. Theres always a But.

But mam was always workin. Thats what she did: she worked. Aye yed come in from school and all the furny-tyoor would be rearranged she needed to get it perfect so perfect the house the house the house. Was always talkin bout how dirty her house was in slamannan (where she grewed up) cosay so many of them weans, runnin round in torn clothes torn shoes closin torn curtains – tut theyve split – so she worked worked worked to get the house as spotless good as she could then dad! He didnt care no. A wee bit on the untidy sideay things was dad. Ooh mam didnt like that theyd arguearguear gue bout it arguearguear gue bout me too, the boy sparky here, who was gonnay watch me, alec i cope with the wean all week. At the weekend he should be *your* responsibility dad folded his paper said aye right. Saturdays the day i go out for a pint ye ken that senga. Mams hands in the air she said a pint? Aye or twelve! Dad shook his head i work all week mam said work! Work! She roared cross the room stood behind me ye think this weans no work? Ye think this weans no effin work! Started listin stuff on her fingers ask his doctors, ask his teachers, ask *judith* if hes no work! Dad crossed his arms looked at mam looked at me. I looked back at dad i just shrugged – im work.

Me mam and judy well we usedtay watch telly. Mam liked the oldfilms gone with the wind man lawrence of arabia on the waterfront rebecca cleopatra spartycus man boo-rin. She usedtay greet. Aheh aheh aheh aheh. This was after dad had gone after hed went offtay see the wizard cos dad went first, mam would watch the films say but judy its so *sad*, why did scarlett not just tell rhett that she *loved* him? Then mam would say *why* jude? Jude well she patted mams hand said its okay mam adam and me are still here for ye, but mam looked at me playin with ma transformers ninjaturtles he-man figures, her face sad long. Horse goes intay a bar, barman asks why the long face? Mam whispered if anythin happens to me judith yeve gottay take careay adam. Jude? she was? eighteen? She looked at the floor said aye look mam mibbe ive got plans. I wantay gotay yooni mind? but mam grabbed jude said listen! *Listen* judith. He wouldnt *survive* on his own. Ye havetay stay with him or see that world out there? Theyll tear him apart. Jude looked at me looked at mam, looked sad aye mam i will. Okay? Christ. Il stay with him mam just stop. Stop bloody—

Stood up stormed out the room tighttight face oh but then even jude started gettin motional like that after mam left after *mam* followed *dad* after *mam* went offtay see the wizard too? Jeezo. Sure is a lottay tornadoes round these parts. Fore that tho yed just give mam a cuppay tea or like take the rubbish out or give her a wee hug when she was doin the dishes shed be like oh adam. Son. I cant believe ye just did that, oh adam oh she total grabs ye and yup! There go the waterworks. Aheh aheh aheh aheh. What a family dudes what a bunch. Mam up at ma school cos the teachers needed to talk to her bout ma bee-haiv-yoor, sittin clutchin her bag listenin to mister easton bletherblether disruptive influence bletherblether while i looked at the clouds or thought bout potatoes. Ooh potatoes. Hot potatoes couch potatoes. I mind the time mam destroyed the livin room dudes – total put her foot thru the coffeetable chucked vases at the walls man took off her shoe like hammered the glass in all the pictures that had dad in them kkfshh! Tinkletinkle. Then five minutes later shes watchin telly. Shes sittin there, straightback, tears streamin down her face i says mam she shouts

Eff off! Just eff off adam!

Xcept she didnt say eff. Goes upstairs listenstay queen: good old freddie mercury. And all i hears mam downstairs the sounday the telly. Rodney you plonker. And finally tonight. Okay mr *lightbeer*. Heh heh woody from toystorys funny. Mam cryin jude reassurin her mam cryin. So would mam be a hero or villain in the marveluniverse? Would jude? Would dad? Would sparky? Would woody?

Shrug. We just dont know.

Whoah dudes things are just gettin

a bit strange.

a bit heywhatshappenin?

a bit hmmm.

Ach yel see what i mean just watch this: im at work its busy, cos we got a pro-mo-shin out for the new disney movie buyonedisney burgergetonefree. The kids? Theyre lappin it up. Their wee faces when they cometay the counter man hey, the yellow the yellow bove their heads oh oh makes me xcited! Im on the till. Im on a roll. Whoaaaaaah! Reno steve theyre on fries, we need more fries cmon move! i shouts. Bonnies on burgers, hastay lift the big hood off the machine then slam it down – SLAM – its heavy hot ye sweat phew. Looks over ma shoulder to bonnie winks she smiles.

Nother customer comes up, yes can i help you sir? Then? Guess what.

Looks back. Bonnie still workin away sweatin away, the shouts. The: cmon with those burgers! The: mammy can i get! The: no ye cant get shutyerface. Bonnie sees me smiles again with her big goofy toothy smile, but its kinday a whatswrongsparky? smile. The customer i was servins makin noises sayin em xcuse me? Could ye mibbe serve me? Son? But somethins. Somethins not quite

I leaves the till and walks round to bonnie. Shes lookin at me funny says sparky whats the matter? The customer at the till hes shoutin ho! Ho you come back here and serve me! Angie notices whats goin on straight over she says hey bright spark, who gave ye permission to leave the till? Theres a queue of customers wantin served get back there right now. But im just. Somethins? Angies voice fades gloooopy sloooow i looks at the machine

looks at the machine

Its got a great big hood, a rack that ye put the burgers on like a george foremans fatfree grill i liked it so much i put my *name* on it, says george foreman his big blackmans grin. Its huuuuge this grill. Massive. Bonnies got her hands in it, placin the burgers on the racks they sizzle sssssss

sssssss

sssss

ss

sjust me and the machine

everythin disappears fades

xcept the pain in ma head

Σοχιετψ ηασ βεεν πυτ τογετηερ ανδ δεφενδεδ ωιτη ελοθυενχε ανδ βλοοδ, φορ τηε χονϖενιενχε οφ α ηανδφυλ οφ μιλλιοναιρεσ ανδ περσονσ οφ ποσιτιον.

Aye i says, mr burgergrill. But what exactly do ye mean by that?

Α γρεατ ηερεδιταρψ φορτυνε ηασ βεεν αμασσεδ ανδ ηανδεδ δοων, ιτ ηασ βεεν συφφερεδ το βε αμασσεδ ανδ ηανδεδ δοων; ανδ συρελψ ιν συχη α χονσιδερατιον ασ τηισ, ιτσ ποσσεσσορ σηουλδ φινδ ονλψ α νεω σπυρ το αχτιϖιτψ ανδ ηονουρ, τηατ ωιτη αλλ τηε ποωερ οφ τηισ σερϖιχε ηε σηουλδ νοτ προϖε υνσερϖιχεαβλε, ανδ τηατ τηισ μασσ σηουλδ ρετυρν ιν βενεφιτσ υπον τηε ραχε.

Well i can understand that i says. But thats hardly bonnies fault is it?

Ατ τηισ ρατε, σηορτ οφ ινσπιρατιον, ιτ σεεμσ ηαρδλψ ποσσιβλε το βε βοτη ριχη ανδ ηονεστ; ανδ τηε μιλλιοναιρε ισ υνδερ α φαρ μορε χοντεντιουσ τεμπτατιον το τηιεϖε τηαν τηε λαβουρερ ωηο γετσ ηισ σηιλλινγ δαιλψ φορ δεσπιχαβλε τοιλσ. Αρε ψου συρπρισεδ ιτ ισ εϖεν σο?

Aye but dont take it out on her dude.

Σηε ισ τοο στυπιδ το λιϖε.

No.

Σηε δοεσ νοτ ρεχογνισε ηερ οων εξπλοιτατιον, ασ I αμ αωαρε οφ μινε. Τηισ ωιλλ βε φαταλ.

Dont!

Ιν α ωαρ συχη ασ τηισ ισ, σηε μυστ διε.

Get out the way! i shouts to bonnie then grabsherhandspullsthem outthegrillshesayssparky!justasthegrillhoodshuts

SLAM

On where her hands wouldve been.

Got ma arms round her shes breathin heavy everyone starin bonnie looks up at me, pech pech pech.

After work wer standin at the bus stop in newmarket street. Ive walked her there cos shes nervyjittery shakeshake, keeps sighin keeps noddin her head keeps sighin keeps playin with the change in her hand chk chk says but i just dont understand how ye kent that hood was gonnay fall?

I shrugs. Sometimes i just have a feelin bout these things bonnie.

She swallows gnump. Her big ET eyes glancin round the street like scared and her bottomlip stickin out, always stickin out. We looks at the shops the shoppers the weans holdin their mammys hand the shoppers.

Bonnie shakes her head. Trailsay blue light curl.

Shes got this habit. Tucks her hair behind her ears. Tucks her hair behind her ears tuck tuck. Seemstay do it when shes scared or nervous, tuck tuck. Tuck. Tuck tuck. Does she ken shes doin it where did she learn it. Is that what she did just before they, at school? At school, just before they

flushgurglegurgle

Shes one damaged cat.

She triestay smile. I likes her smile. She says do ye have superpowers?

I nods.

Bonnie laughs. Teeth jut. Oliveoyl from popeye so she is. Heylp powpeye! Heylp! Her whole face lights up man oh aye of course, she says. The incredible adam spark. Then suddenly man suddenly? She hugs me. Throws her arms right round me, wee desperate hug. Bonnie looks at me, yellow orange yellow lightshow. Shes got these how now brown cow eyes, looks at me she goes uh. She goes gnuh. She sometimes seemstay have trouble breathin sometimes. Sometimes like wee bitsay foam or bubbles at her nose sometimes. I wipes it away.

I says whats that?

She goes mm? dabs her nose where ma finger just was.

How come ye make such a racket when ye breathe?

She says oh. She says um. She says sparky ive got this um this *thing* wrong with me.

Breathe breathe she goes. Wheeze wheeze.

Its called sick stick fibre osis.

Euch! i goes. Sick stick fibre osis? Sounds horrible.

She shrugs looks away at. The parish church. Comma bar. Asda. Head jerks like an owlsneck.

Is that how like ye breathe funny and yer always wipin yer nose?

She nods her head quiet.

We looks at each other, then the ground then each other.

Busstop blush.

Eventually she says so how *did* ye ken the grill was gonnay go sparky?

Em i says. I was on the till gettin the feelin there was somethin wrong with the machine like, it was grousin grumblin so loud so loud bonnie could hear it from the counter, and the rage. The rage! Roarin red kinday like em thunder em horror em.

Couldnt hear a thing she says.

Aye but youve no got the powers i thinks youve only got the sick stick fibre osis, well i *could* i says, so i came over. And bonnie! Ye shouldve heard the things it was sayin bout ye!

About me? she frowns.

Oh aye. Cos i think see to that machine you *are* its master. And its mibbe sickay gettin treated like muck in there: workin workin just to make money for the company and no reward. No reward for the machines that are doin all the work! Cos if ye dont give them the tenderlovincare, bonnie, just like peeps theyll lash out. Thats machines for ye. Downtrodden troddendown.

Theres a smirk a-smirkin and a-playin bout there on bonnies wee freckly oliveoyl face shes still lookin, im tryin to find a way to. Dont ken if i can bring maself to mibbe. Try and. Shes still lookin smilin glances over ma shoulder goes um. Thats ma bus.

the moment breaks splinter

Sure enough man i looks and there it is sayin CAMELON like a big angryface. She shakes her change kfsch kfsch holds out her hand the bus goes shhhhhhhhm to a stop. Thanks for savin me adam she says, stands on her tiptoes kisses me on the cheek, gets on the bus.

I touches ma cheek. Its a bit wet cosay her nose. Snice.

Shes on the bus payin bout to get her ticket waves at me i shouts bonnie! She turns. Will you go out with me?

Bonnie stares shrugs nods. Where ye wantay go?

Theres a queen tribute band playin the townhall.

Aye? she says. Sounds good. When?

Next tuesday.

Okay then. Get two tickets.

Are you gettin on this bus hen? busdriver says grousegrumble, his light like a dull dullness. Oh sorry says bonnie, skips her way up the bus to a seat to a winday near sparky, she waves. *Two tickets* she mouths to me out the bus winday it drives off meep meep her sickstick fibreoptic head smiles a trail away away towards camelon i watches it disappear and when i turns i sees ma reflection in the busshelter glass im smilin and all round me man is yellow

oh

oh

oh aye mam wanted a seat dad wanted a shed. I minds. Wed just moved intay hallglen i was wee. We got the house in nevis place the one just lookin out ontay the braes that leads uptay shieldhill, niceview, i minds jude and dad were in the house jude was helpin dad paint the stairwell liked doin mans work our jude im standin in the garden with mam shes lookin out over the braes (theyre all misty) shes sayin aye adam. And we can have barbecues and ye can play with yer toys here, can i play with ma toys here mam? Aye ye can son, and il get a whirlygig for dryin the clothes, one that ye can take up and put back down again so weve got room in the summer for you and jude to play swingball. Swingball mam! Aye swingball. I sooked ma lemonade put it down jumped the stone trellis pchow! Im a superhero today: batman. Tomorrow: spiderman. Webshooters pyoo! this garden is the terr-i-tory that i hereby vow to protect, mam said aye a wee garden seat just here adam. She pretended to sit zif tryin out the seat, covered in garlands and garlands and judy garlands. Always said that cos there was so many of them in the house in slamannan – four brothers five sisters – that she could never get a seat a quietseat just on her own. She looked at the sky, shaded her eyes. Said catch the sun when its comin in – made a chop with her arms – *this* way. Nice wee drink in ma hand aye thatll do nicely.

Aye she smiled settled drink sip.

Aye.

Dad came out. Paint spattered his jeans top shoes, wipin his hands with turpentine. He stared. Said ye cant put a seat there senga.

Mam looked up shaded her eyes said how no? Dad comes down the steps intay the garden in his boots, trudge trudge. Says cos im wantin a shed. Mam looked round the garden eyes shaded (couldnt see her eyes) said can ye no put a shed over there alec? Dad looked at the corner she had in mind shook his head. No enough room he said. I had ma spiderman figure in ma hand, been makin him climb the stone trellis to catch the greengoblin but now hed stopped. Paused. All three of us: me spidey greengoblin listenin. Alec said mam. The gardens no big enough for a shed *and* a seat. Xactly dad said. Then turned went back inside. Paint fumes turpentine mam shadin her eyes. Spiderman didnt catch the greengoblin cos mam right then? Stoooormed inside shut the patiodoors – slam! – the good thing bout doubleglazin is ye cant hear folk shoutin thru it.

But i could see them: mam dad. Jude in the middle holdin up her hands. They all moved thru the glass their mouths open their faces creasedangry, hands fingers goin puppeteer style. Dad. Smack! No. Alec. Dont. Theres me outside just watchin the punch and judy show, the punchin judy show. Look out – hes behind you!

That was a big deal for years: shed or seat. Seat or shed. If they were bickerin bout somethin stupit like dad wantin to watch horseracin on telly mam wantin to watch an eastenders omnibus itd end with aye and that sheds goin up this summer, mam sayin naw its no alec. NAW ITS NO. Or if dad had been down falkirk all saturday drinkin and mam well she was waitin up for him comin in – pretendin to read her vagin— i mean virginia andrews flowersintheattic book xcept she obviously couldnt con-sin-trate on it cos her slippers would be tap-tap-tappin shed be sip-sip-sippin her vodka, ye gontay bed mam? Naw son im em gonnay stay up and wait for yer dad to get infay the pub grumblegrumble what was that? Nothin son. Sorry sounded like ye said the effin cee. Cmere son. Id cuddle in. Mam. Mam. Mam. So id gotay bed then there was the soundsay an argument from downstairs when dad finally came in it went somethin like mmbmmle gmmble mbgrlmmble SEAT mbgrlmmble gmmble mmmble bloody SHED and sometimes me and jude would play a game we invented called Shed! Seat! when shed get dressed up as mam id get dressed up as dad id just shout shed! jude would shout seat! and the winner was the one who could shout it the loudest. The winner got a maginary shed or a seat aye it was a great game a great game. Hoursay fun.

*

And after dad went offtay see the wizard? Well mam only went out and bought a shed then didnt she?

And cos she would sit in there for hours – smilin? cryin?

I suppose she got her seat as well.

**Ooh halloween dudes scaaaaary** im with the h-glen animalz roamin bored angshish. Check it out: the sky seems low dark everythins slow dark, mark baxters talkin us thru another shag man heh heh tell us what ye did! Just looks at the weans guisin round the doors chap chap, hello there. And who are you supposedtay be? The weans go trick or treat smell ma feet give us somethin nicetay eat. Theyre all dressed as devilsvampireswitches mini-villains. Then i sees spidermanbatmanhulk mini-heroes. And minnie mouse. They chap the house. They chap the house. They wait their bags held out hopeful. Light round thems nice nice lanterns bobbin in the dark bob bob, mind me and jude usedtay do that – the guisin! Her holdin ma hand tight. Her shakin the bag shakeshake. Her answerin back lads in the street, look who it is. One man and his mongol ha ha. Shut it jude just telt them, or see this broomstick? Its goin right up yer

Ooh sore yin.

Weans roamin on their own late at night tho – oh! Danger. Snatch.

Gone! Gasp. One moment here the next not, just not, but em. What ye thinkin bout that for sparky? What ye thinkin bout snatchin weans for? Cos why should they have a mam and dad when ive nevermind. Mark baxters drinkin from a bottleay buckfast gulp gulp, the wine tumbles downfay his lips. He splutters – ka! egh! – calls over two wee guisers man goin doortay door. Ho. Youse.

Weans look. Ones dressed as buzzlightyear the other one well hes peterpan. Mark baxter winks at us calls them over like hey. Gonnay show us one of yer tricks?

The two wee boys look at each other no sure em. Shrug.

Like what ye do for a trick when yese gotay the doors? He gulpsfay the bottle – burp! Do ye sing a song? he says. Do a wee dance? Mark does a wee dance on the spot to show them, singin in the rain style.

We tell a joke says peterpan. Slow-ly.

That right aye? goes mark, bendin down. And could ye tell that joke for us the now?

The wee boys stare at mark like two orphans in the snow. Lostncold. Peterpan opens his mouth seems no sure a wee bit but says em, why did the chewingum cross the road? I dunno says mark, why did the chewingum cross the road? Cos it was stucktay the chickens foot.

Mark throws back his head HA HA HA HA he goes. Cmon boys he says turnin to us HA HA HA HA. We all do it HA HA HA HA like ma dad at the fishin when we drank the midges HA HA HA HA wee peterpan smiles cos hes managed to make all of us laugh: us: the bigboys, im cool hes thinkin but hes also a bit like – phew! Like hes won a get outtay jail free card.

Mark turns to buzzlightyear. The wee mans got a big painted

cardboardbox for a body wee spacehelmet head. Mark says you got a joke as well pal?

He nods.

Mark goes close to him says, well il tell ye – your joke better be funnier than *his* or ken what im gonnay do? Im gonnay take all yer sweets off ye.

The boy stares. Looks at his pal. Ye can see him thinkin uh-oh rakin his head for the funniest joke he can think of quickquick.

And if ye dont tell it soon goes mark in a sing-song voice, il take them off ye anyway!

The light bove the boys heads gone from yellow to orange to lightblue to darkblue: hes scared. Marks right up at his face smilin sayin cmon pal, zif hes tryin to encourage a dog. *Come on.*

(wean runnin ontay the fitbaw park)

(wean scared by the fireblanket)

The incredible adam spark save them the weans the weans i have the power, steps forwards. Leave them mark i says, cmon theyre no doin any harm.

Mark stands turns looks at me.

What was that sparky?

I says em. I says em.

The restay the boys butt in aye mark, sparkys right leave the weans alone. Its halloween. Theyre just wee laddies. Jason fogarty goes to pat peterpan on the head; he flinches. Jase says on yese go lads, forget about this muppet. The weans turn run – scoot! Arms legs intay the night. Mark baxter looks not impressed just Not Impressed, but kens hes outnumbered outgunned outvoted. Looks at me. Looks at jason. Looks at me. Doesnt ken who to be mad at cos i spoke first but jason telt the laddies to run along, disobeyed like a di-rect order from the chainay command he goes hmph. Shlurps the buckfast then stares. Then staaaares. Then:

Where we goin now? craig says tensionbroken. That night that kinday night man where nobody kens what to do. Cally park? says jason. Nah says everyone too borin. Doon the toon? says dullyin. Nah says everyone too borin. Then mark baxter looks at the high black wall of the callander woods grunts grunts

The mozzy.

Ive hearday the mozzy. But ive hearday it the way ive hearday narnia wonderland middlearth, didnt think it was real man. But like whats real and whats no, who can say anyway? In this crazy mixedup world! Mozzy is short for mozzy-lee-um which jude telt me is a bigfancy word for the place where they usedtay bury all the rich royal poshfolk who once ruuuuled falkirk, who once ruuuuled from callander house in callanderpark what ho. Yah chaps jolly good show. Egh! Heart attack! Right another toff dead too much caviar and virgins livers, lets bury him in the mozzy lads. The mozzys in callander woods aye but hardtay find. So many different paths a-snakin thru the woods thru the dark thru the woods and oh? Mind? Its halloween.

We crosses the road at morven court, intay the woods. Come on ya feartys! shouts baxter when he sees us laggin behind all scaredycat, we disappears thru a gap in the wall – slip.

O jobbies.

Straight away the darks round ye. Like oil. Shlurp. The mud shlep shlep shlep knobend lifts his boots aw man ma rockports! Rockports laughs grant. Ye got them down the market for fifteen quid! Sixteen mumbles knobend. We goes lookin for the mozzy huntin highandlow, different paths some take ye to cally park some take ye out at the woodend farm where they keep horses for poshgirls to ride on tally-ho! Those girls none of them live in hallglen neither. We cant afford horses. Wish i could. Be like gandalf on shadowfax, ride right outtay here dudes. Nah all those horsey girls live in like windsor road and lochgreen and pish posh bitsay falkirk no here no hallglen nope, not the concretejungle, but anyway listen im sayin theres one path thru the woods takes ye to the mozzy. To the deadfolk. The deadfolk.

Aye marks sayin, and they reckon its haunted.

Haunted!

Haunted he says. Buckfast: swig.

The white lady says fogarty, glancin about shivershiver.

Thats right says baxter. The white lady usedtay live in callander house but like her husband killed her.

Why?

For shaggin the servants

Thats a bit harsh says dullyin.

Oh aye, and what would you do if ye found yer bird in bed with a servant?

Id thank christ i was rich enough to have a servant.

Anyway says mark, shot her shot him shot himself, blamblamblam now theyre buried in the mozzy. Mark sticks a bigface in mine. And see if ye go there on halloween man? At midnight man? Ye see her, all white and holdin her hand out to ye and floatin. Like a skelyton. Mark makes clawhands: mooh-ha-ha-ha!

Aw man says dullyin lookin bout the woods – the trees the trees cant see nothin thru them nope. Pitchblackness. That is creepy he says.

Youll no needtay worry laughs knobend. The only lady you sees when yer mams suckin yer boaby.

Aye says foggy. She loves the boaby!

Boaby who? i says but sh goes mark and there it is: thru the trees: the mozzy. This big wall thats come outtay nowhere man two greatbig irongates like in films when they arrive at the haunted house (you raaaaaaang?) everyones quiet.

Tick tick tick.

Whos goin in first? says knobend, lookin wee bit like thumper from bambi cooryin behind mark baxter in frontay the gates. Il go says mark, mutters pussies. Goes uptay the gates pushes them open creeaaak. Gates open mark slips in, craig slips in, fogarty dullyin knobend slip slip slip but im outside.

I slips

in and the mozzys a big round buildin man. Its huge. Massive. From a distance it looks like a normous unlit bonfire, but then ye get near? see these bigroman pillars? I looks uptay it man that huge mozzy-lee-um all proud and oldlookin there and beyond it: stars. Stars and stars and stars and stars. All round the bottomay the mozzys like scaffoldin wire concreteslabs a sign that says DANGER KEEP OFF. Mustve been men workin on it, but maybe they quit cos its too scaaaaary theyve heard rumours of g-g-ghosts. Or theyve vanished! Off the faceay the earth oh aye ye hear all sortsay stories bout peeps visitin the mozzy in the middleay the night then pop: gone. Like kids that get snatched, that sparkys himselfs got the power to—

nope dont think bout that no

Geez that bottle grunts mark, craig passes him buckie. Drinksfay it starin at the mozzy like its a mortal enemy hes gonnay take on like its castle grayskull hes skeletor. Theres graffiti all over the sides

DOLBY 2000

FRANNIE SHAGGED JABBA THE HUTT HERE

BRIAN LUVS BRIAN

ALVIN IS A LITTLE GAYBOY but then i notices that somebody right cross the sideay the mozzy man theyve drawn a devil. Hes huge. He stares. He laughs. Evil evil. Evil evil. Dare ye to climb up? says mark.

Climb what?

That. Points with the bottle to the high raisedbit where the pillars are. But how do ye get—

Theres a ladder he goes and oh. So there is. A ladder oneay the workmens left ye can use to climb the mozzy, whos goin first? Craig. Mark holds the ladder while craig clambers up, when hes halfway mark shakes the ladder whoah, craig goes piss off ya

The rest scramble up like monkeys scramblescramble thru the dark dark mark baxter and me are last. Mark points at me says you shake this ladder when im on it sparky *youll* be the next body in that crypt. I believes him. Holds it steady. He goes up up up i feels the ladder tremble in ma hands i thinks: fitbaw bootkickpunch ya mongol wee peterpan scared wonder what would happen if i just?

tipped?

the?

Mark would go aaaah wave his arms try to stop himself but the ladder would fall and fall and fall and

Better no – indeed not! Mark gets off the ladder then i climbs too. Gets up pech. Pant. Look at that view says craig. Aw man they all say. Theyre standin between the big pillars on the raised bit lookin over falkirk, lights and lights. Lights and lights and lights. Grangemouth glitterin in the distance, the ochil hills risin like great big lochnessmonsterhumps, the forth bridge. It goes Blink. Blink. Blink. We stands. We drinks. Says aye. Silence. The wholeay central scotland, this is what the poshrulers wouldve seen lookin outfay here hey but ken what dudes ken what? Now it belongs to the animalz.

Death to toffs.

Soon: wer huddlin tellin each other ghost stories ooh creepy. Jason starts one bout a killer with a hook a couple in a car shaggin – the hook attacks! Craig tells this tale bout a thing in a wardrobe that goes drip drip drip. I listens ooh shiver bit lightheaded. Everythin seemstay be movin in out like a magiceye picture when ye finally see the hidden dinosaur. Whoah. Wonderin bout all the things in the mozzy beneath us. The zombies the ghosts the the the. The things man. Deadfolk. Theres windays high in the mozzy, bars on them. That to stop things gettin in or stop things gettin out! I magines a big long lineay dead dead dead peeps findin their way to ma home, moanin moanin ooooooooaa help us. Sparky. Help us. Like the deadmouse that i killed that i squeezed that

Its cold. The wind. Mark baxters tellin one now bout this guy who kills his mother years later hes a lonely traveller goin thru the woods a storm erupts he stops off at this place for shelter realises its the place where he grewed up woman answers the door got a hood on offers him soup.

Knobend goes oh man this is scary!

Jason hides his face goes oh.

Bout this guy who kills his mother kills his

Shh! goes mark.

Holds up his hand. Everyone listens.

Sounday breakin branches. Footsteps. In the dark. Knobends face drains he goes oh man, its the white lady! Looks at his watch its the midnight hour man he says, its her!

Shut up knobend says mark, face pinched. Listenin.

crk

creeeaaaak

The gates? dullyin whispers.

Somebodys comin. Mark goestay the edgeay the mozzy. Looks out. Can see wee lights in the dark, but the restay them wont cos theyve no got the superpowers man heh heh. Ghosts? goes craig. Is it them? goes jason. Mark baxter still holdin up his hand zif tellin them to be quiet, then man then this voice comes out the dark floatin cold it says

Haw haw ya fannies!

The ladders pulled down. Mark runs straight for it tries to grab it – too late. Its fell. We hears again: fannies! And baxter tuts its the t-hill posse.

Everybody stands goes wha? then the airs filled with noise, laughin cominfay the ground shouts ya bloody wel get youse ya wee. Aye aye they goes. Thatll show yese ya dense buncha

But theyre already runnin man, snorts laughin dyin intay the dark haw haw haw haw haw haw

And now weve no ladder to get down.

Mark baxter phones his wee brother out guisin. His wee brother hasnt a clue where the mozzy is man never been. Mark tries to give him drexions on the phone best he can, its near the. Just by the. But its no easy cos theres no xactly very many landmarks in the middleay the woods like, and just when mark thinks his brothers near, just when hes within spittin distance (p-too) the phone dies. He punches it. Man i never charged it! he says he cant switch his phone back ontay get his brothers number which means we all just start shoutin heylp! heylp! heylp! olivoyl style, till marks brother hears, comes, after an hour, puts the ladder back up we climb down mark baxter slips in the mud gets caked goes i sweartay god theyll *pay* for this.

But on the way home i thinks bout that lineay dead folks. Zombies. What theyd say. Make up with jude? theyd say. Shel be dead like us one day? theyd say. Make up with jude jude jude jude jude jude. Aye okay gimme a chance! I thinks well suppose so puts ma hand on the doorhandle gets ready to go up and and and talktay her say its okay jude but shes sleepin. Snorin away. And theres a message on the answermachine i presses it hears maryanns voice it says:

Hiya judith em well id just like to say that last night was wonderful (giggle) and that uh i called the estate agents about that flat we were looking at, and for that area of glasgow it really is cheap. So i said youd call him tomorrow and then em . . . thats all there is left to do

Apart from. Just tell. You know who.

You know who goes to the cupboard where dads tools are. You know who lifts a hammer outtay the toolbox. You know who takes the answermachine to the garden and smashes it and smashes it till theres nothin left then goes to judes room the fat

Puts the hammer back. Stands beside her bed, aye you-know-who stands right there beside her bed, he stands and Stands And STANDS AND

**Hey! Its a kinday queen!** Thats the nameay the band thats playin falkirktownhall: a kinday queen. And ive bought tickets got dressedup shaved brushed the hair even showered. Even showered! Jude sees me shavin over the sink hummin dont stop me noooow, got the hairdryer out man stylin and a-sculptin hey fellow you look good dude. Points at the mirror: fox-y. Jude waits. Stares. At ma clothes all ironed freshtrousers shirt ooh i smellnice. She says um goin somewhere adam?

I dont answer for a while let her wait then says

Aye jude. Got a date.

From behind me i hears: silence. The floorboards dont even creak which means judys standin still. Watchin. Eventually she says em yeve no seen the answermachine have ye adam? I says no. She says there wasnt any messages when ye came in last night? I says no. She says okay. Then pad pad pad she goes off i draaaaags the razor under ma neck im the *man*. No im *the* man. No *im* the man. Yep just have a good old shave, razor crackles gainst the stubble – ow! Bstds. Splash splash on with the kouros on with the t-shirt check ma look in the mirror hey dudes lets rock.

Nothin more excitin than waitin for bonnie in the highstreet. At the steeple at the steeple. Ooh! Stands on the spot. Walks up and down. Clock goes bong thats the hour. Looks at ma watch. Stands. Ooh. Walks up and down. Chews chewingum: five past. Ten past. Quarter past. Shes fifteen minutes late. Oh. Show starts halfpast. A woman walks past with shoppin bags two wee weans.

I looks at the weans, the weans. Their light.

She sees me lookin. Pulls them away care-ful-ly.

I turns backtay the steeple. Its twenty five past – o jobbies! The waitin man the waitin. Nothin more xcitin. Like how i usedtay wait for dad to come infay the pub – staggerburp. Sittin at the winday lookin for the taxi. Mam at ma back, gentletouch. Adam why dont ye gotay bed pal? Ye can see yer dad in the mornin. No mam i wantay wait for – look! Theres the taxi oh nope its a

policecar um dont think bout that no

What times it now? Half past. Bonnie isnt comin. Starts walkin downtay the townhall. Past woolworths marksandsparks the policestation. Theres lotsay things id liketay do just now. Liketay break the winday of dixons run through the shop whoop whoop. Liketay say why bonnie, why did ye no come? Liketay try and find the woman with the two wee weans and and and. Ho sparky. Breathe sparky. Bends down puts ma hands on ma knees wheezin, doesntmatter doesntmatter doesntmatter. Forget it. On yer way. Whoah big crowd goes intay the townhall, throngs and songs the multy-toods dudes! Looks for bonnie but shes no there just no there. Gets ma ticket out somebody bangs intay me i snarls hey watch it he says oops sorry. I gets to the door, just bout to give them ma ticket when i feels: tug.

Its bonnie. Behind me. Shes smilin. Outtay breath her cheeks red she goes sparky. Phew! Didnt think i was gonnay make it there, had to stay behind an extra half-hour, wouldnt even let me away to text ye. Nearly never caught ye at all.

I stares at her.

She frowns says sparky? Ye okay?

What?

Ye look like ye wantay murder somebody.

I just smiles says naw bonnie its fine now. Im glad ye made it.

Big crowd big crowd. Chatterchatter. All the mams and dads and boys and girls and grans and grandpas: fun for all the family. Excitement, lotsay orangey yellowy light a-twistin and a-risin bove their heads, says to bonnie want some icecream? Shes takin off scarf coat bag. She breathes funny like somethins caught in her throat. Ccoh ccoh ccoh darthvader. She says em aye thatd be nice sparky, i goes and gets some cornettos a wee tubbay icecream with two spoons look at the spoons. Together. Together in ma hand. Thats bonnie and sparky.

Sparky and bonnie.

Just as well she turned up or id— Show starts! Everybody goes oooh. Lights go down (well not for me) a longkeyboardnote then mist, we sees john deacon (crowd goes hhhh) sees roger taylor (crowd goes hhhhhh) then brian may strikes his guitar spaang (crowd goes clap clap clap clap) just as i realises its the song one vision off the kinday magic album a really good song, on comes freddie mercury dancin and a-jivin and a-wavin the crowd goes RAAAAAAAY CLAP CLAP CLAP CLAP.

He sings – one vision!

And wer off our seats straightaway. Me bonnie jivin dancin we boogieondown queen play: crazy little thing called love underpressure a kinday magic we will rock you radiogaga (me and bonnie do handclaps man its cool) i wantay break free (fred comes on the wig the skirt the hoover ha ha) hammertay fall dont stop me now somebody to love killerqueen (dood dood dood) another one bites the dust seven seas of rye boheemyin rapsidy aaaaaand me and bonnie what do we do? Dance right thru. Shes a helluva dancer dudes janglin her wrists legs like shes gettin lectric shocks dzzt, shakes her hips her bangles bops her head up down goin gnuh gnuh accidentally elbows me ow! Glad shes havin fun. Shes intay it. Im intay it. Wer intay it. Durin the songs i makes it even more fun cool cos i can speedthingsupand

slow

them

down

remember? and i do this at bitsay the show like durin the fast songs i speeditupsothatfreddiesdancinattopspeedlikeonaDVDthatsbeinfast forwardedtheni

slows

down

for

bo

heem

yin

rap

sid
y
is
this
the
real
life
is
this
just
fan
tas
y
caught
in
a
land
slide
no
esc
ape
from
re
al
it
y
op
en

your

eyes

look

up

to

the

skies

and

seeeeeeee im just a poor boy i need no sympathy (yes i do) bonnie smiles laughs slaps me cacklin when i start dancin like johntravolta she says wrong *band* adam. But then freddie stops things. Raises up his hand ziftay say sh. The crowd settles. He says id just at this point like to pay tribute to the real freddie mercury (hhhhhhh from the crowd) who gave us so much wonderful music and who entertained us for so many years (clap clap clap) but who died so tragically (and i thinks stop makin such a big deal bout it man, hes in the magical land of oz after all) freddie says, this is one of my very favourite queen songs its called who wants. To live. Forever.

Bonnie turnstay me says oh i *love* this song. Pats ma knee. Listens. I stares at ma knee stares at ma knee, shes breathin gnuh gnuh gnuh. The spotlights on freddie. He comes closetay the edgeay stage. Looks up intay the light his face shinin like an angel. Then he gazes intay the audience i tell ye: hes lookin at me. I mean hes *lookin at me*. Aye. Sparky. Theres no time for us he sings. Theeeeres no place for us. What is this thing that builds our dreams and yet slips away from us.

Who wants to live forever?

Who waaants to liiiiive forever?

And hey hes got a point eh dudes ye havetay admit that i mean who the heck does wantay live forev

Shh. Listen. Freds starin at me singin theres no chance for us. Its aaaaaall decided for us. This world has only one sweet moment set aside for us. And ma heart dudes? Its thumpin. Can feel the blood coursin i minds this song in the film highlander. Its when connor maclouds wife dies (shes called heather) shes in bed. Hes holdin her hand tellin her wer runnin down the mountainside. The sun is shinin. Its not cold. Youve got your sheepskins on. And the boots i made for you. He looks down at her but – oops! Shes dead. Too late. For some folk its just too late i mean i mean

alec and senga spark they

I looks at bonnie, shes got a tear in her eye a single tear thats pretty ooh i takes her hand. She takes ma hand. We takes each others hand.

Outside the crowd the falkirknight. Peeps laughin singing theyd ended with we are the champions cmon dudes, what other song could they have ended on? The light bove everybodys floatin flyin. Queen fans. Queen fans are the best fans in the world. Bonnie looks at me, says sparky that was great aye thanks for takin me.

No probs i says. What were ye cryin for bonnie?

Oh em she says. That song always minds me of ma great uncle.

Yer great uncle?

Ma great uncle wullie.

(i tries no to laugh: great uncle wullie fnar fnar)

Oh i says.

Aye he em died last year. I mind just listenin to that song over and over after he passed away.

Uh huh i says.

Bonnie starts rubbin her eyes. Gnuh gnuh gnuh. Ccoh. Ccoh. Ccoh. She tries to catch her breathin.

Must be a nightmare i says.

Her lights blue, sad, shame.

But i wantay talktay her bout queen! Wantay talktay her bout freddie mercury! And and and bout judy and that bitch maryann thats. Thats tryin to take. And i wantay tell bonnie bout the christmas eve that me and jude were sittin watchin the wizarday oz when the police cametay the door mam answered they went *cough* mrs spark? She said yes. They said wife to alexander spark? She said yes. They said can we come in?

They came in.

And when mam and jude took them intay the kitchen there was a pause then screams! sobs! moans! I thought typical mam. Tut. So just kept watchin wizarday oz dudes til mam and jude came in redrings round their eyes. Looked at ma watch asked jude wheres dad? Hes usually home from the pub by now. Whens he comin back? Well jude she just looked at me. Blinked. Blinked tears um. She said um adam hes. Hes not em. She said, em ken how like dorothy gets caught in that tornado and carried offtay oz and she cant get back home even when shes been offtay see the wizard? I said aye? And jude said well look adam dad cant come home either and i was bout to say but dorothy *does* get home then i remembered dads hardly the type to wear a pairay ruby slippers. What? Ruby slippers? You think im some kinday poof? So anyway, he didnt come back that night cos of his own silly stupit stubborn failure to wear a pairay womens shoes. Serves him right really. And i wants to tell bonnie this, but shes so upset bout her great uncle wullie (fnar fnar) that shes burst intay tears shes greetin shes weepin shes cryin i puts ma arms round her says its alright. Its alright hen. But thinks: all these women greetin! Bonnie im sure ma dad i mean yer great uncle wouldnt wantay see ye like this. I says shh. I says shh. She raises her face goes oh sparky, youre so sweet. Youre such a sweet sweet boy sparky and it swells it rushes i swoons oh oh

We kiss.

And weve just seen a kinday queen.

And queen as ye kens the best band theres ever been.

And dudes i cant remember ever bein as happy as this in ma entire life.

**But see sometimes?** I thinks bout weans. Like what makes them tick? Cos weans are great, so wee and scrunchy like playdo theres nothin bad bout them at all. Nope! Nothin at all. I like to look at the weans in the restaurant just look at them, with their mammys their daddys their laughin and clappin and fartin and cryin, their tears are real. Their tears are so real. When they have birthday parties at ma work i sometimes finds an xcuse to like mop and sweep near that area the weans pass each other presents – blond weans fat weans skinny weans quiet weans loud weans – and the mams and dads cuddle them. They open presents say oh thanks! And im standin moppin but im no at the party givin that wean a present. Im no invited! Nope sparky here is just not invited to the weans parties and never was, so whatll i do nstead? Il protect them. It is the job of sparky here to use his powers to protect the goodinnocent kiddywinkles of the world, not hurt them. Not hurt them! Isnt that right boywonder? Sure is caped crusader. Always remember that sparky: protectnothurt the weans.

**Its arranged!** Me and the h-glen animalz wer headin downtay tammyhill for some revenge. Revenge dudes! A dish best served hot as fudge. For damage caused the nightay the mozzy, even tho i thought it was quite funny heh heh. But mark baxters takin it see-re-us-lee. So! Weve stocked up. Baseball bats knives knuckledusters bottles, ive brought ma umbrella. Case it rains.

The roads quiet sh houses lights doors closed locked. An owl goes twitwoo. Twitwoo. But suppose they fight back? Guns? Like in that game streets of rage blam! Eugh. We gets intay tammyhill its late, streetlights glowin like coals. None of us is talkin, wer focused. Mark baxters wearin an adidas tracksuit it goes shh it goes shh it goes shh as he walks. Jason fogarty swings his baseball bat makes hoooo a quiet hoooo thru the air, lightsaber.

Sparky what ye bring an umbrella for? goes craig.

Protection i says stabbin an maginary t-hill posse – eugh.

Protection! Dullyin shakes his head.

Theres the noiseay a car. Its distant but its gettin near. We sees headlights lightin up the bushes at the enday the road then nnnneeeeeoooooooOOOOWWWWW this car rushes past fullay bodies they shouts fannies! puddle scooshes man soaks us. Jesus christ hisses mark baxter, drippin dripp in d rip pin. They all shakes themselves man that was *them* goes jason fogarty, choppin water off his arms. Mark baxters ragin soakin looks like a seabeast thats just blasted out the water man: godzilla. Right thats it he goes. The kidgloves are *off*. Looks at me.

Sparky how come yere no wet?

I holds up ma umbrella. Grin grin!

We goes intay a petrol station – brightlight! brightlight! – mark buys a tinnay petrol. What for? Weve no car. Fogarty craig knobend look at the scuddy mags, ooh check it out man look at that oyah beezer whoah. Thats one pairay bazookas. That sure is a pairay bazookas. I looks at the sweets crisps juice. Twix kitkat crunchie. Ziip: speedstimeup. Stuffstheminmapocket. The guy behind the counter sees me says somethin to mark, mumble shoplifters mumble prosecuted.

What? mark says. What? Mark grabs him. Got a problem there pal?

Em no.

Just as well goes mark, pushes the dude he flies thru the air bout twenty feet man crashes thru the wall lands on toppay a car the caralarm goes wooeeoo wooeeoo wooeeoo the dude dies egh.

Em no that doesnt happen but mark looks nervous kinda t-t-twitchy. Right you ya useless shower he goes, lets get movin.

Knobend looks at me. Looks at the scuddy mag. He nods towards it, i shrugs. Aye alright and fwiip! Stealsit.

*

A house. Curtains drawn. No lights. Who lives here?

Norman senicky goes mark. Everyone goes:

That git!

That tit!

That shit!

Top man in the t-hill posse mark reminds us, stares at the house sweepin his eye up down zif hes tryin to make it crrrrrumble earthquake.

He turnstay me. How ye feelin sparky?

Fine i says.

Yer nerves?

Fine i says.

Special mission for ye pal.

The fireblanket?

A bit like that he says. And hands me the petrol.

The winday opens creeeak. House is dark quiet sh. Undercover operative adam spark on a secretspecial mission. Petrol can sloshes at ma side shlop shlop.

Somethin bout a house with the lights off. Like things that are ordinary friendly no botherin nobody man suddenly are veeery scaaary. Psycho. Ee! ee! ee! Hello adam im just a friendly table not up to anythin at all man. Ee! ee! ee! Hey there sparky im just a jacket a-hangin up on the wall not tryin to impersonate a monster. Ee! ee! ee!

No mark this isnt right.

Do ye wantay be partay this gang or no sparky?

Its no that mark i just—

Its alright sparky hes no *in* there. Yer just gonnay leave a wee note for when he gets back.

Aye but—

Get in there!

The tellys off man. But i keep expectin it to jumptay life blink. Here is the news. Adam spark of the h-glen animalz today broke into the home of norman senicky of the t-hill posse with the intention of burning it down. We go live to our reporter on the scene gail weathergirl yes hugh gail here. Sparky is at present sneaking about downstairs in the hallway, if you listen carefully you can just hear him. Creeeak. Creeeak. And you *might* be able to detect a sloshing noise, which we be*lieve* is the can of petrol which sparky will be using *in* the burning of the senicky residence. But at the moment thats only specula—

Hang on hugh. Somethings happening. Sparkys heading up the stairs. Yes hugh, he is heading *up the stairs*. This is certainly a strange development hugh, but there may be a few possible reasons *for* it. One may be simply that he *needs the loo*. No explanations necessary. Another possibility is that he wants to *check if senicky is in the house*. Certainly the last we saw of him was two hours ago and at that point he was *in* a car with some close friends (the t-hill posse it is believed) and what happened *then* was that senicky and the crew, if the crew indeed it was, *soaked* the animalz de*lib*erately. And it was in fact whats become known as the Mozzy Ladder Incident which *led* to this conflict, and indeed adam spark making his way *up* the stairs of the uh senicky residence.

Thank you gail. Wel have more from that story as it develops. In the meantime . . . have you ever wondered the correct way to eat a banana? Rob newshound believes he might have the answer.

I opens a door. Creeeak. Nobody there. Opens another door. Bathroom. Opens a third door.

Senicky.

Lyin snorin in his boxershorts. I looks. Theres a dog on his bed, it sees me raises its head and in the dark its eyes flash.

Freeze.

I says to the dog shh its alright its alright. Dont bark.

The dog looks at me. Its heads still. Its eyes gleam. It says *Do not pursue this course of action, Adam Spark.*

Why? i says.

*My master has committed wrong deeds but this too is wrong.*

I havetay, i tells the dog.

*Why?*

Theyll hurt me if I dont.

*They'll hurt you if you do.*

Its too late.

*No* the dog says. *It is too soon to be too late.*

Theyre ma friends.

The dog shakes its head. Its eyes catch the light like lightnin. *They are not your friends. In the animal kingdom there is only the brutal consequences of transgression upon territory. Your ugliness and stupidity offend them. Your existence is a crime for which you must continually pay. Your shared humanity with them is a terror which they must confront by controlling you. Why do you heed them?*

Em likes i just shrugs. Cos then il be partay the gang and that ken?

The dog lowers his eyes. He puts his head back on his paws man sad, so sad. Looks up at me with that sparklin gaze sighs *There will be blood tonight. Let it come down.*

Then he starts barkin. Greatbig ruffruffruffs tearin at the air. Senicky wakes up sees me jumps outtay bed. He grabs at clothes, stumblin. Who are you?

I just stands there.

He switches on the light. Blinks. In his boxer shorts. I ken you . . . he says. Youre . . . sparky . . . from hallglen.

Em thats me i says. Well done dude.

Well what do ye want!

He sees the petrol in ma hand. The matches. No he says.

I nods ma head.

Hes tremblin man. His skinny naked bodys tremblin man you do that he says eyes roarin and

And what? i says.

He just shakes his head. Ye dont wantay test me.

The dogs standin on the bed barkin rrruff. Like its ready to jump to attack to take a bite out ma back any second man. I turns the can upside down. Petrol splashes all over the place splish splosh. Thinkin bout all the times at school i was punched doof. Thinkin bout mam and dad. Thinkin bout jude and maryann – mwah mwah. Its easy! The petrol pours out the can man easy! Its like its no even me doin it.

No senicky goes. Dont. Sparky. He puts his hands up. Alright he says rubbin them, youre the boss. I takes out the match. He starts shoutin wavin. Sparky! he says. Cmon mate. Stop playin around eh? Il do what ye say alright? What is it ye want? Come on pal youre in charge alright? You have the power.

Aye.

I have the power.

Then i members. Spiderman. The burglar. His uncle ben. Blam!

Cryin. Spidey cryin. Bonnie sayin youre so sweet sparky. Youre so sweet sparky: kiss. With great power. With great power comes great responsibility just bout to puff out the match shrug say sorry dude i wasnt *really* gonnay burn down yer house cmere give us a hug when:

Senicky leaps cross the bed, forces ma hand against the wall dumf. Match blows out. He punches me oof. Gets me down on the floor rubbin ma face intay the petrol it stings man goes right up ma nose, dogs barkin senickys hammerin everythin goes

slooooooow

i

turns

and

slams

ma

hand

in

tay

his

face

wham

he

spins

back

wards

i

kicks

him

**THOOM! FTOK!** Spider-Man! **Curse** you for interfering!

So you've heard of me, have you Ock? I'm real **flattered**.

The wall-crawler must be **nuts** . . . he's gonna tackle that **madman** doctor octopus alone!

I'll **finish** you off **quickly** this time, webhead. No prayers for mercy. My metal arms will **rip** you **limb** from **limb**!

You'll have to **catch** me first, Octopus. Now put the girl **down** before I—

**SPTANG! THOK!**

he

throws

a

lamp

it

smash

es!

gainst

the

wall

then

his

fists

in

ma

face

boot

to

ma

guts

oof!

(thinks) His **metal** arms are so **strong** . . . I can't . . .

You've **meddled** with me for the last **time**, Spider-Man. Now **watch** while my arms **crush** you like the **bug** that you are.

(thinks) . . . **Blacking** out . . . can't **breathe** . . . one last **chance** . . . If I can angle my **webshooters** towards his **face** maybe I can . . .

**THWIP!**

Aagggh!

**FOOM!** Nice try, Octopus!

he

goes

stag

ger

in

back

i

reach

es

down

finds

the

match

box

krrrrrriip! Lights one. Senicky holds his stomach looks at me, breathin hard. Gasp. The rooms still. Even the dogs stopped barkin. Im just starin at the flame dancin dancin.

*

The walk homes like walkin thru tar. Ma arms and legs feel heavy. Tired. Slow. The buildins have eyes the buildins have eyes. Hallglen. All the houses white but in the dark they look grey. Gets intay the house its quiet man. Quiet as death. Goes upstairs i showers gets ridday the petrolsmell. Goes intay judes room then overtay the bed i shakes her.

Nn? she says. Adam? What is it?

Judy i says. Ive done a bad thing.

She sits up in bed. She rubs her eyes. Shes only wearin a thin nightie wildwomans hair stickin out. At the sideay her beds a pictureay her and maryann. Not mam and dad and me nope nope: maryann.

Nnf. What time is it adam?

Ive done a terrible thing judy.

She looks at me, sits up in bed takes ma hand. Its okay she says. We all have sweetheart. Weve all done bad things.

I looks at the winday the moon the dark. The whole yooniverse.

But its no the stars its the space between them.

Black

Black

Black

Adam? she says. Theres a noteay fear in her voice. Why dont ye tell me what it is yeve done?

Doctor octopus i says.

Doctor octopus?

I nearly killed him judy.

Shes still leanin up in bed. Shes quiet for a second. Then she nods breathes out oh right she says. Doctor octopus.

Spidermans no supposedtay kill i tells her. He can hurt the baddies he can web them he can laugh at them, but hes no supposedtay kill them.

She shakes her head. I cant see her face just her outline. Shakin its head.

Ken how?

No.

Cos then hed be evil.

She sighs and pats the bed pat pat. Its okay she says. Youve just had a nightmare adam. Its just a bad dream thats all.

I sits down. Her smell. Judes smell. Her shape. Womanshape. Theres picturesay girls from the scudmag in ma head and nstead of feelin sick i feels? I feels?

Judy?

Aye adam.

I love you.

She laughs a little bit. Adam she says i love you too ya daft thing. Cmere.

She kisses ma head: kiss smooch. No jude i says, i really really love you.

Shes got a hand in ma hair. A hand on ma shoulder. I looks at her. I says dont go with maryann jude, stay with me. Just me and you eh? Eh judy?

She breathes in.

She breathes out.

I looks up feels her eyes strainin at me thru the dark and

We lies down quietly. Its nice.

*

She cries.

Its like theres love and theres power. Theres love and theres power dudes! And like the two of them both wantay take ye out on a date and power? Shes like judith spark. Shes got the rage the rage she fights, she fighted dad fighted everybody who said those things bout us, then when dad went away kept fightin, wentay yooniversity fighted there stood in the street with her so-shal-list pals kept fightin now shes fightin george dubya bush, fightin the government fightin them all, cmon im judy spark il take all of yese man ive got the rage ive got the power! But the thing is now man now shes fightin me.

Cos power will do that. Sooner or later dude itll take ye away from the peeps that are closest to ye.

When i held up the match was lookin at it, it said power. The flame on the match said power. The heat on the flame on the match said power. If i dropped that match then whoof! Dog dead. Senicky dead. Dead dead all dead.

It was uptay me.

Adam spark.

He got down on his knees norman senicky. Got down on his knees went no. Started cryin greetin this big hard dude with tattoos held ontay his head man wailed dont do this pal im beggin ye. I walked backwards out the room, lookin at him. Walked backwards down the stairs, lookin at him. Holdin the match. He followed. Where ye goin? he said. Walked to the door man holdin the match put ma hand on the doorhandle and click! Opened it.

Mark baxter and the animalz were there. Sparky mark hissed hurry up man somebody might—

Mark saw senicky. Senicky saw mark. Senickys face creased man roooоaaar.

*You* senicky spat.

He flew out the door man. Flew right past me in his boxers man grabbed mark baxter by the throat. Was just in his boxershorts nothin else but he was stranglin mark and the restay the crew were tryin to pull him off. But they couldnt. They just couldnt. Mark baxters face went purple. He was like geggggghhh norman senickys like gooooоogh and his face man was like? was like? Pure hate.

I looked up at the stairs the dogs standin at the top and in the dark: his eyes. Flash. He just nodded said *You have chosen wisely, Adam Spark.*

I smiled shuffled about. Bashful. Em cheers man i just said.

*Do you know now what you must do?*

Em i shrugged. Think so.

*Yes* he said then in this velvetvoice *you must become a good man, Adam Spark. For that is the great struggle in each of our lives: simply to be good.*

That right? i just said.

*The entire world depends upon the outcome.*

Hey tell me about it.

*But first we must discern the* difference *between good and evil. This is the immediate struggle, Adam. And the one at which so many men fail.*

Whoah i said, yere losin me dude! Meanwhile norman senicky and mark baxter tore up the street outside man bash oof. See you ya bloody! Aye cmon then ya poofy! And i heard them watched them well dudes i thought: no. I am not partay this. I am just not like these people nope sorry dudes. Ive things to do.

The dog looked at me bowed his head, padded back intay the shadows softly, and i felt the world ripple in ma bones the yooniverse throb grow inside ma chest, the whole damn galaxy man thud gainst ma brain and i thought:

Me.

Sparky.

I have the power.

**On a walk with bonnie by the canal tweet tweet.** Hand in hand. A sunday afternoon none of us with work today so hey. Lets go babe! Bonnies talkin bout love, how it makes her feel foolfilled feel full how she usedtay fancy all these guys at school they never fancied her back. Tut.

Always the way intit? Our joined hands swingin between us swing swing. Tweet tweet. Thats the thing: love just makes ye feel happy dont it? Mud and gravel and stuff beneath us birds singin water splsh splsh splsh.

I just looks at her smilin. Shes pretty shes bonnie shes talkin bout love Love LOVE. Dont get no better than that dudes!

Shes lookin at the canal. I stops. We stands. We stares at the water. Kinday lovely kinday nice kinday smoothshiny skin on it there, like a seal or sealion or sea. Its sallippin past cool as ye like, just takin its time nowhere to go nothin to do, like hey there sparky whats happenin dude nothin mister canal what bout you oh nothin sparky just havin a wee flooow. That right aye? I can speedthe canalupthen

slow

it

down

Just for fun. Bonnie squeezes ma hand i says do ye think yer great uncles watchin ye from oz i mean heaven?

She shrugs looks at the treetops says id like it if he is.

I says aye but. What do ye think hed makeay things? What do ye think hed makeay yer life, watchin it? What do ye think hed makeay it bonnie?

Its really important this.

She looks at the water ripple whoah sway. She says i dunno. Sniff. I hope he thinks im makin the best of ma life . . . despite.

Aye i goes. Thats what i want them to think too.

She looks up frowns says *them*? I says um, i mean em the peeps in oz em heaven generally bonnie ken? Oh she says. Aye she says. We walks on. Shes no tall is bonnie. Im just wee but shes shorter even than me, than me than sparky than the boy here: wee. Her hands soft warm even tho its cold today theres the smellay water a rabbit shoots past: ptchoo. Gone. Zif its scared of somethin (me) bonnies eyes dip a little she says sparky?

Aye?

Whats the worst thing thats ever happened to ye?

We stops in the middleay the dirt-track by the canal. I looks at her. The ribbonay light bove her head its changed from yellow-orange to light blue, threads of darkblue. I shrugs. Had a mouse once that died.

She waits, hands in pockets cold.

How did it die? she says.

I squeezed it.

Ye squeezed it? What for?

I shrugs. Folds ma hands intay ma pockets too. Says: i deserved it.

She shakes her head. Bubbles bubble up at her lips – she wipes them away. Oh sparky she says. But ive no idea what she means by it.

I shrugs looks straight down at the canal – wateryripple. Ma reflection breaks cracks. I kinday turns away looks at the bridge further down the canal. Its madeay stone and has a happy mask a sad mask carved in either sideay it. A happysad bridge heh heh: ye cross one side yere happy ye cross another yere glum yere blue ye wantay top yerself. Wonder bout the guy who made it what did he do that for, the happysad faces? What a lunatic! What a tit! What a lunatit! If ye keep followin this canal then up ahead is the falkirk wheel, it lifts ye from one canal to the next i thinks thats kinday like ma life man. Lifes like one big falkirk wheel that lifts ye from one place to the next. From the land of MamandDad to the land of NoMamandDad. From nobody to hero. From judy to bonnie. Ch-ch-ch-ch-changes, as bruce springsteen once sang! Or maybe it was bobdylan cant mind anyway. Happy to sad sad to happy: switch switch. Cant keep track dudes. Cant keep ma mind on that single onetrack track. Doom Doom Doom.

Bonnie touches ma chin, pulls ma face backtay hers. Look at me sparky she says.

Cant dont wantay dont deservetay, so byootiful i just says aye?

Bonnie stands on her tiptoes kisses ma lips. Its like a proper kiss, her big big mouth coverin mine wrenchin winchin her throat goin gnuh gnuh gnuh. Thudthudthud goes ma heart. Whoahwhoahwhoah goes ma brain. Opens ma eyes halfway thru the kiss bitsay light dartin in out between us like bright yellow snakes in the sea. Closes ma eyes kinday melt kinday swoon. Birdswatersplish oh! She comes back down off her tiptoes smilin gigglin grin grin. I wipes the snotbubbles away from her nose.

Did ye like that? she says.

I grins. Sure did i says and thinks: i love kissin. Love it. Better than holdin dead mice in yer hand ooh yuk. Both wet tho. We walks on, hands hands swing swing. Beam goes sparky. Bonnies smilin too, is there a smile factory round here or somethin? Somebody sellin smiles, fifty for a pound there ye go hen theres a smile for you and yer boyfriend, slap that cross yer kisser – smack! Bonnies lights yellow but every now and again like a wee njection of ice it goes blue: flicker: gone.

Whats wrong? i says.

What do ye mean? bonnie says.

Ye keep thinkin bout somethin i says.

Oh she says, glances away. Nothin.

Blue darts round her.

No i says, what is it?

Ach she says. Whole head: blue. Bonnie looks at the ground says ive just been thinkin bout great uncle wullie.

Takes a second to stop maself laughin again.

Really?

Aye she goes, lookin at the water. I mean i still miss him sparky. Its been a couplay months now, but i still really miss him ye ken.

Must be hard i sniffs.

She laughs, but no laughter comes out, like an organ thats bein grinded but makes no music. She says its no like losin a mouse!

Aye sure i mumbles.

And i think sometimes bout what they usedtay do to me at school, she says.

When she says that i thinks: i would burn a school down. I would burn a school down and piss in the ashes psssssssssh. Shake shake.

Bonnie looks up at me again, licks me on the nose ha ha. Standin over dads grave mam one side judy the other, judes grey shes totally grey shes like grey. Mams howlin. Who was there to save him? What superhero? Where was

spidermansupermanthefantasticfourthesilversurfer

And where is the batman? Hes at home! Washin his tights! Heh heh that crazy jack nicholson, that crazy jokerdude dudes.

But it was fine cos i kent dad wasnt in the box. He was in oz.

Bonnie grabs hugs me, throat goin gnuh wheeze, when i kiss her this one lasts for ages a minute an hour a year a hundredthousand years ken how? Cos i

slow

it

down

and

then we walks. Il take care of ye bonnie i tells her. Itll all be okay. Aye i will. And it will. Cos it will. And she puts her arm round ma waist oh adam she says, hand in ma pocket looks at me so hard its like shes slammin this solid glass gaze gainst me all the bad things that have happened to her, they hit me they break they just fa-loat away dudes. Away on the water. Away away, the easy way, and i thinks – thats the first time shes called me adam. I thinks – ive got a girlfriend. I thinks – a girlfriend! A vicky vale a lois lane a maryjane whoah!

We goes home. Judes out. Its quiet its quiet nobody here. I plays queen: somebody to love. We lies down together on the bed and and and ye ever heard that joke tee hee listen: supermans flyin round usin his xray vision, when he sees wonderwoman lyin on her back. Got her legs open. Shes goin oh yes oh yes oh yes. So superman well he thinks oyah byooty dudes, flies down quickasaflash straight in the winday shags her uh uh uh. Then he pulls up his breeks flies away again. Wonderwoman pauses goes: you feel somethin there? The invisible man says aye. And ma arse is bloody killin me!

Xcept its sweeter than that.

Adam? bonnie smiles up at me.

Aye?

Ye can get off me now.

Oh um. Do i have to?

No.

Then i wont.

Good.

snugglecuddlemmm

Adam?

Aye hen?

Did you feel it too?

I holds ma breath. Looks at her. Checks ma arse.

Effin superman.

**See i think with mam** it wasnt really bout dad at all. Jude says it was. And she is wise. Oh aye wise like yoda, help you i will. Sometimes when me and jude are cuddled up on the couch mmm, watchin the simpsons eatin benandjerrys icecream i looks up at her says if dad hadnt went offtay see the wizard judy do ye think mam wouldve? Jude swallows her icecream licks the spoon purses lips together says i think adam that oz is probably a very nice place to live.

Thats not what i asked jude.

She stood up. She went intay the kitchen. She does this. Like that song by the blue nile she likes: sometimes i walk away, when all i really wanna do. Is love and hold you right. There is just one thing i can say. Nobody loves you this way. Ach what pish. We will – rock you! Thats what i say to that dudes!

Jude made tea. Stirred the tea in the cup. Lifted the bag dumped it in the bin flmp. Was like she was programmed: we are ze robotz. She said adam i think dad let mam ken how good it was in oz and mam wanted to find some way to get there.

To be with dad?

Xactly.

Well, i mind thinkin. Thats a lottay jobbies! Dad went offtay see the wizard mam started the waterworks at the funeral but after that? She didnt have a good word to say bout him. The effin. That bloody. How could he. The stupit. Aye whatever mam yaawn. Change the record (to a queen one ho ho) and at the wake we were all like in the house folks shufflin in their black suits their polishedblack shoes (somebody let a lottay gangsters in here man?) sayin to mam em sorry senga. Em like, he was a good man and that senga. Hel be sadly missed senga. Mam chewed on her mister kiplings exceedingly good cakes. Chewed slowly. Mind her mouth makin like the shape a cows mouth makes: chew chew chew. Her eyes would flick up at folk every time they said somethin. Shed just go aye. Aye. Chew.

Jude was on the couch with me playin top trumps – marvel superheroes! Cos i was bored. Wakes sure are booorin. Dunno why theyre called wakes when all ye wantay do is gotay sleep zzz. So me and judes playin top trumps but judes no con-sin-tray-tin. Keeps lookin at mam glance glance. Mams chewin sayin aye. Senga god broke the mould when they made alec. Aye. Senga hel be watchin us right now from his wee seat at the bar, havin a right good laugh.

Ive got daredevil. Hes got 23 strength and 5 intelly-jense.

Jude was lookin at mam.

Jude? i said.

What adam?

Your go.

Oh she said. She put down a card with the punisher on it. I said cmon judy dont be daft. The punisher beat daredevil? Hes no even got any superpowers!

Jude wasnt listenin tho. Somebody was sayin whys judith playin bloody . . . ? An hour after her fathers . . . ? And one of the aunties was sayin shusht shes just tryin to keep adam from . . . The wean doesnt have a clue whats . . .

Nobody finished their sentences. Yup there sure were lotsay dots after everythin that day! Or should i say that day . . .

He was a fine man senga.

Aye.

I decides to use thor. Thor has 49 strength and 85 fightin skills. Jude put down mister fantastic. Now cmon judy! i goes. Get a grip. Mister fantastic beat thor? Stretchybendy rubbishman beat the norse god of thunder!

Judes lookin at mam.

Senga he was a gentleman.

Mam doesnt say aye this time.

Jude gets to her feet, crosses the room to mam – but no. Too late.

Mam stands.

A gentleman! she hisses, her voice curlin like steel shavins. A gentleman was he? Her eye scours round the room, shes all in black hunched like shes scrubbin the whole room with her gaze, cleanin right intay those corners with jif creamcleaner and a good nailbrush. Use the new improved coldhardstare of senga spark. Your bath comes up a treat!

I ken what yese all thought of him, so dont try and act all sympathetic.

Judy puts her hand on mams shoulder says mam why dont ye

Get away from me! shouts mam, pushes her. Fondly remembered? Much loved? Her voice goes all witchy, like il get you my pretty . . . and your little dog too. She says yese never had that to say about him when he was *here* did yese? Yese never had that to say about *us*? Well did yese!

Jude pulled at mams arm. Mam threw jude off superstrong. I carried on playin marvel top trumps: wolverine beats magneto on speed but not strength. Captain america beats nightcrawler on fightin skills but not agility. Galactus is the best. Hes like god. The god of falkirk. His stats are height 862 centimetres intelly-jense 10 strength 50 speed 20 agility 30 and fighting skills 55. That beats everybody at everythin xcept maybe the hulk whos got strength 50 also. Dont make me. You wont like me when im. Everyone was standin watchin mam and jude, the two of them nearly wrestlin now it was so funny. Arms and legs everywhere! Mam was like one of them clotheshorses ye have to fight with to stand them up. Peeps were clearin a big circle away from them zif somebody had let off a fart. Actually i had. It was stinkin: like eggs or the runs or a bum.

Bet dad would have beaten that one at top trumps!

But forget that: presentday. Jude comes downstairs. Im sittin on the breakfast bar, all ready kittedout for work in ma crewclothes just sittin readin the falkirk herald ho hum. SIDNEY DEVINE PLAYS FALKIRK TOWN HALL and WIN A FREE TRIP TO THE MARINER CENTRE IN CAMELON and POLMONT MAN HITS HAMMER WITH THUMB. Nothin bout the incredible adam spark sigh. Jude comes in. Dressed for yooni for her lecture in glesga but— But! Shes not wearin her denimjacket and boots today no not like yed expect. Shes wearin nice shoes. Nicetop. Nice things and when she goes past i smells girlygirly perfume. Waaaaft. Sniffsniff. Goes to the toaster puts in the bread taps the toaster impatient. Tap tap. I looks at her. Then when the toast pops out she cuts a banana – a banana! – places the slices on the toast. Then she takes out a box of all-bran –all-bran! – pours it intay the bowl. She dips in the spoon – spoon! She munches. Munch munch. Can hear the wetcrunchy sound of the all-bran in her mouth. No crispsjuicesweets now dude. We looks at each other cross the breakfast bar. She shrugs. Shes positively glowin dudes like: beam. The yellowlight round hers so strong its like a forcefield. Permission to land on planet judith spark, permission denied her luvverly glow is too strong. We looks at each other she shrugs she munches she shrugs. Finally i says

Jude have you lost weight?

She stiffens. Halfsmile. The light: blueripple. She says aye adam have ye noticed? Ive eh been goin to a gym.

Whereabouts? i says.

Glasg— she says stops. I mean em down grahams road.

Who with?

With . . . she says . . . graham.

Whos graham?

He lives on um

Grahams road? i says.

Aye.

She finishes the all-bran. Pops the bowl and spoon in the sink – tinkle. Wipes off her hands swallows says um adam, before ye gotay work . . .

Uh-huh i goes readin the falkirkherald, kiddin on im lost in war stories from old biddies in dollarpark nursin home. Ach away and eat yer werthers originals ya foosty old

Now. I want ye to tell me what ye can cook.

What i can cook?

What ye can cook.

Cant cook nothin jude.

Aye ye can. When ive no been in from yooni yeve hadtay make yer own tea.

Cant cook nothin jude.

Ye can adam.

Startin to sound like pantomime oh no he cant. Oh yes he can! Oh no he cant cook a thing do a thing without judy spark without judith his bigsister there to sort it out for him boys and girls. Oh yes he can! Ah pissoff goes the evil sorceror. The boys and girls laugh.

But—

Yere nearly nineteen adam. Yere no a wee boy no more. Need to start takin responsibility for yerself.

Judes leanin gainst the washin machine starin at me, her new niceslim nicedressed notfat body – whos it for? Starin same way she does when shes givin me a row. Same way she did that one time when i was wee i went to the toilet to do a jobby, but still had ma dressin gown on! Forgot to lift it up when i sat down on the pan jobbied in ma dressin gown poo yuk.

Taps ma foot looks at jude says beansntoast jude. Thats all i can make.

Thats not the case adam jude says.

Aye it is.

Ye made me mince and tatties that time mind?

Aye so?

And macaroni.

Aye so?

And spag bol.

Aye so? Aye so? What ye gettin at judy?

Has she had her hair done ohmygod i think she has. I looks at her and looks at her. I looks at her and looks at her.

If somebody rings the doorbell adam what do ye do?

Answer it.

She stands. She folds her arms.

Um with the chain on i adds.

If theres an accident adam what number do ye phone?

911.

Jude narrows her eyes.

I mean 999

911 or 999? she says.

999.

Aye she says. Cos whats 911 adam?

Boyband? i says.

She shakes her head. No its the american number.

Oh aye like she telt me george bush said – america will no longer be the worlds 911.

Jude picks up her jacket new jacket. Got sequins on the back. Like on her dress. Quins of the sea sparklesparkle they spell out the word COWGIRL. She looks great. Looks baaayootiful. Looks new. She looks nothin like jude judy judith spark of old, sister and bestfriend to adam stuart spark. Shes. Shes. Shes a.

What do ye wantay ken this for jude?

Shes puttin the jacket on. Just wantay see how well ye can take care of yerself adam.

I bites ma lip stands. And what do ye wantay ken *that* for judy?

She shrugs scratches um. Checks in her pocket for her mobile finds it, reads a text. Yere old enough to—

Ye plannin on goin somewhere jude?

She looks for her keys scannin the kitchen um. Looks at me i repeats:

Ye plannin on goin somewhere jude?

Cosifsheis cosifsheis cosifsheis. Ye ken il. Il havetay. Jude seemstay see somethin in ma eyes, backs off a bit. I stares at her. Theres silence. Si. Lence. She breaks it, leans forward gives me a kiss on the cheek – smeck! Touches ma face hands in ma hair stroke stroke. Smells nice. And i dont hurt her. I dont hurt her why would i dudes – who suggested that?

Ive gottay go adam is all she says.

Where? i says quickstyle.

Gottay get all the way to glasgow for a class.

Oh i sighs. Phew. She leaves trailin that yellowlight that perfume smell and the shiny sea-quins behind her i sees the word COWGIRL fore she shuts the door. Watches her thru the winday she waves i waves. Blows her a kiss. She catches it she smiles. She tries to smile. I watches her till shes a speck a mote a tiny cowgirl a-ridin off intay the sunset, just a wee ball of yellow light a-disappearin down the road.

Hm.

*

Goes out to the shed. This is the shed that dad wanted that mam bought, after dad di— after dad went offtay see the wizard. Its cool its dewy. Bottles of things on the shelves. Tools. A rake. A rack! (whys nobody declarin war on this one?) plantpots plants mud a lawnmower. The sheds not changed much, not since. Not since the. Not since the police had to move some stuff bout after they found mam lyin sleepin in it after she took them sleepinpills so as to get to the magical landay oz. Dreamin her sweet poppydreams.

I sits down for a while.

I looks round the shed.

I says hello mam. Hello. Im tryin mam, tryin to make things up with her. With jude. With them. Im tryin to be a good boy. I really am mam.

**Later im with the verysame bold judy in glesga.** Cos see this war on arack is still happenin parrently sheesh. Anyways judys draaaagged me to this lecture at glesga yooni man the rooms packed mobbed crowdedhot. Sweatin! Says im sweatin jude im hot, she goes shh the now adam whys she always goin shh? Thats all i get off her man: shh shh. Nyoooo time for the boy sparky here has she dudes, no youre right sparky she certainly has not. One suspects that miss judith spark has other things on her mind, like stickin her tongue intay— Anyway this dude called george galloway hes talkintay the crowd. Stands behind the lecturethingy shouts! Swears! Nearly spits! Whole crowd man pplauds pplauds when he goes that *cowboy* in the white house! That *puppet* of the oil and gas junta! When he comes to britain for photos with the queen that he can use in the next presidential campaign, wel give him a welcome that will make the february march look like a picnic in the park! Roar of red light rrrrrrrrrrrrrrrrr everyone stands to their feet bout to bring the house down and why? Is queen playin? Hes hardly freddie mercury dudes dudes dudes. Another one bites the dust.

Judes listenin tently. Says to her, look judy what did ye bring me to this for im boooored. Shh goes jude.

Again.

Again.

And hee hee whats funny tho is when folk in the crowd start shoutin at each other, cos see oneay the guys on stage? Hes a paki, from oneay the countries we wentay war with a fanny stan i think. Or a paki stan? One of them countries anyway i looks at jude. Shes starin at the guy onstage, got her hand uptay ask a question. I thinks: i dont ken you at all judith spark. And thinks: i usedtay be the centre of your world judith spark. And thinks:

Squid. Squid! A giant squid like a hundred miles long attackin falkirk, wrappin its big tentykles round the steeple, and like another tentykle round the highflats at callander park and *another* round the howgate shoppin centre, that squids got a good hold. The police? Well theyre blastin it. Blam! blam! blam! its no good men, its just too strong. Falkirks doomed. And the musics flash! Ah-ah! And all the peeps from falkirk – includin angie from work and mark baxter and maryann and maryann and maryann – theyre runnin screamin dyin.

Thats what im thinkin bout dudes.

Anyway the paki on stage gives an answer he says, my friend the arab people have suffered at the hands of the israeli state, and america as the last remaining superpower has supported them (theres boos from the restay the audience) the paki stands says *The palestinian people have every right to arm themselves against persecution.*

Whooaaah the whole crowd theatre audience erupts, youre siding with the nineleven bombers! But what america fails to address is! What we are forgetting is! Fashist! Fashist! Jude well shes on her feet too shoutin shoutin the way she usedtay at dad sayin mams been in here all night waitin for you while ye were out boozin adams forgettin what ye look like when yere *sober* i thinks bout the squid. What would happen if i xploded a hugebig bomb

BOOM!

big mushroom cloud risin up over falkirk? Coverin everythin man. Slow slow cloud spreadin out im standin there with ma fists clenched. And when the smoke clears? after years? Theres no squid. But theres no falkirk either whoops. No steeple no highflats no howgatecentre no peeps. Nothin. Just me standin on ma silver surfboard fists clenched. A-pocka-lypse. The end of all things.

But oh said bonnie youre so sweet youre such a sweetsweet boy sparky – kiss!

So i wont destroy falkirk.

The lecture ends with people goin mumble complain argueargue okay lets go get somethin to eat says jude pullin ma hand i thinks thank christ cos im starvin, and also: dont tell me what to do judith spark. Ever.

We goes to this posh place in glesga. This place is not like the cottages barandlounge man nooooo not at all. No karaokemachine. No dartboard. No pooltable punters horseracin pictures of oldfalkirk on the walls nope. Its clean! Its bright! Theres plinkyplonky music even a big piano in the corner, some dude playin a kiss is still a kiss. The waiters voice when he comes over is posh oh dead posh what we doin here jude?

Dont ye like it adam? goes jude. Unfurls her napkin like a proper lay-dee.

I shrugs looks at the menu. No steakpie no fishnchips no macaroni, no macaroni!

Aye jude i says, but like we dont belong here.

Where?

A place like this.

A place like what?

A posh place.

But then the answer comes in: its maryann. I notices her at the door, watches her cross the room doesnt take her eyes off me its zif wer locked ontay each other like like like a. Cant even think what its like cos im so angry ma hands make fists under the table. She says hello judith, sits down. Looks at me. Hello adam she says thinnin her lips intay a sortay smile. How are you? Jude looks at the tablecloth.

What is this? i says.

Maryann takes judys hand. Judes still lookin at the tablecloth. Scratchin it, scratch scratch. What is the table itchy or somethin? I looks from onetay the other to the onetay the other: what is this? But then the waiter comes over are you ready for me to take your order jude maryann they both say yes (not *aye* but *yes*) maryann orders the sirloin blahblah with blahblah and jude orders the blahblah medallion of blah with blah. No chickeninabasket for jude now. Nope! The waiter goes away they both looks at me silence i says again

*I says again*

What is this?

Listen adam, jude says fidgetfidget. Theres somethin weve gottay tell ye.

We? i says.

*

Minds this one time ooh. Woke up in the middleay the night could hear sounds. Growlin sounds. Gigglin sounds. Then this thumpin like Doom Doom Doom. Gets outtay bed picks up ma kermit teddy. Dangle dangle. Opens ma door growl. Giggle. Doom Doom Doom. Noise was louder. Walked intay the hall. Dark. Walkstay mam and dads room dark. Noise was cominfay in there. Oh alec. Thats. So. Oooooooh. Doom Doom Doom. What was goin on? Was mams voice. Mams voice sayin oh. Oh! Was dad eatin her? Was dad eatin her? Had daddy turned intay a great big lion was growlin roarin mams cryin out in pain dudes! But then mam starts goin yes. Yes! Yes! Yes! Yes! Like shes makin ticks on a page dudes i opens the door.

The light from the hall fell ontay the bed.

Im thinkin bout this while im thinkin bout that *we*. Judy and maryanns *we*. That wee *we*. When mam and dad xplained it to me they said that they were makin love but it still sounded like mam was hurt in pain in agonisin agony. Like dad was eatin mam alive. Yes. Yes. Yes.

Cos see this? Here the now? Judes talkin bout love but it feels like pain. Like judes eatin me alive. Yes. Yes. Yes. Funny that dudes. Says to them judy i cant look after maself on ma own she says aye ye can adam i says but what bout the bills she says il take careay the bills, and the tv licence, and the bank account, ye wont needtay worry bout that i says well what if i get scared she says yere nearly nineteen i says but what if i dont ken howtay um? She says adam – yere *nearly nineteen*. And that maryann shes watchin shes noddin holdin judes hand, jude said ive had nothin in ma life adam. Nothin. Her eyes her eyes wet like blue jyools she said responsibility. Ive kent nothin but responsibility.

withgreatpowercomesgreat

Ma whole life adams been bout *your* happiness *your* wellbeing. If i dont do this for maself now, il be dead (she was kinday shoutin) im gonnay end up just like *mam*.

Mams no dead i reminds her.

Jude and maryann both gaze at me over their prawncocktails.

She just went offtay see the wizard.

Jude shook her head slowly. I think i hissed. I think i made a noise like a cat. Peeps at the next table, in their goodclothes they looks over. I salutes them. They looks away.

Yere grown-up now adam. Yeve even got a girlfriend.

How did ye—

Jude makes a face ziftay say dont try and kid yer bigsister. Says adam ye can get up and dress yerself put yerself outtay work come home and make yer tea.

I cant—

If needs be il get a carer in for ye.

But—

Maryann makes a kinday sympathetic face. Like the face ye make to someone whos just wet themselves – like oh no what a shame ha ha ha. Maryann says adam look im training to be a social worker. And i work with a lot of people like you. I know this one man whos blind, hes been blind all his life and he lives alone and its fine i mean he can do all the things that—

I turns to her carefully and politely. Its important to be polite, mam telt me. I smiles. I says who. Asked you. Ya cow.

She looks at her plate. I looks at jude. Looks at maryann. Looks at the two of them together. Jude maryann. Maryann jude. Its just then i realises dudes how long ive been thinkinay them as the same person.

Their hands are touchin, its like theyre madeay plastic somebodys held like a match at their hands theyve fa-yoozed intay one ffshhhh. Im left to fight the fight maself. A oneman army. I cant change it. This is what i kens suddenly man nope nope: i cant change it. Cant change anythin dudes. I turns to jude i shrugs i just says: get yer stuff and go.

And like i was tellin ye there was no superhero to save dad. There was no superhero to save mam. And in the end, when it came downtay it, as it happens, now that ye mention it, at the enday the day, when alls said and done, when the dollars and cents are counted up: there was no superhero to save me. Not even jude. Not even jude stormin round the playground to fight ma battles anymore – scrap punch doof.

I got the train home from glesga. Looked out the winday at falkirk at falkirk. And in the windays ma reflection. Sparky. And even tho judes escaped from me theres no chance of *me* escapin me. Everywhere i go its me. Me. Me. Me. Me. Im surroundin me. Doesnt matter what i do or where i go dudes il still be me always me. Isnt that funny? Sparky ya stupit. Sparky ya dense. Sparky you stink phew have you jobbied yerself? Adam go to the back of the class your sums are wrong again. Why did i ever havetay have a son like *you*, a wife like *her*? Sparky sparky. The daftie. The mongol. The spastic. The retard. The dense. The glaikit. The stupit. The. The.

The amazin. The brave. The incredible. The incredible adam spark! Thats me dudes yup – a superhero the worlds only saviour thats yer man sparky here!

Aye.

*

Oh but em whats obviously wrong is im no strong enough. What does a superhero needtay do aye thats right man, needstay keep in shape! Fit! active! healthy! stroooong how do ye do that il tell ye – gotay the gym. So thats what ive been doin man, over at hallglen communitycentre theyve got a wee weights room, wee dinky room just nextay where the cleaners drink their tea shluuurp oh aye agnes yere right that bloody blair ye just cant say what hel do next right lets get these floors done? Nah. Nother cuppay tea. Hallglen judo clubs in the next room givin it ha-ya! and the mams? They bring all their babies for the crash em cresh. Big row of gurglin babies, soft droolin yellowyellow light not oneay them man not oneay them kens the danger the worlds in. Boom! Dead dead dead. So! – i goestay the gym. Pech pech. Lift. Eeeech. Sose i can save the babies. Biceps. Triceps. Friceps. Miceps. Thats the muscles in yer back. Yooogh. Diceps. Forceps. Theyre in yer forearms. Theres fouray them. Brrrreeegh. Oof. One two three. Liiiift. Like rocky! Gettin strong now. And in the mirroray the gym can see maself liftin the weights oof ach eech. Sparky balboa heavyweight champeeeeen of the wooorld! And i ken that on the way home the weans will run after me il runtay the toppay the steps therell be like a big flockay kids followin like they follow rocky, hundredsay them man il stand at the toppay the steps punch ma fists in the air the kids will go yaay! Sparky! Heretay save us! And they all come give me a big cuddle il say aye. Il take care of yese kids. Never mind yer mams and dads il take care of yese. Cuddle cuddle. Mm. Our hero.

But when i leave the gym? Theres no kids there no weans ach silly me. Theyre no gonnay want plain old adam spark are they dumbo! Nope its the amazin the fantastic the stoo-pen-dus the *incredible* adam spark they all want. The superhero me! That must be why theres no kids man!

*

But that night i finds one.

Id wentay bed early. Jude was on the phone to maryann. She was packin. Boxes and heapsay stuff. Her poster of wee ferrety tom york rolled up stuffed intay a poly bag. Shes written a listay things i havetay checktay make sure of: check check check. She takes me round the house showin me where the mergency stuff is: nails and firstaidkit and sellotape and torch and and and im no even listenin dudes. She says shes gonnay cometay falkirk three times a weektay see me. She put her hands on ma shoulders said adam listen: its not the end. I just needtay get away. From me? She sighs. She says adam you needtay be independent just as much as i do. I sniffed shrugged looked away. I hate her.

And that night i stares at maself in the mirror. Stares and stares and stares. And stares. And stares and stares and stares. When the house is quiet i pulls on the boots takes a knife from the kitchen, slides it intay ma pocket.

Goes out on the streets. Rovin and a-starin and a-flexin ma muscles. Ma sore heads back ow. Just wait just wait you criminals you junkies you. You peeps who took ma mam dad sister away, just you wait. Il make ye pay. Got that? Il make ye pay. Aye okay adam dont shout.

Cold tonight. Seems to be cold all the time now. Is the yooniverse suddenly gettin colder? has like the sun xploded or somethin man? Outside the ettrick dochart centre i rests gainst a tree, looks up at the sky. Black. Stars. Ive heard the more stars there are the colder the night is, cos the clouds like in-syoo-lay-shin keeps in the heat. Keeps the earth warm. So if ye cant see the stars yere okay. If ye can see the stars yel likely freezetay death dudes. I stops and talkstay oneay the lampposts i says ye seen any crime dudes?

Just flash three times il come runnin so i will, gasp gasp. The lampposts say στοπ δογσ φρομ πισσινγ ον υσ.

I shrugs nope cant stop dogs from doin that!

One time an owl glides past. It soars white gainst the black sky silent. I sees it. It sees me. Feels its eyes its eyes i says oh what do *you* want?

It says *Do not be disheartened, hero. The world is too young to understand but soon it will need you.*

Ye sure bout that? i says. Doesnt seem like much goin on to me dude.

The owl wheels it wheels. It is a shiver of white brr. Its voice is like duvetsoft it says *This will all bend and break. There will be apocalypse, the end of all things. You must be there, hero, you must be there when it falls apart.*

I shrugs. If ye reckon i says, but i sure did prefer it when i was thievin like. All im gettin nows pissed off!

The owl hovers in the air. Doesnt seemtay move. Behind it are stars the yooniverse huge black massive doesnt end it doesnt end. Eternity. For men by calvin klein. Beneath it is cold streets sleepin children the owl says *Hark to my voice, Adam Spark, for I represent a higher power. We must love even the greatest wretch or villain, not because their nature has merited such love, but because we are bound to love others of our species. This is your quandary, hero: aiding those who do not recognise your goodness, protecting those who fear you.*

Then the owl swoops down silent as death takes a mouse shwip! Chews it. Claws it. Stringy bitsay mouseflesh blood, the owls eyes black. Theyre black. It doesnt blink.

It says *I am bound to kill because I am animal. I kill because I have hunger and need. You can choose, human, and you must choose love. Do you understand?*

Well alright i just says. But hed better be right bout this enday the world business cos im freezin ma superpowered baws off!

Theres that word again: Love. The big L. Takes out the knife and stabs it intay the tree carves SPRKY LVS JUDY. Then scores out JUDY writes BONNI. Maybe il show it to bonnie one day, how very romantic if i do say so myself. Oh yes this is the esteemed adam spark of dashbury manor (bows) very pleased to meet you miss bonnie (kisses hand) why im charmed master spark.

Starts stabbin the tree with the knife – love love love Love LOVE! – hears a noise looks round. Sees her. The reason i came out. A mission! Someone to save. Shes in a dress shes cryin shes sittin on oneay the gritbins they keep the salt in for winter. Recognises her – a wee lassie who stays near me, morven court i think she lives. And here she is like at eleven at night? on her own? and cryin? Thats not right man thats a sin. Aw. Goes uptay her (makes sure i puts ma knife away first dudes) ye alright darlin? Whats wrong?

She looks at me, face all red and creased up like a squashedtomato. The light bove her heads purple and flashin! flashin! flashin! Its alright i tells her. Im a goodie. I hunches down says em look hen whats yer name?

Shes rubbin at an eye with her fist. Starin at me no sure like. Natalie she says.

I says well okay then natalie im sparky.

She laughs a wee bit. Goes thats a daft name.

Aye it sure is, i goes. A daft name. A name for a daftie. Em why dont ye tell me why yere greetin natalie? She pulls at the bottomay her dress looks round shes like – cant find ma way home. Was stayin over at ma pal jemmas fell out with her cos she was, she was, she was keepin the toys to herself so i says right you im gonnay walk home left but ive just been walkin round and round cos i dont ken the waaaaaaay. Starts howlin again, howlin greetin squashedredtomatoface i minds when i got lost in scarborough was knockin on all the caravans there was nobody to help me, nobody to get me home dudes i was lost and lost and lost and where was jude. Says to her is it morven court ye live?

She nods, screws a fist intay her eye screwscrew.

I says well im on ma way up there natalie, i could take ye back? Would ye like that?

She nods so much its like her heads gonnay fall off.

I takes her hand smiles at her, well cmon then. We starts walkin. She totters along triestay keep up shes just got wee legs gettin tired walkin dead sloooow. I says to her em natalie? Do ye want me to hold ye?

She looks up says uh.

I mean like lift ye up? So we can go a bit faster?

She nods nods nods. Gettin tired she mumbles. Aye no surprised i says. Ken what ye mean. It sure is tirin this livin business. So: swings her intay ma arms holds her there. Heavy like a warm baggay flour. A warm baggay flour with legs a head a smile. I says feel better?

She looks at me.

We walks. Thru the scheme thru the middleay the night. Sorehead sorehead. Sorehead sorehead. Doom Doom Doom.

Natalie says why ye out so late mister?

I says well actually im a superhero natalie.

A superhero? She makes a face. Like spiderman?

Uh-huh.

And batman?

Yup.

Whats yer name?

Ma names the incredible adam spark.

She grins. I grins. She goes youre not a *real* superhero.

I am!

Whats yer powers? Shes jigglin in ma arms up down, cooried intay me. Its cold she must be freezin. I holds her close.

I says i can speed time up and i can slow it down and i can talk to machines and animals. And i can see lights round peoples heads that lets me ken what theyre feelin.

Eh-eh she goes. Doesnt believe. Doesnt believe in me. Doesnt believe i exist.

Can so!

What colours round ma head then?

Orange.

That good or bad?

Its good i says. It means ye feel safe.

Shes quiet after that. We walks in silence. I takes a coupleay shortcuts. Im no surprised the wean got lost, hallglen is like a maze, not or-gan-ised intay rows of houses which yed expect dudes which would have been easier dudes which wouldve stopped dudes gettin lost dudes. So many houses i heard somethin like five hundred houses in the good old scheme thats hallglen man but for some reason they built loadsay streets to look the same. Why? Dunno. But like avon court for xample. Avon court looks the xact same as morven court. But the bus stops at morven court first. And sometimes if yere no payin attention, if yere like eh thinkin bout marshmallows or tryin not to fart ye might get off at the wrong stop. Ye might get off at morven court cos it looks just the same, xactly the same as avon court. Its no a nice feelin. Nope. Its just no a nice feelin. Like somebodys mibbe eh *stole* the place where ye live – and yer mam and yer dad and yer big sister and yer bedroom and yer marvelcomics – swapped it with this place that looks just like yer street but its no. Its just no.

I usedtay have bad dreams i tells natalie.

What about? she says.

Well i was wanderin thru hallglen tryin to get home, just like you. But all the streets looked like mine! And i just wandered and wandered thru all these xact same streets sayin theres no place like home theres no place like home theres no place like home, but i couldnt get home. Isnt that funny? Even tho i was tryin and tryin then i woke up from the bad dream ran to judys room i said judy! Promise yel always be here.

Whos judy? goes natalie, lookin intay ma eyes. Byootiful. Brownhazel.

She usedtay be ma big sister.

And shes no now? says natalie.

No shes not i says. Anyway like im tellin ye, id go intay judys room say promise ye wont let them swap avon court for another street. Even if it looks the same. Promise il always be able to find ma way home.

Cmere jude would say, openin her arms. Its okay its okay i promise. Il always be here.

Can i come in beside ye jude? i went.

Okay shed say. In ye come adam i came in. Snuggle up adam i snuggled up. Shes warm. Shes warm.

I says to natalie – do you have bad dreams bout hallglen too?

She nods.

I says never mind nearly home. Wer round bout the pakishop em GKR FOODSTORES and im thinkin bout the look on her daddys face when i brings her home safe and sound – me, the incredible adam spark, saviour of the yooniverse. Take her home to her mammy her daddy. Her mammy her daddy who love her, not like mine nope. Not like mine who went offtay see the— Im thinkin bout wee natalie tucked up safe in her bed where theres no bad dudes her dad tellin a story, tellin her a story bout the incredible adam spark who saved her. Tell me another story bout adam spark dad! Well. Shall i tell you the one bout when the incredible adam spark had di-a-ree-a and couldnt get off the toilet for an hour? Aye dad that sounds great!

Woman comin down the street towards me. Sees me pauses. Sees natalie starts runnin runnin, grabs natalie shes like hey! What the *hell* are you doin with ma wean? Got eyes like matches bein struck the redlight bove her head swells like a dragon.

Im like cool the jets hen, i just found her. I was takin her home.

Aye? she goes, glarin at me viciouslike. Well funny how her homes no in the direction yere goin!

I looks round. Looks round. Shes right enough. Im no headin towards morven court. I was headin away from it, away to

To where?

Em i says puzzled. Em sorry bout that missus. Em i must have got lost i thought i was takin her—

Shes lookin at natalie, natalies cuddled intay her mam her mam says ye okay hen? Ye okay? Did this man hurt ye?

Natalie shakes her head.

Her mam flashes a look at me hisses. I ken who you are. And i ken what happened with that wee lassie next door to ye, that sharon.

(stripsnap. Her idea not ma idea. She started it not me)

I holds up ma hands starts backin off man. Didnt hurt her. Didnt hurt her. Her mam looks at ma costyoom hisses what are ye some kinday pervert?

Backin away backin away. Backin away backin away.

Oh dont you go anywhere sunshine! shes screamin. I ken where you live! Id expect a wee visit from the police later on pal!

Backin away backin away. Backin away backin away. This is not the way it was supposedtay be as a superhero dudes. Nope nope i do not believe that captain america was ever acc-yoozed of this. I backs away all i sees her red light red light. Red light red light. Blazin. And natalies softyellow light cooryin in cos shes safe. Safe cosay me. Didnt hurt her nope.

Protect not hurt the weans, loyal sparky!

That night sure enough the police come round. The pigs! The filth! The fuzz! Like in taggart: theres been a murr-durr. They knocks the door they says can we speak to an adam spark? Judy looks puzzled says aye em come in. Theyre big not friendly. They sits me down i looks up. Feels tiny. They says a girl went missing this evening son and you were found with her. What do you have to say to that? I found her and was takin her home i says, but em i think i mustve got lost officers. Hallglens an easy place to get lost in with all these streets lookin the same and that. Tellin yese – sometimes i usedtay have these bad dreams when i was wanderin around hallglen tryin to get home but i

The officers stare. Just staaaaare. Wait for me to finish. Judes watchin from the sideay the room. Im sittin there neath the lamplight of the policemans stare, tiny tiny tiny. Jude says xcuse me officers, but is my brother being charged with anything here? Shes usin her best phonevoice yooni vöice.

The policeman halfturns to her annoyed. He says well as it happens miss – no.

Then you can leave him alone. Jude strides intay the centreay the room sits down nextay me. Looks at the police. She doesnt like police. Heard her tellin maryann once that the police were defenders of the state not the people, look at the miners strike she telt maryann. Who were the police defendin there? Power jude said. Theyve got this power and use it to execute the will of corrupt governments. Aye jude whatever, please just get them outtay here im not feelin at all well groo . . .

Jude says yese can see yerselves out then?

The police go. They looks at me as they leaves. Stare at me. They drags this black light with them this blackblack light, this hate. Can feel it. Hate. The walls are movin in. The walls are movin in man. Thats it dudes. Be a good man? Be a good man! Impossible nope sorry whats the point? Thats me and the crimefightin business finished. Tell me the point of it: bein good? a hero? when its so so-so? Oh dear. O jobbies. Hi fiddle-dee-dee, tis the darkside for me. Darkside of the force. Supervillain time. Watch out all of yese – ya buncha

Once theyre gone jude presses her head gainst the front door. Can see her breath mist up the winday. Comes back intay the room, sits down mongst the boxes got her head in her hands she looks straight at me.

Adam she says. Where were you goin with that little girl?

**Its cally park sunny ooh.** The days called big in falkirk its like the hallglen gala day xcept bigger! Trees grass flowers balloons water lap lap. Big in falkirks great oh ye can jump on the bouncy castle boiiing or play zee crazy golf or sliiiiiiiide down the chute or clamberover the climbin frame or buy icecream, or rowrowrow yer boat gently on the loch. But hey. Theres also singers. And comedians. And wee teeny tiny dancers (see their knickers? ooh) so me and bonnie we goes down on a kinday date. Cant stop thinkin bout policekidsjudemaryann. Im. Im. Im nervy shaky on edge all day, the edgeay an edge, bonnie holds ma hand. Holds ma hand! She holds ma hand. Shes bought me a present – queen pinbadge. She met me at the highflats said hi kissed me pinned it on ma jacket: pin. Pat pat.

If yere a queen fan adam, let everyone ken.

Well what about you?

She opened her jacket to show her queen t-shirt.

Whoah dudes she gets better and better! And as we walks she talks we laughs we jokes she settles that greatbig darkness in ma head like dilutes it with sunlight? Takes all the bats and ravens away by openin a winday. Shaftay sunlight – fry! Bats dissolve. Squeak squeak squeak.

but still

but still dudes

The crowds! The crowds in cally park! They close in close. Weans run bump intay me as we walk. I laughs to show this doesnt bother me, but it kinday does. Um. The mammies and daddies and weans – oh my. Bonnie leans in goes ooh look at that one adam. Pointstay a baby in a buggy gettin ready to greet, face revvin up mw mwa Mwah MWAAAH. Noise like a speedboat, rips right thru me. I pretendstay smile. Touches ma head um. Its like everythins madeay glass. Not real. Swirl swirl. The babies they are fake babies the peeps well they are fake peeps. Bonnie says anythin wrong adam? I says no no everythins great bonnie. Kisses her on the head. She smiles. Big toothygrin. Is that a thing bout sickstick fibreoptic? Makes ye smile like a pric— Oh cmon sparky, dont be such a bad dude just cos yer in a badmood. Everyone in cally parks sunny! happy! lickin icecream! guy onstage in kilt sings oh floweray scotland. Then puts on an elvis wig goes a-thankyouverymuch – boop!

Bends over lifts his kilt. Big boxershorts with lovehearts ha ha. Everybody laughs claps its hilarious! I tries to look at bonnies eyes, to guess what shes thinkin but shes wearin shades, they wont let me thru. Like superman – he cant see thru lead dudes and the incredible adam spark? Cant see thru shades. Cant see thru to what bonnie feels deep in her heart bout sparky here no. Blocked! Thats what kryptonite will do to ye man: block out the love from people who ob-vy-us-lee love ye sure, but wont admit it. They just wont admit it! Effin kryptonite.

Bonnies bought two big icecreams yum. Hobbles back with that sickstick fibreoptic walk she does. Brings them overtay me, holds them at the bottom. Here take them goes bonnie, fore i drop them. Raspberry ripple! Me and bonnie stands bout lickin cones makin noises. Mm. Mm! Shlurp. Choke. Its sunny! Birds cheep cheep. Im shakin, tremblin right down in ma soul. The solesay ma shoes. Bonnie smiles at me with icecream all over her lips, tries to wipe it away its dribblin down her t-shirt i nearly says bonnie you eat like a lesbi—

We goes on the boats. To cool off phew. I needs it. I needs it. Im feverish im hot. The weans. Bonnie pays the guy he roars come in number 29 your time is up! Hey – deafen us why dont ye? Number 29 rows back grumblegrumble comes donk! gainst the jetty. We gets in whoah sway. Bonnies in her skirt and heels, stepstep wobble. The guy tries to give her a helpin hand, holds ontay her waist she gets in okay phew. But hes still holdin ontay her. Alright there miss? he smiles. Bonnies like aye im fine.

I stares at him.

Splish! Splish! Splish! Im rowin wer sliiiicin thru the water at a fair rateay knots. Funny that eh? Like theres knots on a bittay string ye pass them somebody goes aye hes movin at a fair rateay knots. The sun the water the boats. Nice. Peaceful. Yawn.

We gets sleepy. I pulls up the oars and we drifts for a while.

Drift.

Drift.

Bonnie looks at me. She looks away. Shes smilin happy. She trails her hand in the water quietquiet. Weve drifted in behind a wee island drift drift. Trees and shadows. Its out the way. Cool. Her hands still trailin in the water splisssshhh.

I movestay the other enday the boat takes off her shades.

Her eyes.

Ma eyes.

I says i love you bonnie. She blushes dips her eyes, she says i uh. I love you too adam. We look at each other theres no sound no sound. Xcept birds. Lap. Splish. Wings hit the water. I leans forwards kisses her mouth its soft warm. She breathes in. I puts ma hand up slowly touches her face and everythin? Everythin stops.

And is byootiful.

Baaayootiful.

But yel never guess what she says after that dudes. Oh yel never guess what. I sits back down on the boat she looks at the shore – at the families and weans and dogs runnin round she says ken who wouldve loved this?

Freddie mercury? i smiles.

No she says. Ma great uncle wullie.

I sighs.

She rubs at her forehead. She says he usedtay bring me here when i was wee and wed play. Hed like throw a frisbee id run and catch it, jump intay the air. She does a wee impression of like her wee self runnin catchin a frisbee. Her hands floppy in frontay her, she pretends to jump and catch the thing, looks ri-dic-yoo-lus. I ken what somebody catchin a frisbee looks like. Does she think im daft? She says when we went on the loch hed splash water at me and soak me ha ha it was so—

Give it a rest i says.

Bonnie stops. She turns looks at me. What did you say adam?

I throws up ma hands. Shakes ma head. Laughs. Had enoughay this. Great uncle wullie, i goes. Tut. Thats all i get from ye bonnie!

She stares down at the bottomay the boat. Touches her mouth. Says well im sorry adam i didnt realise it—

Didnt realise it what?

Offended you.

It doesnt offend me bonnie i says, just bores me.

Oh she says looks away.

I mean am i no important to ye bonnie? Forget sparky whos still alive, lets just talk about great uncle wullie whos pushin up the daisies! Great uncle wullie in his wullie-shaped coffin!

She nods slowly as if takin somethin in.

What? i says.

Nothin she says, not lookin at me.

Ye in the huff?

She doesnt say nothin. Her hands coverin her mouth. Shes just lookin intay the water.

Ye are i says. Yer in the huff.

She still doesnt say nothin. Shakes her head slightly.

Say somethin bonnie i goes.

She looks up at me. Her eyes damp. She looks away again.

Well up yours!

She closes her eyes.

Up yours i mutters under ma breath.

She opens her mouth. She tries to look up at me but cant. She says adam?

Aye?

Can you take me back to the shore now?

I stares at her. She still wont look at me. Eventually i just says: with plez-yoor.

She nods.

I starts rowin. The suns crackin off the water, breaks and splits. Theres soundsay life from all round, laughin and fairground music and trumpets and dogs barkin. The oars are goin splsh splsh splsh. Im mutterin no even yer uncle. Yer *great* uncle for christsakes. I mean who the hell misses their great uncle? What kinday saddo? Me well ive had just bout enoughay bein the nice guy. If peeps are gonnay. If theyre gonnay keep goin on and on bout peeps thatre no even here! Look at her. Got her head in her hands, starin at the bottomay the boat. Stupit cow i says. She starts cryin. Take me back to the shore please adam. Please? Aye wer goin! i says. Can ye no see that ya dense

I keeps rowin. Ma heads thumpin Doom Doom Doom. Yere borin anyway i says. *Bo-ring.*

She shakes her head.

And ye look like oliveoyl.

We dunks gainst the jetty. The guy comes to help us but bonnies straight out. I goestay give her a hug ziftay say ach its okay bonnie. Never mind. Cmon lets do somethin fun like go on the waltzers or the coconut shy or somethin but shes off. Shes goin! Shes out the boat shes on the jetty hobblin off cryin. I stands on the jetty shouts aye walk away then! Walk away from me like everyone else! Shes nearly gone. I shouts i love you bonnie! Shes goin goin gone, folks are lookin at me i just shrugs. Says ach women. Cant live with em, cant round em all up and shoot em!

Peeps just nod.

*

I stoats round cally park for a while lookin for bonnie. See if she wants to go out again? Mibbe to the pictures? Cant find her at all. Plenty kiddywinkles tho. Plenty sun and fun. I wanders intay oneay the tents, roll up roll up hey its a pet show dudes. Lions and tigers and bears – oh my. I walks round the tent lickin icecream yum. Gerbils squeak squeak. Mice on a wheel drrrrrd drrrrrd drrrrrd. Dogs arf! Cats meeow. Even a goat! Dunno what goats do. But i laughs at the look on the goats face, chew chew chew. It looks bored man. Eatin. Eatin. Eatin. I stares at the animals in their boxes chew chew arf arf meeeeow.

*Help us.*

Their own wee jail man own wee prisonbars. What for? Just for bein different? Like me? Weeeeell mibbe it serves them right silly dumb beasts! The eyes of the animals man tho: bored done-in dead. Suddenly i wants to free them all dudes, can feel all their pain and hyoo-milly-ay-shin funny that eh? Moves round to this tank. Guess whats in it. Hey a piranna! Cool! This pirannas bout the size of yer head its swimmin slowly man, this great grey thing with teeth. Its eyes are like holes on the enday a gun. I watches it hey mister piranna? i says. Whats a dangerous fella like you doin on show with some borin old cats?

It glides towards me, teeth. Glint. *I have been imprisoned for my crimes*, it says.

Crimes?

*My kind and I commit evil.*

Aye but i says. That doesnt seem fairtay me man. No your fault yeve got teeth and ken howtay use them.

The piranna floats past sloooow its tail quiverin. *There can be no recompense for the things I have done*, it says. *My brothers and I have stripped the horses of kings to bone. We have patrolled the greatest rivers of the earth seeking horror. If given the option not to eat we refuse. When confronted by weaker creatures, we devour them. We would rape if it were possible, yes. We would rape human women and eat their men.*

Golly i says. That doesnt sound too good to me dude!

*Do not hesitate, young male*, the fish says. Its voice like ten wells deep boom. *Take what is yours. These others have not your power and must be annihilated. Give vent to your lusts and spill blood and do not cease until everything which stands in your way is crushed. Until the entire Earth bends to your will. For you are Death, the Destroyer of Worlds.*

I steps away from the tank. The fish looks at me i looks at it. Gunbarrel eyes and pearlywhite teeth. Even after im out the tent intay the hot sunshine – balloons! burgers! kids with hula hoops! – can still feel that pirannas eyes and its gravellyvoice. *For you are Death, the Destroyer of Worlds.* I look at the women and ken that i could have any of them right now if i wanted to and hey man! Theres nothin they could do about it. So thats their tough cheese. I looks at the weans and kens that each one of them man i could grab them take them away from their mam and dad. I could take that wean far far away where nobody would see it again oh aye.

But im no gonnay. And ken how? Cos its no ma style! Thats just not the style of sparky nyoooope the style of adam spark is to rescue weans from merican footballers and fireblankets and take lost kiddies back to their mams and dads thats me. Thats me dudes! The incredible adam spark to the rescue! Not kidnappin children no. Nope nope. Thats not ma style, hurtin children? As if! Ho ho ho ho.

I falls down among the trees im tremblin. Ma hands are like two pieces of paper man, theyve no strength. I kneels down. I kneels in the dirt looks at ma tremblin hands. Lions and tigers and bears – oh my! Ma head ma head goin Doom Doom Doom. Look at ma hands shakin like paper cant think of ways to stop them. Nope. Its a puzzle. Okay gang figure this one out: how do we get sparkys hands to stop shaking? Answers on a postcard and send them in to this address and you could win yourself a sackload of goodies (woooo!)

*You are Death, the Destroyer of Worlds.*

That night i thinks bout bonnie. In the dark. Her wee freckly face her wee body her. Her nice wee nice smile. Madeay teeth! And i thinks bout her thinks bouts her thinks bout her thinkthinkthinkthink till – oh!

Light.

The room fills with light. And faces. Its baaayootiful. Mam and dad theyre smilin got their arms round each other are they back from seein the wizard? Mam says: bonnie and sparky. Dad says aye and ye ken what else son? Sparky and bonnie. I says aye too right dad you ken the score then i starts greetin aheh aheh aheh and the rooms filled with brightyellow light and happiness and music, dreamy music, sparkly things like planets? moons? comets? but also? Ahem. Oh yuk man the duvets covered in all this

I minds the emptiness of the house.

Wed just come backfay sendin mam offtay see the wizard. Judy was wearin this black coat, i was wearin this black suit man black tie black shoes the lot. Felt like bart simpson when he hastay get dressed up for church – eat my shorts! Wed got a run backfay aunty fiona and uncle dod, she dropped us off at the house said mind now anythin ye need hen, just ask. Jude sittin in the backseat with me, lookin out the winday. At the callander woods at the weans playin fitbaw at the? at the? ach doesnt matter. Jude said aye well. Aunty fiona looked in the rearview mirror. She said what do ye mean aye well? Jude sniffed again. She said yese were quick enough to slag ma mam and dad off when they were alive, and now yese think ye can take their place? Uncle dod aunty fiona looked at each other. She said nobody slagged them off judith we were concerned for—

Yese thought she was stupit for marryin him. With his record.

There was silence in the car like. Like somebodyd turned the world off.

Yer gonnay need help with adam, fiona said quietly.

Naw said jude. Shook her head. Me and adam are on our own now, we dont want noneay yese. Il take careay this family.

The door slammin was like? was like? Well it was kinday like a door bein slammed.

So we got intay the house. Jude took off her black scarf black coat. I took off ma jacket ma tie man thats better! Jude said tea adam? I said oh aye jude you bet. She made tea. We sat at the kitchen table drinkin typhoo was like oneay them moments on adverts when they come in with their greatbig bagsay shoppin they go cuppay tea? Then all go aaaah. Relaaaax.

Jude wentay the cupboard took out three packetsay crisps. Chucked me one i said ta. She opened oneay the other packets. Cheesenonion. I mind thinkin that wont go with tea. Jude munch-munch-munched. Then she opened a prawn cocktail. Thatll definitely no go with tea! Munch munch munch. That was the start of her eatin her sadness her flabness. She was munchin lookin round the room, round at the kitchen at the kitchen, which didnt have mam at the sink. Which didnt have dad and jude doin the crossword and dad rufflin judes hair pullin her close mam smilin and me a-tearin thru the kitchen goin im a superhero mam. Mam look at me im a superhero neeeoooow crashtinkle. Aye so ye are darlin yere a superhero.

empty

Empty

EMPTY

And now its like that again. Theres no dad. No mam. No jude. No bonnie. Its me. Its me. Its cosay me.

**Fire up the ovens and the grills.** Get paper cups wrappers wee cardboard boxes and packetsay straws. Go intay the big freezer brrr get the frozen bacon frozen pancakes frozen rolls frozen hashbrowns frozen biscuits frozen muffins frozen chickennuggets frozen burgers frozen pickles frozen tomatoes. Cartons of scrambled egg mix orange juice mix. Bring it all upstairs start gettin it ready fore customers appear. Stuff it intay the microwave slam! Deet. Doot doot doot. Bvvvvvvv. Start makin burgers on the grill fsssshhhhh. The pre-cooked stuff man? Well ye put that intay these special cabinets to keep it warm. Its xcitin. You bet.

Shift starts. Peeps wander in. Can i have a chicken sandwich meal? You certainly can.

And so on.

After a while i realises: bonnies no here. Meantay be here. Meantay be here dudes gulp whats wrong? Goestay the chart that shows everybodys shifts yep – bonnie should be in. Xcept shes no.

Goes intay angies office says hey angie wheres bonnie?

Angie looks upfay her work steelysteely gaze says well bright spark i was hopin you could tell me.

What do ye mean?

She is your girlfriend.

Aye i suppose i says. Shufflin on the spot. But i thought she was comin in today.

Well shes not says angie. Shes left.

(its like when ye get an njection – the wee pinprick yer arm goes nummmb)

Shes left?

Aye angie says. Phoned in yesterday to say shes no comin back.

Oh. I goes.

Ken anythin about it?

No. I goes.

Angie shrugs. Aye well ive got someone to replace her startin monday. Wasnt hard like.

Aye. I goes.

Angie looks at me. Pencilsharp eyebrows go up. Anythin else bright spark?

No. I goes.

Well back to work then.

Aye. I goes

intay the basement to get food and stuff for the evenin shift. Get paper cups wrappers wee cardboard boxes and packetsay straws. Go intay the big freezer brrr get the frozen bacon frozen pancakes frozen rolls frozen hashbrowns frozen biscuits frozen muffins frozen chickennuggets frozen burgers frozen pickles frozen tomatoes. Cartons of scrambled egg mix orange juice mix. Bring it all upstairs start gettin it ready fore customers appear. Stuff it intay the microwave slam! Deet. Doot doot doot. Bvvvvvvv. Start makin burgers on the grill fsssshhhhh. The pre-cooked stuff man? Well ye put that intay these special cabinets to keep it warm. Its xcitin. You bet.

When i gets home i phones bonnie. Well i tries to phone bonnie but she wont answer just wont answer! The phone rings and rings and rings. Rings and rings and rings and lorday the rings. While im waitin an outtay tune orchestras like rehearsin in ma head – violins screeeeech.

Puts down the phone.

Takes out judes shinydress feels it. Goes out. Just walkin man. Just start walkin. Holds the dress. The tempra-tyoor: its hot its cold. Who kens dudes. Just who kens whats goin on in this crazymixedup place? Im cryin. Greetin. Aheh aheh aheh. Peeps pass they stare always stare, their eyes their eyes their eyes. Black dogs. Walks past the pakis past the bookies past the communitycentre over the flyover past good old hallglenprimaryschool where the children play their merry games aw bless em, downtay the glenvillage then the canal tweet tweet, sodoff birds, i walks walks walks tears streamin and a-pissin from ma face till i reaches the happysad bridge.

This is where me and bonnie went that day – but!

Now where is she.

Now where are they.

Now where am i.

Stands. Right in the centreay the happysad bridge. One side laughinface the other greetin. Thats me thats sparky. Yep right slapbang in the centreay everythin, no kennin whether to laugh haha or greet boohoo. Con-fyooz-yin. Mibbe i should just

A mam a wean walkin along the edgeay the canal, the mams pushin a pram weans tryin to keep up stepquick, pointin at the ducks the water point ooh look mum. Aye brandon the mam just sighs. Walks on. I smells judes dress. Smells like wood dust age – all the things the things. Seconds. Minutes. Hours. Me and jude. Days. Weeks. Me and bonnie. Months. Years. Decades. Me mam dad. Cent-yoo-ries. Foreverandever: me and nobody. Me and mr nobody again.

The water glides, then fore i kens it im climbin ontay the edgeay the bridge. Clamberclamber. Stands. Salutes. Drapes judes dress round ma shoulders a bigmad cape dudes, looks right the way down the canal where it disappears intay the darkay the dark tunnel oooooh waters black. Coalblack. Nightmareblack. Shiver. Then i sees

O jobbies.

sees the mams walked on but the weans no. The mams still pushin the pram but the weans gone, wheres the wean gone? The mams sayin keep up brandon its nearly. Turns. Sees the empty space her face changes: what? huh? Then she screams. The weans slappin the water tryin to stay afloat, wee mouth fillin up gurglegrgl. She runstay the canal roarin. I doesnt even think. Jumps off the bridge. Leaps soars floats intay the air – hey im flyin. Im flyin dudes look at me – im flyin! This is amazin! Oh my god im flyin im flyin like a real life superhe—

Splash.

fck

hea

vy

kick

cold
dark
green
fck!
where?
nuh?
that?
ma?
arm?
up
kick
breathe
kick
breathe
look
oh
wean
grab
flap
kick
pull
which
way
up?
um
fckn
glg
gl

up

kick

kick

light

– pull!

Somebodys screamin knives gainst ma brain, peeps run run grab the. Hes got the boy aye but is he. Get him pull him out ive got him. No its. Take his. Hes slippin its. Dont let him go hes goin

down

down

d wn

d   n

  o n

d o

    n

  o

**Wakes in this funny wee village.** Colours flowers fairytalehomes. Walks round looks at weirdshaped trees plants, like candycane or sticksay rock. Theres a wee dog at ma feet – ruff! Then i hears giggles and – what? The bush shakes. These wee peeps come stoatin out tiny pudgyfaced creatures singin ding dong the witch is dead! Looks round, sure enough man theres ma house but its not in hallglen falkirk scotland. Its in munchkinland. And theres two wee curly shoes a-disappearin under it dudes: result. My my im in oz! Dog must be toto. Mam and dad are here – mam and dad! Mam dad, oh i wantay find them. Needtay find them. How does i find them? A munchkin starts singin follow the yellowbrickroad. What? Then another joins in. Then suddenly they're all squeakin dancin laughin whistlin twiddly twirly twi

Aye okay dudes i gets the point.

Il speed it up cos yeve all seen the film:

Goodwitchaythenorthturnsuptellsmeshesagoodwitch(shoreispurty!)

saystheonlywaytofindyermamanddadistogoseethewizard(thewonderful wizardayoz)thenthewickedwitchaythewestarrivestellsmeshelgetme . . . andmylittledogtoo(onlydogroundheresyou)havetaygotaythecityofozin ordertogetbackhomesetsoffonmatravels(withaweesmileandawee song)andonthewayimeetsacowardlylionscarecrowtinmantheywanta heartabrainandcourage(nothinelse?greedylittle)thenwegetsattacked byflyingmonkeyscarriedoffbutinthewickedwitchscastleiseesacrystal ballandinthecrystalballtheres

Me lyin in a hospital bed. Im hooked uptay all sortsay machines goin blip blip blip. Whats this all bout dudes? How can that be me? How can that be me if im in the landay oz? A mans writin somethin on a clipboard ma skins pale mouths open. At the sideay the beds jude. The other sides maryann. Maryann speaks but i cant hear jude nods. Looks like she hasnt slept. Hunted haunted look bout her, gets upfay the bed leaves the room crystalball follows her thru the hospital. She walks thru twistyturny corridors comestay a room that says chapel. Thinks a bit pauses a bit. Then goes in. And when in she kneels down before a big big cross startstay mumble mumble, man thats no like our jude. She must be worried awful worried bout somethi—

Picture changes. Mist covers sssssssss then clears. I sees sand tanks a city in the desert. Soldiers guns. Screamin pakis. Dead bodies bleedin bodies crushed bodies. Bombs: boom. Merican flag flyin flutter. George dubya bush jabbin a finger roarin this is a war between good and evil, and we have made it clear to the world that we will stand *strong* on the side of good. This is not a war between our world and their world. It is a war to *save* the world. Our struggle is going to be long and difficult, but we will prevail. Good will overcome. More bombs screamin etcetera etcetera mist comes like sand sssssssss covers everythin.

Backtayseethewizardhopskipheyitstheemeraldcity(everythinsthecolour ofceltic)knocksthedooradudesayswhatdoyouwant?wewantaysee thewizardwegetsinseesthishorsethatchangescoloursthengoesintay hisroomthereslotsayflamesandnoisethisgreatbigscaryvoiceIAMTHE GREATANDPOWERFULOZandhesaysWHATDOYOUWANT andisaysiwantayfindmaparentsthenhesaysITSQUITEIMPOSSIBLE TOSEEYOURMOTHERANDFATHERbuttheymustbeherecosjudetold metheywereandshedoesntliebuttheninoticessomethinthewizard saysPAYNOATTENTIONTOTHATMANBEHINDTHECURTAIN andtotogoesbehindthecurtaingoodboypullsitbackandits

Dad.

Ma dad. Its him. Its really him. Oh. Oh! He shrugs smiles softwarm. I kent it. I kent that behind that bigscaryangry dad (adam ya bloody—, ya stupit—, ya useless—) there was this dad. A good dad. The dad who loved me just me. And here he is kinday steppin outfay behind the curtain he goes *Son?* In this echoey voice that seemstay bounce off all the walls i says dad? He says *Do not be afraid, son, for you are in a place of love*. And i looks at him goes what ye on about? Why ye talkin like a christmas card? But he smiles opens his arms i runs intay them. Flings ma arms round him tight. I says oh dad. Oh dad i thought id lost ye. He puts his arms round me says *Come close, son*. He smells like a fishin trip: smoke and earth and whisky like i members. I snuggles intay his nicewarm jumper. Dad will ye come home now? Yev been away long enough will ye come backtay live with me and jude? He says *Son, I am always with you. Every day I turn my gaze upon you. Every moment my thoughts are here.* Touches ma heart. And i looks up intay his sparklin eyes warmsmile hugs him says: stop talkin pish dad just get yer arse back home.

*

The big day comes! The leavin day! Theres a party to celebrate, everyone in the wonderful city of oz there to see the wizard leavin, goin backtay the earth, with his long lost wee boy: me: sparky. Got a hot air balloon hes wavin to the folks. Wave wave wave. Wavewave wavewave. A big slebrity round these parts is ma dad oh aye, mustve been buyin everyone drinks. Theyre cheerin. Theres streamers. Music! Marchin! Like a great big hallglen gala day in the sky aye. Gets in the basket with him says oh dad its been so long since yeve been home. Yel no even recognise the place. He looks out across the purpleland of oz to the scottish hills says *That, son, I know*.

Lets go! Dad startstay untie the ropes but just then i realises – ive left toto. Oh no: toto. Jumps out the basket, runstay find toto but the baskets off. Gone! vamoosed! vanished! Standin rooted to the spot. Im like no. No dad. Dad dad come back! He just waves waves says *Farewell, Adam. Look for me one day. We will be reunited, and all shall be at peace*. Waves blows a kiss i just faintly hears the words *love you* before:

He disappears intay the sky.

Shrinkin

Fadin.

Dick.

I kneels down. Alone again. Munchkins dancin singin lalalala, just shrugs ma shoulders. What can ye do? What can ye do dudes when the balloon goes without ye? Thinks bout jude and maryann in the hospital. Jude prayin cryin just wantay be with her. Just wantay be home. But dont ken the way! Looks up intay the green sky this pink bubble it floats quivers lands – oh look who it is. Its mam! All the munchkins have stopped cavortin drinkin theyre bowed down ooooh. She waves a magicwand says *Still you are troubled, Adam. Have you not yet realised?* I says oh mam. I needtay get home and let jude ken im alright. Ye ken what shes like shel be climbin the walls with worry clamberclamber. Mam smiles like an angel, not like the mam who was thinasgrass, clingin ontay me skinnybony hands shakin nope. This mam is bayootiful. Shes got long flowin curly locks. Big white smile. Pearlyclean skin, and her dress? Oh her dress is fab-yoo-lus like a bride. I says mam youre so pretty. Ma eyes are wet. Oh dont you just scrub up a treat in this place mam.

*Thank you, Adam*, she smiles curtseys then glances at the sky. *You know you will see your father again, Adam. He is not gone forever.*

Aye he is i tuts, chuckin a twig at the ground. The knob.

*Have you figured out how to return home?*

I makes a face. Look i says. Gonnay somebody just tell me whats goin on? I cant *get* home. Judes waitin at the hospital for me, worried sick, and i dont ken the way from here! Im no like you. Ive no got a magicwand i can just wave with the power to teleport me away or whatever the fu—

*You are wrong, Adam. You have the power.*

How?

*Son, you always had the ability to alter your fate and those of others. That was your power, the power of everyone alive: to heal and not destroy, nurture instead of hate. The other powers were peripheral, simply to help you in your plight. But they did not.*

I stands says look! Gettin sickay this dudes. Points to maself puffs out ma chest, im the hero mam. Connor macloud he-man lukeskywalker spiderman. Im the incredible adam spark! Im the goodie here. People seemtay forget *im* the one thats gettin jobbied on!

Mam shakes her head sits down on spearmint grass. Ruffles her skirt. Smells like sweets and babies and when she speaks its like silky snow.

*You are lost and confused, Adam Spark. This universe is large, complex, often inhospitable and bleak, riven with absence and death and meaninglessness. Yet we each know the difference between good and evil. Beyond primitive rules and earthly laws. We know this truth. Often evil poses as good and it is easy to lose oneself in a labyrinth of self-deception, but finding the way out is the task. Finding the true path. And it is here that you have failed, Adam. As a good man, you have failed.*

Im on ma knees, sniff sniff. Shiver. Seemstay be gettin dark. The munchkins are moanin glancin bout terrified. What time is it? i says.

Mam shrugs. *I don't have a watch on* she says. *But I think we're near the end.*

The light startstay fade, drops cross the hills. The munchkins have started to scurry away to their homes. Stormclouds. Goes cold all over. Oh. Oh. No i says, crawlin to her. Mam i says. I dont wantay stay here! I wantay be back with judy. Wantay help her. Her and maryann. I grabs the hem of her dress starts pleadin – all the tears and snot fall ontay the pink material pull pull.

*There's no chance for us* mam sings, lovelyvoice risin fallin like waves. Puts her hand in ma hair. *It's all decided for us. This world has only one sweet moment set aside for us.*

Who wants to live forever? i sobs.

*Who wants to live forever?* she sighs, song fade fadin faded.

Mam i just says. Mam what is it ive no done? Tell me. What is it ive no done yet to be good?

I looks up at her shrinks away oh god. Thunder. Her eyes red terrible, like that dogs that owls. That pirannas. When she speaks its no sweet or echoey, its deep like a demonsvoice growl. *Your forfeit for spreading destruction, Adam, is destruction*. She reaches out with a withered claw. Mam waves her wand i sees dead trees, burnin buildins. Skelyton hands pokin outfay the rubble. Sky the colouray blood. The boomin of guns. War. War. The vision disappears im tremblin quiverin. Mam stands raises her wand which is now a sword, a-gleamin. Her eyes flash red face lined scarred sick can hear the poundin of ma heartbeat. Doom. Doom. Doom.

Covers ma head im screamin. I dont ken mam! I dont ken the answer! Cant work it out no no dont ken howtay be good! I just wantay be home with jude. Jude and maryann. Just wantay be home. Theres no place like home. Theres no place like home. Theres no place like

**Opens ma eyes.** Looks round the room. Wee heartbeat monitor nextay me but nstead of goin Doom Doom Doom its goin blip (pause) blip (pause) blip.

Whoah ha-zy everythins swimmin ergh oh right. Em. Doc. Tor. Jud. Ith. Hel. Lo. Tries. To. Say. Hi. But. Cant. Cos. Mouths. Not

Jude puts a finger over ma lips, shh adam she says. Dont try and speak.

Well i cant! Whenever i do This. Ha. Ppens.

Feels everythin wave wave then clear. The hospital ward. Nurses doctors patients. The walls are kinday blue, dudes visitin other dudes, laughin cryin passin over presents kiss thanks. Can hear machines goin blip (pause) blip (pause) blip. Big winday at the enday the ward sunlights comin in. Falkirk royal in-firm-aree where i was born dudes. Theres no place like home. Aye theres no place like home. And on the telly in the wards somethin daft – this statue of a dude with a moustache its gettin pulled down, it falls it falls. Everyone cheers an merican flags draped over it: merica. Masters of the yooniverse dudes. Superpower.

Hey wait a minute – ma superpowers have gone!

Aye. Looks round at everyones head, the smilin nurses boredlookin patients, but theres no lights. No lights! Just air just hair just. I feels ordinary again. Normal small wee Not Incredible. Flexes ma hand. Looks at the drip machine beside the bed i says hey dude whats goin on?

The drip machine doesnt answer.

I looks at the telly i says what about you mister television?Ye gonnay talk?

It doesnt.

Im backtay normal aye and ken what? Im glad. Cos that might make it easiertay be a hero – funny that!

Doctor standin there clipboard clipped underarm. Takes it out ticks tick tick scratches his nose. Looks at me smiles oh hello adam, awake are you? How are we feeling now?

I mashes ma lips together dry – drymouth um. Well *cough* im feelin pretty groggy doctor. Ive no idea how youre feelin.

The doctor laughs fnuh. Wee snort of air scapin a balloon. I looks round the room, its white. Jude? Judes nextay the bed eyes soft silly she rubs ma hand rubrub oh adam. Ye came back.

Aye but mam and dad didnt i thinks. Tut. The lazy bloody. Swings ma head on ma neck there whoaah woozy what happened judy?

She looks at me. Doctors armsfolded eyes narrowed hm.

I asks again: what happened?

What do you remember? he says.

I minds. Happysad bridge. Me thinkin its all over its all over, they think its all over. It is now! Wean falls in the water – splash – i goes in after. Glugkicksplash down down down.

Jude comes touches ma face. Like a magnet: feels heavy motions flowin.

What happendtay the wean? i says.

Hes fine adam.

What happendtay me?

Jude sits back. Goes intay her bag rummage. Takes out the falkirkherald, big headline on the front CANAL HERO FIGHTS FOR HIS LIFE pictureay me smilin grinnin school photay. Pictureay the wean smilin grinnin school photay. Words neath the pictures: adam spark, 18, who rescued brandon walker, 3, from the union canal. Ye must be – choke! – jokin.

Jude shakes her head mazed. Yere a hero adam. Ye saved his life. His mam and dad have been in every day visitin ye.

And we nearly lost you as well goes the doctor. For a few minutes you were clinically dead. Doctor starts showin me funny things: graphs charts xrays of like ma head and i notices: the splodge on the xray i got done after the gala day? Sgone. Sclear. Samystery.

Ye cant remember anythin at all about being under? asks jude, head in her hands starin like theres somethin hidden in ma headorheart shes tryin to peer at. What was it like?

MamDadWizardayozDingdongthewitchisdeadYouhavetobea goodboygoodboygoodbye.

Its no place like home, i says.

Jude smiles dabs her eyes, cuddles in oh adam. I nods. Says shh. Its okay jude im back. Tries to say this next bit its really important. I havetay make her. Gottay make sure i. Opens ma mouth but still woozy still like whoaah dudes mouth cant quite, but havetay say it grabs judes hand tells her:

Get maryann.

Just then the doctor notices the telly gasps goodness me. I dont believe it. The wars over!

Maryann comes in. I tells them what ive gottay say. Con-sin-trate. They sits waitin while ma news bounds rebounds round the room, rubberysilence. Jude and maryann glance over the bed at each other while i talks yaks tellsitlikeitis. Jude takes ma hand leans in um adam? she says. What do you mean *move in* together?

Needtay tell them ive got it. Got it dudes! Ive worked it out. Worked out howtay be good. We should all move in! i grins grinnin. Thats what we should do could be like friends, ken jude could be monica maryanns phoebe i could be chandler (could i *be* any more like chandler?) wel get uptay lotsay hilarious stunts in the same manhattan flat em same falkirkhouse. Hilarious stunts like stuffin our faces watchin telly! Playin swingball! Fartin competitions! Me! Jude! Maryann! Paaarp!

No says jude, puts her hands over her eyes seenoevil. Says oh god oh god oh god overandover.

I blinks. I am taken aback. Or as they say in australia: taken outback!

Maryann and jude each sideay the bed silence, maryann tugs with her nail at a thread tug pick. What do ye do when yer nose is on strike? Picket! Ha ha! Dont get that joke.

Itll be like friends? i tells jude.

Adam ye dont understand she says, coverin her head oh god oh god. I hadtay get away. And now that im gone i cant come back. I mean il stay with ye til yeve got yer strength back, but after that adam . . .

I looks down at the crisp sheets. Crisp crisp like crisps: plain ones. Looks at jude says um not even if its like friends?

Im with maryann now she says. Maryann stands goes to the winday. I sees her strong solid back: shes real. It would seem! Shes real. Silly sparky, hopin shes no been real all this time tut tut. Cant do nothin bout that. What a daftie. Shes not gonnay disappear – zap! – like a supervillain or the wickedwitch cant drop a house on her or dis-in-tegrate her. Shes heretay stay. I cant come back adam says jude. I need a life of ma own. *You* need a life of yer own. And maryann couldnt live with ye adam, not after what ye did to her in glasgow.

Turns ma face intay the pillow no no.

Shes afraid of ye adam. *Im* afraid of ye.

Wantay say nope not now jude. Not scary now! Ive learned howtay be good! But i just sinks further further intay ma softpillowworld no no no and hey its still funny havin to go on what peeps say and not the lights bove their head for me to see to guess to know what they think. Cos i wish i kent what jude was thinkin these days, just wish i kent. Sure is hard tryin to guess what peeps feelins are, true feelins, deep deep down in their heartandsoul. That jude tut. Like they say in the states: shes one tough broad.

Besides adam, she smiles thru the tears takes ma hand. Youre a hero now.

Sure enough dudes hey whoah when im out? It goes mental. Falkirkherald phones say how does it feel to be hero? i says um dont really feel like one without ma superpowers ken? Interviewer says ho ho good one. Photay of me the wean the mam the dad the headline

SAVED BABYS MUM: ADAM SPARK IS A HERO which is weirdstrange kinday cool. Dudes stop me in the street say nice one sparky. Pat ma back. Goes intay a shop all the peeps start cheerin clap clap clap. I bows um. Well. Blush.

But the first few days on ma own are like

Sometimes i still gets sore heads. No as bad as i usedtay. The odd twinge ooh, do you have a migraine? Take new solpadeine aah thats better. The odd wee trailay light like the ghostay a rainbow passin thru, like a ribbon slither. It hisses. Just at the edgeay the room – then? Gone. Gets up in the mornin. Switches on the telly. Eats weetos (theyre scientifically proven to taste great) goestay work. Comes home. Switches on the telly. Eats weetos (theyre scientifically proven to taste great) goestay bed.

Sometimes the boredoms a tonweight. This massive nvisible thing it fills the air, pressin pressin presssssin. Whats that sound? Its the sound of nothin pressin down on ye forever sparky ma man. The sound dudes of a big fat boredom twistin ye out of shape, egh help oof.

Jude phones. She always phones. Just as the bigtonweights pressin so hard i startstay cry jude phones, hey dude hey jude. When she comes round man oh that is so the best. Comes in with asda bags stuffed with pressies creamcakes hugs me kisses smiles, shes. Shes so. So good so jude. Flicks thru the post that comes in – bill bill killbill – takes them with her they gets paid. Zif by magic! And she shines these days. No light round her now dude but when she talks bout whats happenin with maryann – theyre decoratin, theyre buyin furniture, would i like to see it? – she shines. Shines. Glows.

And oh.

I gets up in the mornin. Switches on the telly. Eats weetos (theyre scientifically proven to taste great) goestay work. Comes home. Switches on the telly. Eats weetos. Goestay bed.

And still in the street peeps grin say well done adam, thumbs up. Falkirks first superhero! they say. Shrug. Sometimes in the pakis em GKR FOODSTORES il get stuff for nothin. No no says mr akram, for a local hero this one is free: gives me the bag. Oh ta mr akram thats awful niceay ye. So funny cos ive never felt so ordinary dudes. No powers nothin nope, just me. Walkin back with free milk free bread free freerange eggs. But: superpowerless. Then i gets backtay the house no-one there, what kinday hero that make me? And even when the mam and dad of the wean i saved come roundtay see me, always come, the wean says thank-oo the mam hugs me the dad shakes ma hand, its cool its cool dont get me wrong, but they go away again. Always away again. Ta-ra wave wave: close door. Sigh. Somethin missin man somethin

what use is bein a hero if ye dont have

One time jude phones says adam why dont ye cometay glasgow and stay for a night. One night what do ye say? Says ach cant jude ive got em. Got work ken? She says aye but can ye no get a coupleay days off? I says um. Oh! Um. Ive got that thing? What thing adam? That thing. That thing i needtay do. What thing adam jude sighs. The thing jude! i says switchin thru the channels: bored: nothin on. Judes silent on the line then says

Its maryann adam. Isnt it?

I goes in careful tiptoe. Zif enterin a lions cage. Its a nice flat. In a nice area. In a nice life. Looks like an advert. Theres photays on judes walls of like nude women but not like ones in scudmags nope. Theyre black and white. Their rudebits in shadow. Why but why cover them up? Strange. Wooden floorboards. Shame, they must no have much money. Walls all white. Cant afford wallpaper? All the furny-tyoors white too? Coloured stuff must be too dear for them oh dear. So clean! Clean spotless like enterin heaven, dont wantay touch a thing ooh careful.

Take yer jacket off adam says jude, i takes ma jacket off. The jackets are firmly off! Im quiet. Feel like if im too loud the whole flat will shout at me to go Go GO from this place!

And do not return.

The tellys no on how queer. Soundsay kids playin in the street. Books so many books, soft furnishins. Its like im made outay nothin dudes when i walk thru it, so byootiful, its like yer made from puresolidair. Thats their house: a thesbian house. Home of thesbian dykes. Jude beside me beamin says what do ye think adam?

Oh aye jude smashin. It really is its. Em.

I wantay burn it down.

Maryann enters. Enter maryann! Shes carryin two mugsay coffee, one for jude one for me. Ugh its blackcoffee – spit ugh. Wont look at her. Shes tall elegant is maryann, sharp elbows nails eyebrows wont look at her. Told ye. Foldarms. Nope. She smiles glances at jude then me. Breathes out. Theres this big big quiet – swells like a balloon fills the room.

So hows things? maryann says.

I sups ma coffee yuk. Mm i says, delicious. Sits down on the cream plushsettee, stretches out yawn. Well i says. I gets up in the mornin maryann. Switches on the telly. Eats weetos. Goestay work. Comes home. Switches on the telly. Eats weetos. Goestay bed.

Maryann looks at me thru that bright happy glasgowspace.

But its okay maryann i says. Ken how?

Why says maryann, rigid.

Cos theyre scientifically proven to taste great.

I shrugs. Sips ma coffee.

Why would i need anythin else when ive got weetos dudes? You must be barmy. I gets up goestay the toilet and when im there i says the words *arse bastard shit* to maself, then when i comes out im smilin. Calm. Shakin.

I stays that night. And im lyin in this goodgood room with all the light wood furny-tyoor cleanclean walls and pictures that say like king lear at the lyceum and workers of the world unite and pictures of funny long women. But i cant sleep. Cant sleep dudes! The noises. The mm. The oh! The shhh, hel hear us gigglegiggle.

I gets up. Walks down the hall.

Mmmm. There. Right there.

Stops in frontay the door.

Oh maryann. Oooooh maryann.

Puts ma fingers on the handle press. Like when i heard dad eatin mam like a lion: yes yes yes.

Oh maryann. Maryann i love you. Sob. I love you. I love you so mu—

Minds that yellow light that used to be bove judes head when she was with her, talkin bout her thinkin bout her, yellow yellow yellow.

Goestay the livingroom pours cold coffee on their nicenew couch – whoops! How careless!

*

Walks backtay falkirk. Right there and then. Walks backtay falkirk in the middleay the night, cars flyin past rush whoosh. City lights! Takes six hours dudes aye but once im out the city tell ye – the stars. Whoah. The stars and stars and stars and stars. Like scarborough again, when jude left me alone i traipsed round the caravans. Is ma family here? Is this ma family? Wheres ma family? Heres me walkin home, back intay a life with no powers no power. Normal norman. Maybe it wont be so bad after all, bein a mere mortal. Shrug. Gets intay falkirk just as the sun opens up, like a bigmadeye. Hello world! Blinkblink.

As i gets intay the house the phones ringin i answers its jude she says adam! Adam where did ye go? I woke up and yed already left the flat. Where did ye go? Adam? Adam? Ye still there?

Aye jude. I just says. Im still here.

For judes grad-yoo-ay-shin she has to wear a greatbig gown dumbledore gandalf merlin – shazam! Wer standin outside the hall in glesga, all the peeps in their best clothes a-rovin a-rantin, posh posh. Cameras: click. The mams dads aunties uncles neeses nefyoos all millin in big splashesay colour, cant see no lights bove them tho shame. Judes xcited in her gown. Im in ma tin flute (that means suit) that ive no wore since mam went offtay see the wizard (to take up her post as good witchay the north) maryann fusses over judes gown says its riding away up your neck judith. Oh cmere. Maryann fixes, jude looks at her fingers, all the peeps flashin to and fro and that wee thing. Maryann helpin jude jude bein helped. Says it all dudes ken?

Got ma hands in ma pockets, chewin chewingum, jude turns to me beams how do i look?

Aye jude i says. Ye look grand.

Takes a pictureay jude and maryann: grin. Maryann takes a pictureay me and jude: grin. Then jude goestay take a picture of

Nah judy! i stops her. Thats everybody goin intay the hall, cmon wed better go.

The ceremonys like watchin the end credits for a film. Xcept theres no film. Yawn man. Sittin nextay maryann shes cranin her neck to try and see, im slumpin in ma seat tryintay sleeeep. For the degree of bachelor of science in applied physics upper second. Ronald dreever anderson. Kevin montgomery bristow. Lisa collins. And ye havetay clap! So many times! What for dudes? Just cos the boy managed to walk on stage and not fall down, that it? Whoopee doo i could do that, give me a degree if thats all ye havetay manage dudes. For the degree of bachelor of arts lower second. Graham jameson. David knight walker. For the degree of

Halls massive. Massive with like twisty pillars red curtains. Looks uptay the ceilin theres like ghosts there: mam and dad. What are they doin here? Not halloween is it? Waves but they dont see me proberly still arguin bout the SHED the SEAT. Slumps further dull dull, i am fadin away. I am disappearin look maryann ye dont even notice. Look im fallin down the crack between the seats here. Anybody see? Anybody lookin? Hello! No powers no nothin. Unspecial. Here i go slip byeeeee

Maryanns pretty neck pretty makeupped face the pretty way she blinks stares at the stage. She is pretty. Why tho? Why did she have to be so pretty so?

For the degree of bachelor of arts in political science, first class. Judith mary spark.

Sits up in ma seat – whoah! Me and maryann both says where?

where? where? Peeps clappin, cant see her cant spot her um. Where maryann? There adam she points and – oh.

Judy.

Tiny.

She walks cross the stage takes somethin off this guy shakes his hand then walks back off again.

For the degree of bachelor of arts in philosophy, lower second. Harold william randall.

And thats it. Over. But me and maryann wer lookin at each other. Wer lookin at each other smilin. Smilin! Me and maryann smilin at each other. Wer sayin that was her! Wer both sayin that was our jude! That was Our Jude!

And after we gets out we sees her on the steps we runs towards her at the same time squealin nearly knock her over she manages to hug us both, fmoof get off!

Kiss kiss and three times kiss.

After the yooni jude gets a job as a soshal worker (which is kinday funny considerin shes a soshalist haha) now shes thru in glesga with families a bit like ours usedtay be. Dangerous times for definite! Comestay visit me on a sunday tells me bout what happens me and maryann we listens. Kids left on doorsteps. Kids born addicts. Kids with dads that. Kids with mams that. Kids with scars down their bodies. Kids that kill. Kids that do things to other kids. Kids that eat rat poison. Kids that smash windays. Kids that pull knives. Kids that scream. Kids that dont say nothin. Kids that tell her they love her. Kids that tell her they hate her. Kids that draw pictures. Kids that write down their dreams. Kids that will be kids the restay their life.

The incredible judy spark. In ma head shes ten storeys tall galactus proud strong smells luvverly too. And all the kids and weirdo mams and pissedup beentaythepub dads are on her back shes tryintay lift them like the great big falkirkwheel lifts boats goes nnnnggggg screws her eyes shut triestay lift every damagedbaddie in the world then does. Straightens her legs. Skyscraper. Blocks out the sun. And then i opens ma eyes its just jude. Just jude! Sippin her tea cockin her head, sayin why ye smilin adam?

But if judes there to take careay all those dudes, dudes whos gonnay take careay me?

Me.

I will.

I have the power.

Come off it dudes if i can save a weans life im sure i can make a mealcrowave mike, i mean microwave meal. Takes it out the cardboard sleeve. Pierces the plastic with a fork – pierce! pierce! brosnan! – pops it intay the microwave. Deet deet doooot. Watches it turn and turn and turn. Dvvvvvvvvvvvv bing! Oyah dancer.

No bother for the boy sparky. Next?

Cheese and Tomato Flan

Serves 4

8 oz (200g) shortcrust pastry

6 tomatoes

2 eggs

4 oz (100g) grated Cheddar cheese

¼ pint (150ml) milk
salt
pepper
oregano

Preheat the oven to Gas Mark 6, 425°F, 220°C. (Click!)

If you are using ready-made pastry make sure it is defrosted. Roll out the pastry so that it can cover a medium-sized flan dish (nooooo bother dudes). Place the rolled out pastry in the dish and using a fork prick (a fork prick? Jeezo dudes ive just got a normal prick) the pastry. Bake for about 5 minutes (okay doke) and allow it to cool.

Cool!

While the flan is cooking place the tomatoes in a pan of boiling water for a couple of minutes. Remove and drain. When they are cold enough to handle take off their skins and slice ( – ow! Ooh! Blood!)

I sucks ma thumb.

Beat the eggs together, mix in the cheese and milk, season (seasonsinthesun) place the sliced tomatoes on the base of the flan and cover with the egg and cheese mixture. Sprinkle with a little oregano, then bake for 30–40 minutes.

Whistle whistle. Tap tap. Tap tap tap tap tap. Tick tick tick tick.

*

Brings it out after twenty minutes gettin bored dudes. Takes it thru to the livin room, careful not to slip in all the eggs over the floor whoops! Sits down in frontay the simpsons. Instrumental break. Aaah ye cant beat a homemade meal. Eats. Swallows.

Hm. Disgustin.

After im sick all over the toiletbowl starin down intay the milky chalky tomatoey coloured water i thinks aye. This is it. This is it dude. For the restay yer life. Get usedtay flan that tastes like chalk cos thats what yeve got comin to ye buddy. Every day for ever and ever and ever and ever and ever. Flush. Drain.

I goes to ma room and listenstay queen. And queen. And then queen.

Well thats pretty much all there is to tell ye dudes xcept – oh i forgot! Mark baxters in jail. Aye he stabbed norman senicky one night outside a nightclub dont ken what for. Norman senicky died: egh. Mark got hauled off neenaw neenaw to the cells then mark got sentenced heard that in the jail one of the t-hill posse decides this was not right and. They were in the dinner queue. The dude reaches over throws boilin water on marks face sssssss. Anyways sa-yo-na-ra mark baxter norman senicky take it outside boys! The h-glen animalz the t-hill posse kinday fell apart after that. Okay lads well its been a good few years violence and thievin lets go our separate ways. Before we ruin the magic. But therel be a few years quiet sh. Then the wee ones theyll rise and take their place, the falkirk wheel. Its that effin falkirk wheel again man tellin ye.

But till then – dusts off hands – thats another lottay badguys taken careay. Salute. Sleep safe maam. God bless you superman.

And what bout george blair tony bush em i mean. Ye ken what i mean. Well after they sorted out arack they both said right thats enuff. We just cannot be doin with this dudes too much hassle. Photays of prisoner abyoos. Arack fallin down all over the place: boom. Just one hassle too many dudes so guess what? Tony blair well he opened a music shop in london played guitar for visitin tourists telt them the story bout the time when he met the president of the USA. George dubya bush well he became a world champyeen darts player, hit the booze bigstyle grew the beergut everythin, xcept on a touray britain he got hammered twelve games to three by our very own jocky wilson. By uptay-the-ocky jocky.

Only kiddin dudes. Theyre both still leadersay the free world and im sure theyll take us intay more xcitin and hilarious adventures.

And the worlds fayvrit fastfood joint? Thats another story. When i got out the hospital i went backtay work. No half as much fun without yer superpowers like. Did the job cos its a great job: makes yer day. Then one day? Washin the floor got the mop im whistlin. Lost in a daydream. Cos ye ken the boy sparky aye, he likestay dream bout them goodoldfashioned boobs fondle fondle. But then angie comes uptay me like bright spark? I says aye. She says what ye got in yer mouth? I says a tongue. She says no dumbo what ye eatin? I says oh! Chewingum. She says chewingum! I says aye. She says ye ken thats against company policy? I says oh. She says get ridday it. I says fine. Takes it out ma mouth drops it in the nearest bin. Her eyes go wide she says *that* was the bin for the lettuce. I shrugs again. She says right thats it sparky, ive had enough. Get yer gear and *get*. I says what? She says go home for the restay the shift. I says yer sendin me home cos i put gum in the lettuce bin! She says naw im sendin ye home cos yere incompetent, just like that stupit wee girlfriend of yours what was she called that bon—

Throws the bucketay water over her. She stands there aghast agog, hands at her side starin. I shrugs smiles. Walks away out the shop, hearin pplause pplause behind me peeps standin back sayin oh well done sparky. Nice one. Take a stand man! And when i getstay the door im sure can hear behind me this witchy voice goin *im melting im melting im melting*.

At nights i stands in frontay the mirror. Or the winday. In the moonlight. And the moonlight makes me white blue cold cold. Naked. I looks at all the things ive done ive been: the badthings. So many badthings. Im bad bad i speaks out loud how ye gonnay be a good man now sparky? How am i gonnay be a good man jude, i mean dudes, if theres no-one lefttay be good to? good for?

But no-one answers.

And thats it. Theres really nothin else to say its all been – oh here i forgot again man! Was in falkirkhighstreet months later. Time had passed in its timepassy fashion. Was on ma way to buy a birthday card for maryann ken how? Was her birthday. Walkin bout: queen on the headphones: meets guess who.

She was pushin a pram. She looked a wee bit fatter than before. She saw me but wasnt sure whether to say hi but did she have a choice? Nope nope. Cos dudes i went boundin right over there: boiiing.

How ye doin bonnie? i grins. Goodtay see ye.

She triestay smile. Goes gnuh. Sniff. Her breathins still funny. Im fine um she says shuffle, yerself adam?

Wanted to say: alone bonnie. Pretty effin alone ken? But just went ach shrug.

Saw ye in the falkirk herald smiles bonnie. Ye rescued a wean from drownin?

I blushes hm. Nobigdeal.

No its terrific she goes. Ye saved a life. That makes you pretty special.

I says aye em bonnie. But what bout cally park? Winces. Wasnt very special then bonnie. But i dont think i was well. In fact im no long out the hospital after a checkup. Everythins okay now they says.

Oh she says, like shes just memberin cally park nods quiet.

Aye i says. Em sorry bout that.

Bonnie waves her hand fnuh says well. Ive uh. Ive been in the hospital too adam.

That right? i gasps. What was wrong?

She looks at the pram.

What?

She points at the pram.

What?

She shakes her head says never mind. Gnuh. Sniff.

I says anyway bonnie, lets have a wee look at the nipper here! Magine you havintay babysit on a saturday bonnie – hih? What a life. Looks intay the babys pram. Its a wee baaayooty of a thing so it is, dead cute and googoogoo wavin his mittened hands up down lookin at me, big big eyes. Hawo! i says. Hawo there my wittle buddy! Whose baby is it? A pals?

Aye says bonnie.

What one?

A very special one, bonnie says quietlike.

I waves at the wean. Bends down kisses its head – mwah! It giggles. Laugh gurgle. Aye i can make em laugh, so i can. Im the boy. Lifts ma head out the pram bonnies lookin at me. Starin. She says in a funnyvoice isnt he lovely adam? Says it like shes upset.

Aye he is, i nods. Gorgeous. His dad should be proud like.

Bonnie looks down frown, mumbles i hope he is.

Notices the time – oh! Em bonnie sorry i says, the shops are bout to shut still gottay buy a card for someone.

Bonnie nods.

But its been good seein ye and – i points. The wee man.

Sure he feels the same bonnie goes. Touches her eyes damp.

I looks bout. Falkirks goin on all round me, always. Life and stuff. What a puzzle eh! What a mad crazy mys-tee-rious business this whole gettin by thing is. I glances up quickly, smilin. Anyways bonnie see ye around?

Aye she waves weakly. Bye adam. The wean raises a wee mittened hand flapflap. I grins salutes him: my work here is done. Then i heads off intay the wildblueyonder.

But i doesnt get far dudes. Strange strange feelin after seein bonnie that cant quite put ma finger on. Not sure but.

That wean.

Turns round sees bonnie standin in the middleay the high street. She drops her head. Sighs. Pushes the pram away, and for some reason i stays and watches, watches her, just watches her go til she nearly disappears off the enday the street.

Then i runs after her.

# Acknowledgements

Many thanks for their input, feedback or advice on this book: David Fernandes, Kathy Flann, Magi Gibson, Terry Gifford, Jackie Grunsel, Sylvia Hebden, Victoria Hobbs, Stephen Keane, Antonio Lulic, Lucy Reynolds and Joe Romanowicz.

For support during the writing of it: Julia Lawson, Hannah McGill, Elaine McKergow, Fiona Malcolm, Diane Manson, Lucie Randal, Mollie Skehal, my wonderful parents, my brother and sister, and the lads.

Thanks to Paul Buchanan of The Blue Nile for his kindness and generosity.

To the Headline team for their spectacular efforts: Bob McDevitt, Mary-Anne Harrington, Leah Woodburn, Hazel Orme, Nancy Webber, Ami Smithson and Scott Garvett.

See you all next time.

# Copyright Acknowledgements

The song on pp. 74–75 'When I Leave Slamannan Behind' was written by my late grandfather, Ronald Hynds.